THE LISTENING EYE

The morning was a pleasant one. There was a hint of spring in the air. His fancy occupied itself with thoughts appropriate to the season. When eventually he turned into Cranberry Lane they distracted his mind from the fact that another car was doing the same thing.

Before he realized that anything was going to happen the two cars were abreast and he was being forced off the road. He braked, ran scraping along the hedge, and came to a stop. As he turned, between fear and anger, he saw the other car at a standstill too and the driver already out.

He had time to see the revolver in the gloved hand. After that there was no more time. He may have heard the shot which killed him, or he may not. Evidence on this point is not available.

Bantam Books by Patricia Wentworth

THE FINGERPRINT
THE LISTENING EYE

THE LISTENING EYE

PATRICIA WENTWORTH

BANTAM BOOKS
TORONTO • NEW YORK • LONDON • SYDNEY • AUCKLAND

The characters and situations in this book are entirely imaginary and bear no relation to any real person or actual happening.

This low-priced Bantam Book has been completely reset in a type face designed for easy reading, and was printed from new plates. It contains the complete text of the original hard-cover edition. NOT ONE WORD HAS BEEN OMITTED.

THE LISTENING EYE

A Bantam Book / published by arrangement with Harper & Row, Publishers Inc.

PRINTING HISTORY

Lippincott edition originally published in 1955

First published in Great Britain 1957 by Hodder and Stoughton Limited

Bantam edition / July 1980
2nd printing ..... June 1980
3rd printing ..... May 1985

ISBN 0-553-24885-5

Bantam Books are published by Bantam Books, Inc. Its trademark, consisting of the words "Bantam Books" and the portrayal of a rooster, is Registered in U.S. Patent and Trademark Office and in other countries. Marca Registrada. Bantam Books, Inc., 666 Fifth Avenue, New York, New York 10103.

PRINTED IN THE UNITED STATES OF AMERICA

H 12 11 10 9 8 7 6 5 4 3

1

The gallery was well lighted. Paulina Paine had a vague feeling that it was too well lighted. A good many of the pictures might have looked better if it had not been possible to see them quite so clearly. Everything about Miss Paine declared that she was a sensible person. She was fifty-seven, and she wore the kind of clothes which she considered appropriate to her age and her position in life. Her sturdy form was comfortably and sensibly attired in a thick tweed coat, grey with a black and white fleck in it. She wore sensible laced-up shoes and a dark grey felt hat with a plain black ribbon. She could not, in fact, have looked a less likely person to be visiting one of those small winter shows which display the kind of picture more calculated to shock than to sell. Unless, of course, the artist suddenly becomes famous, in which case art critics embark upon lively praise, dispraise, and argument, and millionaires begin to compete.

Miss Paine was not here because she admired this type of work. Far from it. She did not. But if someone paints your portrait and it is put in an exhibition, you do feel obliged to go and see what it looks like there. As a matter of fact she thought it looked very well—much better than it had done in David Moray's studio, which was the rather flattering name he had bestowed upon her top attic, a bare untidy room in which he cooked horrid-smelling messes and slept on an iron bedstead several sizes too small for him. She stood in front of the portrait and was gratified on two points. It wasn't labelled with her name. It wasn't even called *Portrait of a Lady*, or, more realistically, of a landlady. It was just called *The Listener*, and she could see what David meant by the name—there was the kind of look about the eyes, and the turn of the head. It vexed her a little, because she thought she had got rid of looking as if she were trying to hear all the things that she would never hear again. The second thing that pleased her was that the picture was marked "Sold." She couldn't imagine why anyone should want to buy it. Even when she was quite young she had had no pretensions to anything beyond pleasant, sensible looks. At fifty-seven—well, she hoped that she still looked pleasant, but she couldn't think why anybody should want to hang her on a wall. There had been quite a flattering notice in an Art Journal, but she still couldn't understand why the portrait should have sold.

Her own picture was not, of course, the only reason why she had come. It wasn't even the chief reason. Her cousin Hilda Gaunt's son had two pictures in the gallery, and her sense of family duty required that she should come and see them and write and tell Hilda that she had done so. If it was possible to find anything to admire in them she would say it, but she was not prepared to tell lies, which in her opinion very seldom deceived anyone and were apt to lead to complications. Wilfrid's first picture puzzled her. She thought she might perhaps describe it as enigmatic. There was a broken tombstone looming up out of a kind of blue fog, there were some bones that looked as if they might be human, there was an aspidistra in a bright pink pot. The aspidistra was really quite well painted. It was in fact immediately recognizable as an aspidistra. She had known plants of which it was the spit and image, she had known pots of china in just that shade of pink. She thought perhaps she might say that she found them lifelike, but it was difficult to suppose that this would satisfy Hilda's maternal pride.

She moved on to Wilfrid's second picture, and it was Worse. There was, unfortunately, nothing enigmatic about it, it was plain Nasty. She had taken a seat in front of it because her feet were killing her, and until she had taken her weight off them and drawn several deep breaths of relief she didn't realize just how nasty the picture was. She simply couldn't imagine what she could possibly say about it to Hilda. The word daring presented itself. Anyhow, now that she was sitting down she wasn't going to get up again—not until her feet had had a rest. But go on looking at that revolting picture she could not. What she could do and did do was to avert her gaze and look down the room. There was a seat away to the left and quite a long way off. A man sat there. He had a catalogue in his hand, and he appeared to be studying it. She had a vague impression that he had been there for some time.

Just as she looked round, another man came in through a door at the far end. He too carried a catalogue. Paulina watched him idly as he consulted a page and stood looking at what suggested the explosion of an atom bomb. She had excellent sight, and she couldn't imagine that it could possibly be intended for anything else.

Presently he transferred his attention to a greenish female who appeared to have had several of her bones broken, after which he stepped backwards in the direction of the seat and sat down. So there they were—two ordinary men on a shiny seat with a civil distance between them. Paulina found herself wondering whether their reactions to the dislocated lady would be strong enough to induce them to exchange views on the subject. If anyone had come to sit on the same bench as herself, she would have found it difficult to refrain from speech. She sat and watched the men. They were to all intents and purposes as much alone as if she had not been there. It would not have been possible for her or for anyone else to hear what they might say. In point of fact even if she had been sitting on the same seat she could have heard nothing. The last sound which had reached her, or would ever reach her in this world, was the crash of the bomb which had brought her office down over her head in 1941. She had been buried in the ruins for twenty-four hours, and when they got her out she was stone-deaf, and had so remained. With characteristic energy and fortitude she had learned lip-reading, developed a talent for cooking, and taken a post as housekeeper at a school in the country. Just before the war ended her uncle, Ambrose Paine, died. He was a very cross, determined old man whose motto through life had been "When I say a thing, I mean it." In the course of a long and rather dreary life he had said a number of disagreeable things, and at least one courageous one. He said he would see the war out in London, and he had almost brought it off, dying only a week before the Armistice in the big old-fashioned house where he had been born. He left it, with what remained of his capital, to his niece Paulina, and she came back to town and let off all the rooms except two on the ground floor, which she kept for herself. Ambrose Paine would have been outraged and scandalized, but Paulina hadn't really liked school life or communal cooking, and she loved London. It was odd at first to walk down familiar streets where the traffic had roared and see it go by as silently as if it were no more than a picture on the screen at a cinema. But she got used to it, and she got very good at her lip-reading. Practising it continually, it had become second nature. Interesting too. She had read some curious things from lips whose words were pitched for the ear of a friend, a lover, or an enemy. She could sit in a restaurant and know what people were saying at some table isolated by a barrage of talk and music—

She looked along the gallery and read what the man who had just come in was saying.

2

Sally Foster had two rooms at the top of the first flight of stairs in the house that Ambrose Paine had left to his niece. One of the rooms looked to the front over the small square and the rather decayed-looking garden in the middle of it where the laurels and lilacs which had survived the war continued their struggle for existence. No bombs had fallen amongst them, but most of the windows in the Square had been shattered when a land-mine fell in the neighbouring thoroughfare. The houses were all about a hundred years old, and had been designed with basements and attics for a numerous staff. Nothing could be shabbier, more inconvenient, and less adapted to modern conditions. Ambrose Paine had always refused to move with the times, but Paulina had contrived a couple of extra bathrooms. Sally cooked on the latest baby gas stove, shared a sink with Paulina, and thought herself lucky. She had a job as secretary to Marigold Marchbanks, whose publishers confidently asserted that her sales ran into millions. In private life Marigold was Mrs. Edward Potts, with a vague husband somewhere in the past and a couple of daughters, one of whom had just made her a grandmother. When she felt like it Marigold dictated to Sally from ten to half-past twelve. Added to which there was typing, checking of proofs, and fan mail. Sally answered the fan mail, and Marigold appended a flowing signature. It wasn't a bad job at all, and with what her parents had left her Sally lived comfortably enough. On occasion she drove the car and they got out into the country.

Whilst Paulina Paine was trying to make up her mind what to say to her cousin Hilda Gaunt, Mrs. Gaunt's son Wilfrid was lounging in Sally's most comfortable chair and hindering her. She had already told him so in no uncertain terms. There never was anything uncertain about Sally, from the bright chestnut of her hair, the bloom of her complexion, and the sparkle of her eyes, to the forthright manner in which she dealt with a time-wasting young man.

"Look here, Wilfrid, I can't do with you—not when I'm answering fan mail."

"Darling, you've said that before."

The typewriter clicked.

"And I shall go on saying it until you go."

Wilfrid extended himself into what was practically a straight line. He was long and slim, and he had sleek dark hair.

"You wouldn't be so harsh."

Sally laughed. Even when she was preparing to be harsh it was an uncommonly pleasant sound—one of those laughs that go with a kind heart and an even temper. She turned her brown eyes on him and said,

"I can be *fierce!*"

Wilfrid produced a slightly supercilious smile.

"Not with me, darling."

"And why not?"

"You wouldn't have the heart."

She frowned, typed an exclamation mark in a perfectly uncalled for place, and said,

"You're wrecking this letter—and it's rather a special one to a professor who has taken a cross-section of twenty-five of Marigold's books and counted up how many times she has split an infinitive, so it simply won't do for me to provoke him by making mistakes in my typing. Please do go away."

He slid down another inch in the capacious chair, closed his eyes, and said,

"I don't feel strong enough. Besides I'm just working up to a proposal of marriage."

Sally planted an asterisk in the middle of a sentence and took her hands off the typewriter.

"You proposed to me yesterday."

"And the day before, and the day before that. I'm just wearing you down, darling."

"And how many times do I have to say no?"

"I have no idea. You'll get tired of it some day."

"Look here, Wilfrid—"

He waggled a hand at her.

"Let us change the subject. I don't feel strong enough to wrangle. Besides I've got a grievance. Against Paulina. Or does one say with? A grievance with—a grievance against—anyhow it's still with or against your Aunt Paulina."

Sally's colour rose becomingly.

"Wilfrid, she is not my aunt! She is your mother's cousin, and that is all there is about it!"

He moved his head in a slight negative gesture.

"I am not talking about cousins, I am talking about aunts. If a helpless girl finds shelter with an elderly female, the elderly female automatically becomes an aunt and is so addressed. It is what is known as a courtesy title. You would not be discourteous to Paulina? Anyhow this is no time for idle badinage. As I started out by saying, I have a Grievance, and I wish to enlist your support in getting it removed. Are you any good at sabotage?"

"Now, Wilfrid—"

The hand flapped again.

"Don't hurry me. It weakens the system, depletes the energies, and makes me come all over a doodah. As you may have guessed, the grievance concerns the attic. Why should Paulina have allowed David Moray to intrude himself into her top floor? It has an excellent north light. If she was prepared to let it as a studio, why in the name of the tables of kindred and affinity should she let a stranger have it rather than her own cousin's son?"

"What on earth are the tables of kindred and affinity?"

Wilfrid opened his hazel eyes sufficiently to allow a reproachful glance to travel in her direction.

"Ah—you weren't brought up in the bosom of the Church like I was!"

"No. What are they?"

"A compendious list of all people you mustn't marry and no one in their senses would want to. In the Book of Common Prayer." He closed his eyes again and intoned, "'*A Man may not marry his Grandmother*—' But we digress. At least you do. I return to the point, which is Pressure to be brought on Paulina. By you."

Sally's eyes widened in the way which had in the past caused a good many young men to be emotionally disturbed.

"My good Wilfrid, what has it got to do with me?"

"You will be the agent for bringing pressure to bear. Paulina is fond of you—she eats out of your hand. If you were to burst into tears and say that life without me in the attic would be valueless, or words to that effect, she might be nerved to the point of giving David Moray the push."

Sally said briefly, "It wouldn't be."

He drew himself up about an inch.

"What do you mean, it wouldn't be? What wouldn't?"

"Life. It wouldn't be valueless. In fact quite the contrary. Why on earth should you try and turn David out?"

He looked at her maliciously.

"Being a little stupid, aren't you, darling. I'm coveting my neighbour's studio. What I have is only a room, and a foul one at that. The stair smells of cabbage-water, and Mrs. Hunable smells of drink. If I am laid low, nobody holds my stricken hand or smoothes my stricken brow. I would, in fact, be a good deal better off with Paulina. Added to which there are the sacred claims of relationship. An inspiring thought that we shall be under the same roof! Who was it who said, 'If propinquity be the food of love, play on.'?"

Sally was betrayed into a faint engaging giggle.

"I suppose you mean Shakespeare—only I should think he would be a good deal surprised, because he didn't say propinquity, he said music."

"He said such a lot of things," said Wilfrid in an exhausted voice. Then, sitting up another inch or two and brightening a little, "Consider what it would be to wake in the morning and think, 'Wilfrid is only two floors up,' and to sink into slumber at night with the same beautiful thought! Only, of course, there might be times when I should be burning the midnight oil elsewhere."

"I can well believe it."

"Oh, I always get home in the end—sometimes a little the worse for wear, but no matter. And as already stated, Paulina would be there to soothe the anguished brow next day. Or you, my sweet!"

"No."

The word was pronounced in a peculiarly firm and resonant manner.

Wilfrid sighed deeply.

"Not a womanly nature."

Sally said "No" again, and then spoilt the effect by a little gurgle of laughter. "Wilfrid, *will* you get out! I've got to concentrate on the professor, and then get on with a kind 'No, I couldn't possibly' letter to a woman who says she has written a novel, and she's afraid her writing is dreadfully bad and she can't afford to have it typed, but will Marigold read it? And that's only a beginning, because there are three people who want autographs, and one who wants advice, and two that I'm saving up to the last who just say how grateful they are because Marigold has given them a lot of pleasure. So will you please get up and go away, because I'm not getting on, and I've got to if I don't want to sit up half the night, which I don't."

"Why don't you?" said Wilfrid in his laziest voice. "If you don't sit up at night, when do you sit up? All my best ideas come to me then. No distractions, no interruptions. The mind just floating—not quite detached, but almost imperceptibly linked with the abstract. There is a rhythm, a sense of the imponderable, a kind of floating haze."

"It sounds like drugs or drink," said Sally frankly.

"There might be some flavour of alcohol. But not drugs, darling—they are lowering to the Moral Tone so conspicuous in my Work."

"I hadn't noticed it."

"Dim-witted of you. However one can't have everything, and your looks are pleasing. I did ask you to marry me? These things slip the memory. What is much more important at the moment is the matter of the outing or ousting of David Moray. You wouldn't like to wake up in the morning and read in the paper that I have been driven to the violent elimination of Mrs. Hunable. My nature is one of peace, but I have an exceptionally sensitive psyche—if that is what they call the thing that takes charge and nerves you to murder the people who have been annoying you. I don't think it is, but no matter. What emerges is the horrid fact that I am being driven to desperation, and that if I can't oust David and have Paulina's attic, almost anything may happen at almost any moment. You will notice that I have now decided upon oust rather than out. It is more forcible and has a richer flavour."

Sally was about to raise her voice in a final "Wilfrid, will you *go*!" when there came a rapping on the door. She said "Come in!" instead, and Mr. David Moray walked into the room. He was a large, uncompromising young man of Scottish appearance, with blunt features and fair hair burnt to the colour of dry grass. His eyes were between blue and grey, and his eyebrows and lashes very fair and thick. He viewed Wilfrid with disfavour and addressed himself to Sally.

"Are you busy?"

"Frightfully."

"With him?"

Wilfrid said, "Yes," and Sally said, "No."

David Moray frowned.

"Because if you're not, there was something I rather wanted to ask you about."

Wilfrid pulled himself up a little farther in his chair.

"Not another word. You wish to give up your attic, and you want somebody to break it to Paulina. Don't worry—it doesn't really need breaking at all. You want to give it up, I am ready and willing to take it. The whole thing is as good as done. Except for the mere physical transaction you have already moved out and I have moved in. Blood is thicker than water and a nod is as good as a wink to a blind horse. Paulina will be delighted. Sally walks on air."

David looked at him bleakly.

"If you know what you are talking about, nobody else does."

Wilfrid's tone became tinged with malice.

"Sally and I do. The proverbial two hearts that beat as one. A stroke of the wand and we change over. I to Paulina's attic, and you to my Mrs. Hunable, now mine no more. I have bestowed her upon you freely. I will go and pack."

Under a particularly menacing look from Sally, he rose, kissed his hand to her, turned a charming smile on David, and drifted out of the door, which he left open behind him.

David didn't wait for his footsteps to die away. He gave the door a push with his shoulder, and derived some satisfaction from the fact that Wilfrid must have heard the resulting slam.

Sally raised her eyebrows.

"It *is* my room," she said.

"And my studio isn't mine—is that it? Is there anything in what he was talking about, or was it just blethers?"

Sally Foster had a very charming dimple. It showed now as the corner of her mouth lifted.

"It was just blethers. He doesn't like his place, and he would like to come here. I should never get any work done if he did."

David scowled.

"Why do you let him bother you?"

"Oh, well, there isn't very much I can do about it—he just gets into a chair and sticks."

"You could tell him to go."

"David, *darling,* if you think that makes any difference you just don't know our Wilfrid."

There was an angry jerk in his voice as he said,

"Don't call me darling!"

"But it doesn't mean anything."

He gave her a look of concentrated dislike and said, "That's why."

Sally said "Oh—" on which he continued in the same forbidding strain.

"I suppose you call him darling—too!" The last word was ejected with considerable force.

Sally said, "Sometimes."

"And what have you left to say to the man you love, if all this frittering stuff has left you any feelings worth the name? Tell me that! And I will tell you that when I call a woman darling it will be because I'm thinking of her for my wife, and because she's everything in the world to me and a bit over!"

Sally said, "Oh—" again. Afterwards she thought of quite a lot of things she might have said, but at the time nothing came out but that "Oh—" Because something hurt her at her heart and there was a pricking behind her eyes. It didn't get quite as far as anything you could call a tear, but it did impart a softness and a brightness which were quite extraordinarily becoming.

Mr. Moray may have felt himself slipping. He may have felt that he had been harsh, he may have decided that he had gone far enough. He stopped looking at her as if he might be about to proceed to violence, allowed his features to relax, and dismissed the subject.

"That will be enough about that. If I'm not interrupting you—"

The fan mail might not have existed. That was the bother about David, when he was there. Sally found it quite dreadfully difficult to remember things like being a secretary or having work to do. Afterwards she would kick herself and work overtime to make up, but for the moment she couldn't have cared less about the professor and his split infinitives, or the other people who were waiting for autographs and advice. She said quickly.

"Oh, no. This is just Marigold's fan mail,"

"Well then, I came down to talk to you. About that picture of mine. *The Listener*—it's all right about its being sold. I went round to the gallery and met the man who was enquiring about it, and he asked what I wanted for it, so I said two hundred, and when I heard myself say it I thought I'd gone out of my mind. But he just nodded and said that was all right, and he liked it very much, and I'd got a future before me."

"Oh, *David!*"

It was naturally meat and drink to have Sally looking at him like that, but he kept his head.

"His name is Bellingdon, and Masters—you know, the Art Gallery people—they say he has one of the best private collections in the south, and when he buys any new stuff it means that other people are likely to be interested too. Anyhow there it is, marked "Sold" and the cheque in my pocket, so I thought it would be a good plan if we were to go out and celebrate."

The faint stirring of a usually competent sense of duty prompted Sally to say, "I oughtn't to."

"Why oughtn't you?"

She threw a reluctant glance at the typewriter.

"Work."

He picked up the letters, pulled up a chair, and straddled it.

"I'll dictate them to you. I suppose they just want tactful answers."

Sally gave her delightful laugh.

"And you would be so good at that!"

"Oh, I can be tactful when I choose. It's mostly waste of time, when it's not plain insincerity." He used the back of the chair to prop the professor's letter and regarded it with a gloomy eye. "What this man wants is to be told to go and boil his head. If he's got the sort that can be bothered to read twenty-five of Marigold's novels, it's all it's fit for. I'd like to tell him so."

Sally said, "We can't!" She very nearly said "darling" again, but stopped in time. She typed rapidly:

"How nice of you to have read so many of my books. I

am so grateful to you for your kind interest. I think it is wonderful of you to spare the time.

Yours sincerely,"

She left a space for the signature, withdrew the sheet, and read it aloud.

David relaxed into a grin.

"That's a good score! He sends her a ticking-off, and you've turned it into a compliment. I'd like to see his face when he gets it. He'll be foaming."

Sally said,

"I hope so. And now I really have got to be tactful with a woman who wants Marigold to read a book she's written on odd bits of paper and things."

"Is she going to read it?"

"Nobody could! I shall have to pack it up and send it back, and I really think I had better just say straight out that Marigold can't undertake to read manuscripts, and that no publisher will look at anything unless it's typed. You know, I really can't think how they managed in the old days. I've seen manuscript pages of Scott, and Dickens, and people like that—photographs of them, that is—and I just can't think how anyone read them."

"You had better be quite firm about it."

"Oh, I will."

They were not getting along very fast, but time didn't seem to matter any more. They talked about the letters, and all the nice ones got such warm answers that Marigold's stock went up appreciably.

When they were nearly through, Sally suddenly stopped typing and said,

"Did you say that man's name was Bellingdon?"

He nodded.

"Lucius Bellingdon. Why?"

"Because I was at school with his daughter. And I've just remembered there was something about him in the paper—no, it wasn't a paper, it was a magazine—an article about who had the most valuable jewels—you know the kind of thing. And it said he had given his wife a most wonderful necklace which is either supposed to be the one Marie Antoinette had and there was all that fuss about it because she didn't really order it, or else it's a copy which was made when the original was broken up."

David produced a frown.

"I haven't the slightest idea what you are talking about."

"Nonsense—you must have! Everyone knows about the

Affair of the Diamond Necklace. It was one of the things that brought on the French Revolution, and I don't remember all the ins and outs about it, but it was part of a plot by a woman called Lamotte to get hold of a lot of valuable diamonds which the King's jeweller had tried to sell him to make a necklace for the Queen, only she wouldn't let him and said much better spend the money on a battleship. And I really do think it's a shame that everyone remembers the silly story about her saying if the people hadn't got enough bread to eat why didn't they eat cake, but practically no one remembers about the battleship. Anyhow, when she wouldn't have the necklace, the Lamotte woman persuaded Cardinal Rohan that the Queen had changed her mind, and that she really wanted it. There were a lot of forged letters which he thought were from Marie Antoinette saying she wanted him to put the matter in hand, but there mustn't be any talk about it. Lamotte and her husband got a girl called Oliva to dress up as the Queen and give the Cardinal a secret audience in the palace gardens after dark. You wouldn't have thought they would have dared, or that he would be such a fool as to be taken in, but he was. And then when M. Lamotte had got away with the necklace, the jeweller sent in the bill to the Queen and the whole thing came out. There was the most colossal row. Marie Antoinette said she didn't know anything about any of it, but a lot of people didn't believe her, and it did the Royal Family a great deal of harm."

David had his impatient look.

"And what has it got to do with Bellingdon?"

"I told you—he gave the necklace to his wife. At least some people say it's that one and some people say it isn't, because the real one disappeared, or was broken up, or something. But if it isn't the same it's exactly like it and it's worth goodness knows what. There was a picture of it, all festoons of diamonds looped up with big ones, and the woman who was writing about it said Mrs. Bellingdon had never worn it because of the war, and then she got ill and died. But Mr. Bellingdon is letting his daughter have it to wear at a ball he is giving at the Luxe next month. It's a fancy dress ball, and she is going to go as Marie Antoinette. I told you we were at school together. She was a bit older, and of course even a year makes a lot of difference when it comes right in the middle of your teens, but she knows one of Marigold's daughters and I've run across her a good bit lately. She got married a year or two ago, but he was killed motor-racing. I can't say I think being Marie Antoinette with a lot of diamonds is really her line. Only I suppose most girls would rather jump at the chance. Diamonds do seem to go to people's heads."

David Moray frowned.

"I can't imagine why you should take an interest in this sort of thing."

The dimple came out again.

"Well, I do. You know, David, I'll tell you something—just for your own good. If you ever come across a woman who isn't interested in the sort of odds and ends that you feel all haughty and despising about, she'll be one of the earnest ones who'll want to run you and everything else in sight, and you'll get so bored with her that you'll probably end by doing her in. Because you know what it would amount to—it wouldn't leave you anything to feel superior about, and you would hate that like poison."

She found him looking at her in rather an odd kind of way. If it had occurred to him that there was something in what she said, he would certainly not give her the satisfaction of admitting it, and then all at once he was saying,

"Well, I'm not denying that's a point of view. I wouldn't say a woman was any the worse for taking an interest in what you might call the frivolities, always provided the solid stuff is there underneath—like having a good sound cake under the icing. For instance, you mightn't have noticed it but I've a sense of humour myself, only I make it my business to keep it in its place." He reached across for the last two letters. "It's time we were getting on," he said.

3

Paulina Paine came out of the gallery upon the street. She had sturdy legs, but they were shaking under her in a way that had nothing to do with the fact that her shoes were new. She was, in fact, unconscious of the feet which had been hurting her so much only a short time ago. There was just this feeling that nothing was quite steady, and that the pavement appeared to be going up and down. Not enough to make her fall, but enough to be troublesome and confusing. She came to a small tea-shop—one of those that still linger in London, where they sell cakes and buns in front and there are half a dozen tables at the back. She sat down at the first one she came to and ordered that British panacea, a cup of tea.

She began to think what she was going to do. Suppose she had just gone on walking till she came to a policeman. She could picture the conversation—

"Now, miss, let's get this straight. You say you heard this man make a statement to the effect—"

"No, no, I didn't hear him. I can't hear anything—I'm deaf—"

It would be quite hopeless. There had been experiences which resembled it closely enough to assure her of that. Besides, the next question would be as to the identity of the man she had watched, or at the very least a description of them. Of the nearer one she had seen a turned shoulder, a dark raincoat, a black felt hat, and a profile. Of the other man she had had a better view. She supposed he could have been called quite goodlooking, but by the time you came to make a list of anyone's features, what was there left of that or of any other impression? The features themselves would sound so exactly like those of a great many other people. She had often wondered how a clever writer managed to convey the living presence of some character in a book. She had no such talent, and when she thought of herself trying to describe the man in the gallery all she could think of was a bare inventory—a drab raincoat as against the first man's dark one, height medium, age somewhere about thirty, hair neither fair nor dark, eyes neither grey nor blue, no beard or moustache to blur the line of the lips when he spoke. Of course she ought to have waited and tried to see where he went. But equally, of course, it wouldn't have been any good, because he would have soon found out that she was following him, and he would only have had to hail a taxi or walk into an hotel to get away from her. Detectives followed people, but she hadn't the least idea how they did it without being seen, and when she thought about the man seeing her and knowing that she was following him the tea-room floor began to shake under her just as the street had done. She took a sip of the strong tea and leaned back until the shaking stopped. Then she went on sipping, and when her cup was finished she had another. It would have been better to have had a pot of tea straight away, but all she could think of when she came into the shop was just "a nice cup of tea."

When she had finished the second cup she was feeling herself again. She really couldn't think how she had come to be so upset. She thought that she had been very stupid. What she would do now was to go back to the gallery and ask the attendant about the men. Even if they had left, he might know something about them. She paid her bill and walked back along the way that she had come.

When she came to the gallery she had to make it clear that she had no intention of paying a second time to go in. It went against her conscience to ask whether she had dropped a handkerchief on or near the seat from which she had contemplated Wilfrid's nasty picture, but it would have gone against it even more to pay a second entrance fee, a thing which would come under the heading of sinful waste.

Mr. Pegler said no, he hadn't seen any handkerchief.

"It was the next seat to where the two gentlemen were. About half an hour ago—I don't know if you noticed them."

Mr. Pegler was a little rosy-faced man with a flow of conversation. So far from resenting Miss Paine's hypothetical handkerchief, he welcomed it with enthusiasm.

"Now if that isn't a funny thing, your mentioning those two gentlemen, miss! Proper interested in you one of them was, and you can take it from me that's a fact."

Paulina had to take a grip on herself.

"Interested in me?"

"Well, miss, it was this way. One of them he got up and went out, and after a bit the other one got up too. Walking along looking at the pictures he was, and all of a sudden he come to the one that's marked "Sold," and the spit and image of you, miss, if you don't mind my saying so, and I couldn't help thinking whether it was done from you, and glad to get a chance to ask you if it was."

"Yes, it was done from me."

He beamed.

"I thought as much! The only thing—if you'll excuse me, miss—the gentleman as painted it, Mr. Moray, he was here a bit earlier on with the gentleman that's bought it. Well, what he said was that the lady he painted it from was deaf. Stone-deaf was what he said, and so be there was a good light, he said, no one would credit it, the way you could do this lip-reading—not unless they saw it. Well, if you'll pardon me, that's a thing that interests me a lot on account of my daughter's youngest. Shocking deaf she is and getting worse, and they said it would help her if she learnt this lip-reading, so when I seen you I thought I'd ask you about it, only you went out so sudden."

Paulina found herself embarked on advising Mr. Pegler about his grand-daughter. Oh, yes, of course the child must take up lip-reading, and at once—the sooner the better.

"It was much harder for me than it would be for a child. Children learn very quickly."

It was a little time before Mr. Pegler came back to the gentleman who had been so much interested, but he got there in the end.

"I took the liberty of telling him what Mr. Moray said about you not hearing anything but how quick you was with the lip-reading. 'What!' he said. 'You don't mean to say she could be standing over there'—and he points back to the seat what he'd been sitting on—'and that she could tell what you and me was talking about just by looking at us!' 'Well, sir,' I said, 'it's funny you should put it that way, for that's just the way Mr. Moray put it—him as painted the picture—when he was talking to the gentleman as bought it. Pointed to that very seat he did and said, "I give you my word," he said, "if she was there and we was here, and you was looking her way, she'd read the words off of your lips as fast as you said them." ' You wouldn't credit how interested he was, miss, when I told him that."

Paulina found no difficulty at all in believing him. She went out of the gallery and began to walk towards her bus stop. All the way home she was thinking what she had better do, and the more she thought about it, the more certain she was that she couldn't cope with it alone.

She came in at her front door just as David and Sally were going out. She thought it was as if they were in another world—a safe, pleasant one where young people could meet and be happy. It wasn't a world that had ever come her way, but she liked to think that Sally and David were in it. They went by her with a pleasant word, and then suddenly she had her hand on David Moray's arm and was speaking to him.

"It was so kind of your cousins the Charles Morays to ask me to their party the other day."

He said, "It wasn't kind of them at all. They wanted to meet you."

"Because of your picture?"

"No, because of you."

She felt herself flushing with pleasure. But she mustn't keep them—She said in a hurry.

"I was so much interested—there was someone I met there. I wonder if Mrs. Moray would think me troublesome if I were to ring up and ask her for the address. And I was wondering if by chance you could remember the number."

He said, "Four two's in a row and the same exchange as this. Would you like me to ring up for you?"

She was scrupulous.

"I mustn't delay you."

"It won't take a minute. We'll go back to Sally's room."

Margaret Moray was in. Her voice came pleasantly along the wire. David said,

"Miss Paine wants to speak to you. She'll say what she wants to, and I'll repeat your answers so that she can see them. Now, Miss Paine—"

Paulina took the receiver.

"Mrs. Moray, I wonder if you would be kind enough to give me the address of your friend Miss Maud Silver—"

4

Miss Silver was reading a letter from her niece Ethel Burkett, the wife of a bank manager in the Midlands. The subject of the letter was a distressing one, the foolish and frivolous conduct of Ethel's sister Gladys Robinson, who had taken the unjustifiable step of leaving an excellent husband whom she complained of finding dull.

"As if anyone in their senses expects their husband to be exciting!" wrote Mrs. Burkett. "And she doesn't say where she is, or what she is doing, so all we can hope and trust is that she is *alone*, and that she hasn't done anything which

Andrew would find it impossible to forgive. Because what is she going to live on!" There was a good deal more in this strain.

Laying Ethel's letter down on the left-hand side of her writing table, Miss Silver addressed herself to answering it in a neat legible hand.

The table stood out in the room by reason of its plainness, most of the other furniture being of the mid-Victorian period—chairs with curly arms and legs of yellow walnut and the wide spreading laps which had been made to accommodate the crinoline popularized by the Empress Eugenie; curtains and upholstery of the cheerful shade which used to be called peacock-blue; the carpet in the same tone with flowery wreaths; whilst looking down upon what might have been a contemporary scene were reproductions of the masterpieces of the same era—*The Stag At Bay*, the lovely nun of the St. Bartholomew massacre, and *Hope* with her bandaged eyes drooping gracefully over a darkened world.

Miss Silver suited her room. She had the old-fashioned and dated appearance of someone in the kind of family group which young people turn out to laugh at and exclaim over in the winter evenings. In any such picture she would unhesitatingly have been identified as the governess. She had, in fact, graduated into this branch of what she termed the scholastic profession when she left school, and for many years had no other expectation than that she would grow old in it and ultimately retire upon such a pittance as could be saved from her salary. The curious combination of circumstances always referred to by her as "providential" which led to her taking up instead the much more varied and lucrative occupation of a private enquiry agent now lay far behind her in the past. But though the profession had been thus left behind, the professional appearance remained and was an enduring asset. She could not only pass in a crowd, she could—which was much more useful—pass unregarded in a drawing-room. She could melt into the background, she was no check upon anybody's tongue, she could be, and very often was, ignored. She had a good deal of soft mousy hair with only a little grey in it. This she wore piled in a fringe above her forehead and plaited at the back, the whole very nearly controlled by an invisible net. She wore a dress of olive-green cashmere, black woollen stockings, and black glacé shoes. Her features were neat, her skin pale and clear, and her eyes of some indeterminate shade. She held her pen poised for a moment, and then wrote:

Dearest Ethel

I am indeed sorry that you have had this anxiety about Gladys, but let me hasten to relieve your mind. She has acted with inconsiderable folly, but she certainly has not eloped with anyone. She has merely quarrelled with Andrew and gone off to Southend with her friend Mrs. Farmer. You will remember that Andrew did not like her influence. Gladys has written to me and asked me for money to pay her hotel bill, which I am prepared to do provided she returns home before the end of the week. She is fortunate in having so long-suffering a husband.

Miss Silver had turned to the pleasanter topic of Ethel's three boys and of her little Josephine, now nearly eight years old and everybody's darling—a pretty, fair child, though at the moment going through a plainer stage owing to changing teeth.

She had written, "I really do not think the alteration in her looks should trouble you. Once the new teeth have settled down, her expression will, I am sure, be just as sweet as it was before," when she caught the sound of the front-door bell. Since she was expecting it, she laid a sheet of blotting paper over her letter and turned towards the door. It was opened by her faithful Emma, and Pauline Paine came into the room.

She was, as Margaret Moray had described her, good, solid and dependable in appearance. She was also uneasy and nervous. Most of the people who came into this room were that. In many cases the impulse which brought them there had expended itself and they desired nothing so much as to be somewhere else. Paulina did not go quite as far as this. She sat down in a chair with its back to the window, glad to be off her feet again.

Miss Silver took the chair on the other side of the hearth and reached for the flowered knitting-bag which lay on a small table beside her. She drew from it a partly completed baby shawl in a delicate shade of blue, but she did not immediately begin to knit. She was remembering that Miss Paine was stone-deaf, and she was much interested in the prospect of receiving a practical demonstration of the art of lip-reading. She said,

"We did meet at Mrs. Moray's a little while ago, did we not? I do not believe I heard your name then, but as soon as you came into the room I remembered meeting you. But on that occasion I had no idea that you were deaf. We conversed quite easily. What a wonderful thing lip-reading must be."

Paulina said gravely, "Yes, it is wonderful. You are very easy to read from. After I had talked to you Mrs. Moray told me about your work. She said you were a detective."

Miss Silver smiled.

"I prefer to call myself a private enquiry agent."

As she spoke she picked up the needles and began to knit in an easy, effortless manner. Paulina said,

"Mrs. Moray told me that you have helped a great many people."

"And do you feel that you are in need of help, Miss Paine?"

Paulina gave a short, quick nod.

"I think I may be. I think I've got to talk to someone—I don't think I can cope with it alone. So I thought if I came round straight away without losing any time—"

"There is something that has just occurred—something which troubles you?"

"Yes."

"And you would like to tell me about it?"

"Yes. I'm going to."

There was a pause. The room was quiet. Miss Silver knitted. The old-fashioned pictures looked down. Everything was very safe and peaceful and ordinary. Paulina Paine recalled a line which she could not place—"The world shut out, and peace shut in." It seemed a pity to break in upon it. Everything in her quieted. She said,

"I was in a picture gallery—one of those places where they have shows. It is run by Masters, the art dealers. I have let my top floor to a cousin of the Morays who is an artist. Well, he painted a picture of me and he called it *The Listener*. It is in this gallery, and it has been sold. A young cousin of mine, Wilfrid Gaunt, has two pictures there too. I thought I ought to go and see them, so this afternoon I did."

Miss Silver, looking across the cloud of pale blue wool

in her lap, saw the hand in the grey kid glove tighten upon the arm of the chair. The knuckles strained for a moment and then relaxed again. She said,

"Something happened?"

"Yes."

Paulina's sentences came short and jerky.

"There was a man on a seat at the end of the gallery. He had a catalogue. He was just sitting there. Another man came in. He looked at the pictures, and then he went and sat down on the same seat. After a little he turned round and spoke to the first man. I was on another seat quite a way off. I couldn't have heard what he said—no one could. But the light was good and he was facing me, and I could see what he was saying. I want to tell you about it—I've got to tell someone."

Miss Silver said clearly and firmly,

"What did he say?"

Paulina went on.

"He said, 'It's for tomorrow. The secretary leaves the bank with it at twelve noon. Nothing can be done whilst he is on the main road, but as soon as he turns into the lane, that will be the time. It should be quite easy. When I've got the stuff I meet you as arranged, and there we are.' He stopped there, and the other man said something. I could see the muscle moving in his cheek, but I couldn't see his lips. When he stopped, the first one said, 'I'm not taking any chances of being recognized, and that's final. Give me a clear stretch of the lane and no one on it to turn his head at a shot, and leave the rest to me.' The other man spoke again, and the first one said. 'I tell you I won't touch it on any other terms. This way it's a certainty.' The other man put up his hand with a catalogue in it and said something, and the first one said, 'Then there will be two of them for it, that's all,' and he laughed and got up and went over to look at one of the pictures. And I got up too and went away. I didn't know what to think, I didn't know what to do. I was afraid they would notice me. I went into a tea-shop and sat down. They were planning a robbery and a murder, and I felt I must do something to stop them. I felt better when I had had a cup of tea, and I went back to the gallery. Both the men had gone. I talked to old Mr. Pegler, the man in charge there. I said I thought I might have dropped a handkerchief near the seat where the two gentlemen were. He told me one of them had noticed my picture—it's a very good likeness. Mr. Pegler said he had told the gentleman about my being deaf and about the lip-reading. He said I wouldn't believe how interested he was."

Miss Silver was knitting quietly. She said,

"Did Mr. Pegler imply that this man had recognized you as the original of the picture?"

"I am sure he recognized me. He pointed to the seat on which he had been sitting, and he said, 'You don't mean to say she could be standing over there and she could tell just what we were saying by looking at us?' And Mr. Pegler said that he had heard Mr. Moray who had painted the picture put it that very way when he was talking to the gentleman who had bought it?"

"Mr. Moray's name was mentioned?"

"Yes, it was."

"But not your name?"

"No. It wouldn't be difficult for him to find it out if he wanted to."

Miss Silver supposed not. She said,

"You may have to tell this story to the police, but there is, of course, no means of identifying what was to be stolen, or in what locality the theft was to take place. Can you describe the two men?"

Paulina did her best. She had seen one of the men full-face, and the other in profile. One had had a drab raincoat, and the other a dark one. When she had described them, they sounded like any two men whom you would meet before you walked the length of any street in any part of London. All she could say was that she had seen them, that she remembered what she had seen, and that she would know them if she saw them again.

Miss Silver pulled on her pale blue ball.

"Miss Paine, do you think that you were followed after you left the gallery?"

"No—no—I don't think so. You see, I had gone away first. It was only afterwards that one of them saw my picture and Mr. Pegler told him about my being deaf and about the lip-reading."

"I see. And when you came here?"

Paulina looked at her oddly.

"Why do you ask that?"

"Why do you not answer what I asked you?"

"Because I'm not sure. The fact is, I'm not a nervous person, but I've behaved like one. I opened the front door to go out, and there was a taxi just beyond the Square with a man in it. He was just sitting there. I didn't like it. I went back into the house, and I got Mrs. Mount who has the basement flat to come up and telephone for a taxi for me."

"And did the other taxi follow you?"

"It came along after us. I think we lost it in the traffic, but I don't know. One taxi looks very like another, and I couldn't see the man's face."

Miss Silver said in a very thoughtful tone,

"Miss Paine, I think you should take your story to Scotland Yard."

But Paulina shook her head.

"There's nothing for the police to go on, is there? And you know how they would be about the lip-reading—they wouldn't believe it could be done, and they would just think I had been making it up. People do that sort of thing to get themselves noticed. And even if they believed me, what could they do?"

Miss Silver spoke firmly,

"Nevertheless it is your duty to tell them."

Paulina got to her feet.

"You have been very kind, but I think I have been foolish to speak of it at all, except that doing so has shown me how very little there is to go on. It is not like me, but I feel that in this case I have given way to a nervous impulse. I was startled, and I think perhaps I have made a mountain out of a molehill. The men may have been discussing the plot of a book or of a film. I may have been mistaken in a word or words which would alter the whole sense, and of course only one side of the conversation reached me."

The rapidity with which these phrases sprang to her lips surprised her. Whereas all her energies had been bent upon reaching Miss Silver, she now desired nothing so much as to take leave of her without being pushed or persuaded into going to the police.

But if Paulina was surprised, Miss Maud Silver was not. It was not the first time that she had encountered the reaction which follows upon the shifting of a burden. In such a case there is very often an immediate sense of relief and a lessened sense of the importance of what has been described. She did not feel that there was anything she could do about it. It was possible that Miss Paine might return. But she could not force her to go to the police, she could only once more and with the utmost gravity advise her to do so.

Paulina shook her head.

"Talking to you like this has done me good. It was most kind of you to see me. It is of course a professional visit, and you must let me know what I owe you."

"For advising you to go to the police? My dear Miss Paine, since I have done nothing more than that, you do not owe me anything at all. You will let me ring up for a taxi?"

But Paulina said no to that too. The evening was fine, her spirits had risen. She felt quite convinced that any idea that she might have been followed was a trick of the imagination. She said goodbye with a smile and went down the stairs and out into Marsham Street.

5

Miss Silver stood at the window and watched Paulina Paine until she was out of sight. This was quite soon, because she took the first turning to the left, which would bring her out upon a busy bus route. She was uneasy. She did not know when she had felt more uneasy about a case on which she could not really be said to be engaged. Miss Paine had reached out for help, refused to be guided by her advise, and then gone away, leaving nothing between them except the words which, once spoken, could not be taken back. She looked down at the people passing along the opposite pavement, half a dozen perhaps, who had gone by since Miss Paine had done so—an elderly man, a young one, two middle-aged women, a young girl, a man in a black felt hat. From opposite the side street a man crossed over. He turned off as Paulina Paine had done. So did the two women, the young girl, and the man in the black felt hat.

When she had watched them out of sight Miss Silver sat down at her writing-table. But she did not immediately go back to her interrupted letter. There was a moment when she picked up the pen she had laid aside to greet Miss Paine, but it was almost immediately set down again. A few moments passed during which she finally made up her mind to an unwonted course of conduct. A client's confidences were sacred, but in a case where a violent crime might be contemplated there must be an over-riding public duty. She put out her hand to the telephone, dialled Scotland Yard, and asked to speak to Chief Inspector Lamb.

They were old friends, and though he was sometimes conscious of a feeling of exasperation when he found her mixed up in a case, she enjoyed his most profound respect. As always, she was punctilious in her greetings and in enquiries after his family.

"Mrs. Lamb is well, I hope. And the daughters? Lily's little Ernest and the baby? They must be such a pleasure to you."

Lamb's daughters were his weakness. Lily was very happily married, and her children were the core of his heart. Even over his office line he could not resist the temptation to embark upon a fond anecdote or two. Had Miss Silver's interest been simulated, the temptation would not have existed. It was the genuine warmth with which she responded to his family news that made it irresistible.

She passed to his daughter Violet, a pretty girl with a habit of getting engaged to highly unsuitable young men, the more recent of whom had included a South American dance-band leader and a long-haired crank with an enthusiastic belief that only the British Navy, Army, and Air Force stood in the way of univeral brotherhood and perpetual peace. These two young men had almost brought the Chief Inspector to the point of manslaughter, from which only the calming influence of Mrs. Lamb and his other two daughters had restrained him. Miss Silver was relieved to hear that they had now faded from the scene, and that Violet's current boyfriend was an atom scientist.

"And what she sees in him, I don't know. Head full of figures and no thought for anything else. But Mother says not to worry, it won't last. There's one thing, Myrtle never gives us any trouble except that she thinks of nothing but her nursing, and we'd like to see her happy in a home of her own."

Appropriate and sympathetic comment having been made, Miss Silver came to the point.

"You are always so kind, Chief Inspector, so I hope you will forgive me for taking up your valuable time. The fact is, I have had a caller with a story which has left me uneasy, and I thought I should feel happier if I could pass it on to you."

He listened while she repeated what Miss Paine had told her. When she had finished he exhibited some of the scepticism that Paulina had anticipated.

"You're not asking me to believe that a couple of men would meet in a public gallery to discuss a robbery and a murder for anyone to hear!"

Miss Silver gave a gentle cough.

"That is the point, Chief Inspector. My caller's seat was too far removed from the men for them to be within earshot of her, and there was no one else in the gallery at the time. Also the two men were not together. They arrived separately, and to an ordinary observer would have appeared to be merely exchanging a few casual remarks about the pictures in front of them."

"You say she was too far off to have heard anything?"

"That is my information."

"And she asks you to believe that she can tell what a man is saying at such a distance by the movement of his lips?"

Miss Silver said steadily,

"She sat in my room and conversed with me as if she could hear every word I said."

Lamb's hearty laugh came to her along the line.

"And what makes you think that she didn't?"

"Mrs. Charles Moray told me that she was stone-deaf. Charles Moray's cousin, a young artist, rents a studio in her house."

He said gruffly,

"Well, well, it's all one. Seems to me a pretty fancy sort of thing, and nothing we can do about it. Suppose it's all genuine, or she thinks it is, what does it amount to? There isn't a clue to the men, and as she describes them you could pick up a dozen like them anywhere. There isn't a clue to the bank, or to the stuff that's being removed from it. A secretary is mentioned, but there isn't a clue to whose secretary he might be. How many banks do you suppose there are in London alone? And from what you've told me this one could be in Edinburgh, Glasgow, York, Leeds, Birmingham, Hull, Manchester, or any one of dozens of other places. No, no, I'd follow up anything if there was anything to follow, but there isn't. If you give me the address of the gallery, I'll send someone round to make enquiries about the two men who are said to have been there at—what time did you say?"

Miss Silver said,

"Just before five. But they were not known at the gallery. My informant enquired."

"Well, well, that's that, and nothing we can do about it. I'll be surprised if we hear anything further. But I'd better have that address."

Miss Silver gave it to him, after which he said goodbye and rang off. She had done what she could. She could neither do nor suggest anything more. She completed the letter which she had been writing to Ethel Burkett.

The next day was very fully occupied. She travelled down to Blackheath to see Andrew Robinson, the husband of her niece Gladys, and found that she would have her work cut out if a reconciliation was to be effected. Mr. Robinson was nearly twenty years older than his wife and had indulged her whims and condoned her extravagances for a very long time. Gladys was now over forty, and he expected a more reasonable standard of conduct and some peace and harmony in his home. But if this was not forthcoming, he contemplated a separation, and his income being no longer what it had been, the sum he was prepared to allocate to Gladys was one which would necessitate the strictest economy. Miss Silver returned home persuaded that the situation was indeed a serious one, and that Gladys must be made to realize the fact. She wrote a long letter to Ethel Burkett and another to Gladys herself. She wrote to Andrew Robinson.

Her mind, being thus taken up with family affairs, had neither the leisure nor the inclination to concern itself any further with the problem presented to her by Paulina Paine, yet waking suddenly and unexpectedly in the night, she found it vividly present. So much so that it was a long time before she fell asleep again.

6

Arthur Hughes came down the steps of the County Bank at Ledlington, a goodlooking young man and very well aware of the fact. If Lucius Bellingdon was dispensing with his services as assistant secretary after a comparatively short trial, it did not occur to him for a moment that there could be any reason for this beyond the carping disapproval with which Lucius was practically bound to regard a penniless young man who had found favour in his daughter's eyes. He would have to come round of course. The irate parent, stock figure of countless romances and now in these modern times a mere shadow of his former self, always did come round in the end. He would be a laughing stock if he didn't. Besides, even if the worst came to the worst, Moira had money of her own, settled on her when she married Oliver Herne.

Arthur frowned as he walked in the direction of the Market Square, where he had parked the car. He had known Olly Herne, and he hadn't liked him at all. He had actually been at his wedding when he married Moira Bellingdon. He hadn't minded then because he wasn't in love with Moira at that time. There had been a girl called Kitty. She had married someone else, and he could hardly remember what she looked like. And after her there was Mary, and Judy, and Ann, and quite a lot more. But none of them was like Moira. She did something to you, he didn't quite know what. He used to think of her as cold—icy and unapproachable. And then quite suddenly she wasn't icy any more, she was a flame in the blood. Even if she hadn't had a penny . . . No, of course that was nonsense—you can't get married without money. Anyhow it would be all right because she had her settlement. And she might say what she liked, she couldn't very well go back on him now, not whilst he had her letters and those photographs. He wouldn't have to use them of course. It would be quite enough to let her know that he hadn't burned them after all—and a lover's excuse ready to his hand, *"Darling, I just couldn't bear to part with them."* It was all perfectly simple, safe, and water-tight. But the time had come to get a move on. Once they were married his position would be secure. And Lucius Bellingdon would come round. You didn't cut your only child out of your will—not nowadays.

All the time he was walking down to the car and getting into it and starting up he went on thinking about Moira Herne. It pleased him immensely to be taking her the Queen's Necklace. A bit of luck that old Garratt should have had one of his attacks and not have been able to go for it. He had a pleasant picture of himself throwing the sealed packet into Moira's lap and saying, "There you are!" After which she would open the packet and take out the necklace and put it on and he would kiss her. The fact that this pleasant daydream deviated in every possible particular from what was in the very least bit likely to happen had no power to detract from the pleasure it gave him.

He extricated himself from the crowded marketplace as skillfully as if his mind had really been on what he was doing, threaded one of the two narrow passages which connected the Square with the High Street, and began to move with its stream of traffic at the snail's pace dictated by an absence of width and the presence of two famous bottlenecks. Emerging upon the outskirts of the town where the houses were set far enough apart to allow of a wider road and more accommodation for the traffic, he was able to pick up speed. He did not really want to go very fast. The morning was a pleasant one. There was a hint of spring in the air. His fancy occupied itself with thoughts appropriate to the season. When eventually he turned into Cranberry Lane they distracted his mind from the fact that another car was doing the same thing. There was no reason why it should not do so. He just hadn't noticed it, nor had he been aware that it had followed him out of Ledlington.

Cranberry Lane has the twists and turns which are a common feature of the English by-way. When it twisted, the car that followed him would be out of sight. After one such turn the driver accelerated and came up with him. Before he realized that anything was going to happen the two cars were abreast and he was being forced off the road. His near front wheel bumped down into the ditch.

He braked, ran scraping along the hedge, and came to a stop. As he turned, between fear and anger, he saw the other car at a standstill too and the driver already out. He had time to curse, to stop half way, to say "You!" and to see the revolver in the gloved hand. After that there was no more time. He may have heard the shot which killed him, or he may not. Evidence on this point is not available.

7

Of the two newspapers to which Miss Silver subscribed she was in the habit of glancing through the one addicted to headlines and pictures at the breakfast-table, whilst reserving the perusal of *The Times* for a more leisured hour. On the morning following her visit to Blackheath she had no more than sat down and reached for the former than there stared at her from the front page a heading which instantly fixed her attention. It ran:

DARING JEWEL ROBBERY
THE BELLINGDON NECKLACE STOLEN
SECRETARY FOUND SHOT

Like Sally Foster, Miss Silver had heard of the Bellingdon necklace. She had even read the same article about it and its conjectured history that Sally had. She was aware of the intention ascribed to Lucius Bellingdon of presenting it to his daughter in order that she might wear it at the fancy dress ball he was proposing to give. Her eye travelled over a repetition of these particulars and came back to all that seemed to be known about the robbery. It was not much. The necklace had been in safe keeping at the County Bank in Ledlington. Mr. Bellingdon, who had a large account there, had written to say that his secretary, Hubert Garratt, would call for it at 12 noon on the 14th instant. The secretary duly provided with a written authorization, arrived punctually, signed for the valuable package, and left again by car, driving himself. That was the last time he was seen alive. The car was found twenty minutes later on the grass verge of a turning off the London road with the secretary dead at the wheel and the necklace gone. The turning, an unfrequented one, would be a short cut to Merefields, Lucius Bellingdon's country home.

There were photographs of Merefields, of Mr. Bellingdon, a gentleman of dominating appearance with a jutting chin, his daughter Mrs. Herne, and the unfortunate secretary.

Miss Silver read all that there was to read, and had no more than come to the end of it, when the telephone bell rang. It was not with any great surprise that she recognized the voice of Detective Inspector Frank Abbott. Since he announced himself in this manner instead of his off-duty "This is Frank," she was instantly aware that he was ringing up from Scotland Yard. She said,

"Miss Silver speaking."

His voice came back with a touch of formality quite noticeably absent from their private relationship. There was between them a strong tie of affection, and on his side a high degree of respect which did not prevent him from regarding her idiosyncrasies with appreciation and enjoyment. She was, he considered, a period piece, from her Edwardian hair style with its controlling net to her beaded shoes of a smaller size than is usual today, and from her admiration for the late Lord Tennyson to the stock of elevated maxims which he was in the habit of referring to as Maudie's Moralities. What he said now was,

"I suppose you have seen the paper?"

The gravity of her reply informed him that he need not particularize any special item of news. He said,

"The Chief would be glad if you could make it convenient to come round to the Yard. It is with reference to the conversation you had with him the day before yesterday. He would be glad to have a talk with you."

About three-quarters of an hour later she was being ushered into the Chief Inspector's room. It was by no means the first conversation she had had with him there, but as he rose from behind his desk to greet her, she thought he appeared to be vexed and burdened beyond his wont. With the briefest preliminaries he sat down again, filling his chair squarely—a big man of country stock with a florid face and strong dark hair which only the most rigorous cut prevented from curling.

Frank Abbott, standing on the hearth, presented as great a contrast as was possible—tall, slim, elegant, with a long bony nose, fair hair mirror-smooth, and the light blue eyes which were capable of so icy a stare. Miss Silver was one of the people for whom they could soften. They did so now.

She had taken the chair which had been set for her on the far side of the writing-table. She wore the black cloth coat which had seen so many years of service and, the wind being exceptionally cold, an antique tippet of faded yellowish fur. Her hat, no more than two years old, was of black felt renovated last autumn, the trimming being now of black ribbon arranged in loops, with a bunch of violets added recently to mark the approach of spring. She wore black kid gloves and carried a well-worn handbag.

Lamb sat back in his chair and said in a voice that kept its country sound,

"Well, Miss Silver, I suppose you can guess why I wanted to see you."

She inclined her head.

"I have read the account in the paper."

He lifted a big square hand and let it fall again upon his knee.

"And I suppose you've been saying to yourself, 'Well, I told them, and they wouldn't take any notice.' That's what you've been doing, isn't it?"

She said with a touch of primness, "I hope I should not be so unjust."

His eyes, irreverently compared by Frank Abbott to the larger and more bulging type of peppermint bullseye, were turned upon her for a moment.

"Well, I ask you! Ledlington! Who'd have thought of that? You bring me a mare's nest that might have been anywhere in the kingdom! I believe I mentioned a good few places on the telephone when we were talking—and not a clue to which of them would be the least unlikely, or what any of it was about anyhow! And then it turns out to be Ledlington and the Bellingdon necklace! Of course if we'd known what was going to be stolen—" He broke off with a short laugh. "Pity your Miss Paine didn't get hold of something useful whilst she was about it!"

Miss Silver looked at him in a manner which reminded Frank Abbott of a bird with its eye upon a worm. There was nothing contemptuous about it, it was just bright and enquiring.

"I do not remember that I mentioned my caller's name."

"No, you didn't. Careful not to, weren't you? But you

did give me the address of the gallery, and you did tell me there was a portrait of her hanging there, that the artist rented her top floor, and that his name was Moray. And no need for anyone to be Sherlock Holmes for Frank here to get his address and go round and see him. And when you hear a couple of things he walked into, I'm expecting you to have a bit of a shock. There—it's your pigeon, Frank. You'd better get along with it and tell her."

Miss Silver transferred her attention to Inspector Abbott.

"Well," he said, "the gallery identified the picture for me as soon as I said it was a portrait of a deaf woman by an artist called Moray. And a very good portrait I thought it was—streets ahead of most of the other stuff they'd got there, so I wasn't surprised to see that it was marked 'Sold.' What did surprise me, and what's going to surprise you, is the name of the man who bought it. There was an old chap called Pegler taking the entrance money, very friendly and chatty and tumbling over himself to link the picture up with this morning's smash-hit headlines. Because it seems that the man who bought Miss Paine's portrait is no other than Lucius Bellingdon, 'And you'll have heard all about his having his diamond necklace stolen and his secretary shot in the papers this morning,' as Mr. Pegler put it."

Miss Silver said, "Dear me!"

"He had quite a lot to say about Miss Paine one way and another. Told me how she'd been in to see her picture, and how she 'did that lip-reading a treat,' and had advised him about his grand-daughter who was going deaf. He said she was a very nice lady and a lot of people were ever so interested when he told them how good she was at the lip-reading. 'They wouldn't hardly credit it,' he said. So then he told me about the gentleman that was in there the same time as she was, and how he wouldn't believe she could tell what anyone was saying—not the length of the gallery—'but I told him she could, because I'd heard Mr. Moray use those very words, and the gentleman went away and he didn't look any too pleased.' I asked him if he would know the man again, and he said he would, but when it came to a description it was the sort where there's nothing to take hold of. He wouldn't go so far as to say the gentleman was tall, nor yet short—he wasn't to say fair-complexioned, nor you wouldn't say he was dark, but he had a black felt hat and a drab raincoat." Here Inspector

Abbott broke off and addressed his Chief. "I don't suppose we have any statistics as to how many men in Greater London would have been wearing black hats and drab raincoats on that particular day—"

Lamb said curtly, "Get on with your story!"

Frank obliged.

"I got Moray's address, which is 13 Porlock Square, and I went down there. The woman who came to the door said she lodged in the basement, and when I asked for Miss Paine she got out her handkerchief and said Miss Paine had been run over by a bus coming home the day before yesterday evening, and they took her off to the hospital but she never came round."

8

The news was a shock. Miss Silver felt it as such. She recalled the moment when Paulina Paine had terminated their interview and gone out to meet her death. Could she have pressed her more strongly to go to the police? She was unable to believe that it would have made any difference. Could she have insisted on calling for a taxi? She did not know. Would insistence have been of any use? If the knowledge accidentally acquired by Miss Paine was so dangerous as to warrant murder, there were other times and other places where this might have been accomplished. She remained silent for a little before saying,

"I was most uneasy. I feel that I should not have let her go."

Lamb said heartily,

"And that, if you will allow me to say so, is nonsense. You couldn't possibly have expected the woman to be murdered—if she was murdered, which to my mind is a thing there is no manner of proof about."

"She had some idea that she might have been followed on her way to me. There was a man in a taxi at the end of the street. She was sufficiently alarmed to turn back and ask one of her tenants to call a taxi for herself. She was not sure of being followed after that. She says the taxi came after them, but she thinks they lost it in the traffic. It looks as if they had not done so. I urged her to let me call a taxi when she took leave of me, but she refused, saying that she thought she had given way to a nervous impulse and made a mountain out of a molehill. I did not feel easy about it, but I let her go."

Frank Abbott said, "You can't possibly blame yourself," to which she replied soberly, "I suppose not. Yet it is difficult not to feel that she came to me for help and that I failed her."

Lamb said in his most decided voice,

"If she had taken your advice and come to us she would have been safe."

"Are you sure that you would have taken her story so seriously as to give her police protection? If her death was determined on, nothing less would have saved her."

He frowned.

"I'm not ready to say that her death wasn't an accident. She could have been mooning along with her head full of this story, and being deaf she wouldn't hear a bus coming. We've asked for details of the accident, but we haven't had them yet. What beats me is why should they go to the trouble of murdering her? What, after all, did she hear, or lip-read or whatever you call it? Nothing that's the least bit of use to us as far as I can see, or the least bit of danger to them."

Miss Silver looked at him very directly.

"There was the chance that she might recognize the man who spoke."

Lamb laughed.

"My dear Miss Silver—what a chance! Even if she connected what he said with the theft of the Bellingdon necklace, what sort of odds were there against her ever coming across him again?"

She said gravely,

"I do not know. They may have been less than we imagine. In this connection, one thing she reported him as saying has remained in my mind."

"And what was that?"

"It was when he was speaking of the robbery, and what he said was this. 'I won't take any chances of being recognized, and that's final.' From which I infer that he was someone whom the secretary might recognize."

Lamb said with impatience,

"He'd have taken precautions against that."

"So strong a precaution as the murder of the person he feared might recognize him?"

Lamb said impatiently,

"You say he was planning a murder?"

"What else, Chief Inspector, when he said that he was not taking any chances of being recognized, and that all he wanted was a clear stretch of road where no one would turn his head at a shot! There may have been a protest and then the first man said, 'I tell you I won't touch it on any other terms. This way it's a certainty.'"

Frank Abbott said, "Now I wonder if this man really said certainty. If we knew that, it would help to place him, because the ordinary crook would almost certainly have said cert."

Miss Silver gave a slight reproving cough.

"I am repeating Miss Paine's own words."

Lamb leaned forward.

"Yes, yes, we know that you can be trusted to be accurate. But Frank has got a point there, you know. Most men, let alone crooks, would have made it cert. Pity we can't ask Miss Paine whether she prettied it up, but there it is! What would she be likely to say herself? I mean, what was her own way of speaking—schoolmarmish, or plain everyday?"

In the way of business Miss Silver was not apt to take offence. She let the derogatory "schoolmarm" pass.

"Miss Paine was a plain, downright person, and that was the way she spoke. I think she was repeating to me what she believed herself to have read."

"You mean she might have mistaken the word?"

"It would be possible that she might have completed it."

Lamb said,

"Making cert into certainty? Well, there's no means of knowing one way or the other that I can see, and we're getting off the track. Seems to me we were talking about what precautions the murderer would have taken against being recognized. You take what Miss Paine got as meaning that he was planning murder as a precaution. At a guess I should have said he'd have used a motorbike for the job. There's no safer disguise than the goggles and helmet—in fact the whole rig-out."

Miss Silver's features expressed a mild firmness. She said,

"He may have done so. Yet he was still afraid of being

recognized and was prepared to shoot the secretary to avoid any risk of it. In my opinion this may be a valuable clue. Such a strong apprehension that he might be recognized does to my mind suggest that the murderer was someone in Mr. Bellingdon's immediate circle. He certainly had inside knowledge of just how and when the necklace would be transferred from the bank."

"Well, Ledshire have asked us to come in on the job, and Frank will be going down to Merefields. By the way, Mr. Bellingdon will be in town this afternoon. He wants to call and see you. He'll be coming here first. Would four o'clock suit? He wants to have all that lip-reading business first-hand from yourself. I think he finds it a bit difficult to swallow."

His tone informed her that the interview was at an end. She rose to her feet.

"Four o'clock will be quite convenient, Chief Inspector."

9

Lucius Bellingdon was quite a personage. Even in a crowd he was liable to be remarked. In Miss Silver's Victorian sitting-room his big frame and massive features, the jutting chin of the photograph, and an eye decidedly competent to threaten and command, might have been considered overpowering. Miss Silver was interested, but she was not overpowered. She remembered fantastic stories about Mr. Bellingdon's rise to fame and fortune, she remembered that she had listened to them with scepticism. Now, in his presence, she found them less difficult to entertain. He occupied the largest of her walnut chairs, and occupied it as if it were his own. He wore a town suit, but he looked like a man who spent a good deal of time in the open air. His dark skin had a healthy tan and his eyes were bright. He might easily have been credited with ten years less than the fifty-two which the reference-books accorded him. He leaned forward with a hand on his knee, a strong hand admirably kept, and said in a voice not loud but full of resonance,

"Now do you mind just repeating what Miss Paine told you she—well, I don't know how to put it, but I suppose I had better say—read. I take it you are convinced that she definitely could and did read what was being said from the motion of the lips. It is a point upon which I have felt some doubt."

Miss Silver was knitting. The needles moved rhythmically above the pale blue wool in her lap. She said,

"I met her first in a crowded drawing-room. I had talked to her for half an hour without experiencing any difficulty before someone informed me that she was completely deaf. When she came to see me here it was just the same. She did not appear to be at a loss for a moment."

"The police say they have made enquiries and there seems to be no doubt that she really was deaf, and that she had acquired great proficiency in this lip-reading. So I suppose I must accept the fact that she could see what a man was saying thirty or forty feet away?"

Miss Silver inclined her head.

"Yes, I think you must accept that, Mr. Bellingdon. In any art the performance of an expert must seem surprising."

Lucius Bellingdon laughed.

"You used to teach, didn't you? When you said that, I felt as if I were back at school again."

She gave him the warm smile which had so often won her both confidences and hearts, and said,

"Everything seems difficult until you know how to do it, does it not?"

He nodded.

"True enough. Well now, we'll take it that Miss Paulina Paine really sat in the Masters galleries and watched two men on a seat about thirty-five feet away. One came in after the other, looked at some of the pictures, and then sat down. After a bit he turned his head and spoke. Now this is where you take over. I want you to repeat what Miss Paine told you she had read from his lips, word for word just as she said it."

Miss Silver rested her hands upon the cloud of blue wool in her lap. In her mind she reverted to the picture of Paulina Paine sitting there across the hearth from her and speaking. Her own features took on a listening look as she repeated what had come to her in those short jerky sentences.

"These were her words, Mr. Bellingdon—'It's for tomorrow. The secretary leaves the bank with it at twelve noon. Nothing can be done whilst he is on the main road, but as soon as he turns into the lane, that will be the time. It should be quite easy. When I've got the stuff I meet you as arranged, and there we are.' She said he stopped there, and the other man said something. She could see the muscle moving in his cheek, but she couldn't see his lips. When he stopped, the first one said, 'I'm not taking any chances of being recognized, and that's final. Give me a clear stretch of the lane, and no one on it to turn his head at a shot, and leave the rest to me.' The other man spoke again, and the first one said, 'I tell you I won't touch it on any other terms. This way it's a certainty.' The other man put up his hand with a catalogue in it and said something, and the first one said, 'Then there will be two of them for it, that's all!' and he laughed and got up and went over to look at one of the pictures."

Lucius Bellingdon had a retentive memory. Scotland Yard had furnished him with a copy of Miss Silver's account of her interview with Paulina Paine. He remembered it perfectly. He had just listened to a repetition of this account from her own lips. To the best of his belief and recollection it had not varied by so much as a single word. He said,

"The second man—the one who was turned away from Miss Paine—she didn't get what he said. If you had to make a guess at filling in those gaps when he was speaking, what sort of guess would you make?"

She was knitting again easily and fast, her eyes not on the work but on his face.

"I suppose that on the occasion when the first man had spoken of a shot we may presume the other to have made some protest or objection. This would fit in with the first one's reply that he would not touch the affair on any other terms, but that this way it was a certainty."

"He said certainty—not cert?"

"The Chief Inspector raised that point. I agree that it is an important one and might afford a possible clue to the man's identity. I can only say that the word as repeated by Miss Paine was certainty."

Bellingdon nodded.

"And the other gap—how would you fill that? The one

which the first man came in on with his 'Then there will be two of them for it, that's all!' What do you make of that?"

Miss Silver said soberly,

"I think there can be no doubt that the other man had raised the question as to what was to be done should there be a second person in the car. It is, I think, the only explanation which would fit in with the callous response. Had there been such a second person, there would no doubt have been a second murder."

"Not much doubt about that, I should say. Now about this poor woman. Did she run into an accident, or was she murdered too? Just go over all that about her thinking she might have been followed, will you? They showed me your statement at the Yard, but what a thing looks like in cold black and white, and what it sounds like when you hear it, are two different things. Which is why I wanted to see you for myself."

Miss Silver said,

"I can repeat Miss Paine's words, and I can undertake to be accurate in repeating them. What I cannot do is to reproduce her voice, her manner, her expression. I can only endeavour to convey the impression that they left on me."

Lucius Bellingdon was becoming increasingly aware of the impression that Miss Silver herself was making. Scrupulous accuracy, a temperate judgment, considerable powers of observation—of these she was giving him proof. But above and beyond these qualities he was aware of a poised and keen intelligence. It was a thing which he respected above everything else, and he had seldom been more instantly aware of it.

He said, "Just give me as much as you can," and listened attentively to the repetition of Paulina Paine's story about a taxi which had waited just beyond the Square and been lost sight of in the traffic.

"She was sufficiently alarmed to go back into the house and take a taxi herself instead of walking as she had intended. She left no doubt in my mind that her experience in the gallery had been a very severe shock. She undoubtedly believed that she had become cognizant of a plot which involved robbery and murder, and the fact that one of the persons concerned in this plot had subsequently become aware of her deafness and her proficiency in lip-reading could not fail to intensify that shock. She began to fear that she might be traced and followed. Such a course would have been perfectly possible if this man had really believed her to be in possession of the highly incriminating remarks which he had made in the gallery. Do you suppose he would have hesitated over silencing her or lost any time in doing so?"

"I don't suppose he would."

Miss Silver continued to knit and to speak.

"When Miss Paine came to see me she was a badly shaken woman, but she was, I believe, of a very courageous and resolute disposition and she possessed a strong vein of common sense. As soon as she had relieved her mind by telling me of her experience she returned to her normal condition. She was able to dismiss the fear that she might have been followed, and to consider the impulse which had brought her to me as a trick of the nerves. She would not allow me to send for a taxi, and I am sure that when she left this room she had no idea of the possibility that her life might be in danger."

"And you think it was?"

She gave him a very direct look.

"What do you think yourself, Mr. Bellingdon?"

He lifted a hand and let it fall again.

"No proof—probably never will be. One has one's own ideas—" Then, with a change of manner, "And now to business."

She was loosening some strands of the pale blue wool. Her "Yes?" held a question.

With the change in his manner there had come also a change of position. He sat up straight and said,

"I am informed that you undertake private enquiries, and that you are extremely efficient and discreet. Chief Inspector Lamb tells me that you have often been of considerable help to the police."

He received an impression that the distance between them had somehow been increased. She gave a slight formal cough and said,

"The Chief Inspector is very kind."

In the midst of his serious preoccupation Bellingdon experienced a twinge of amusement. He had not got where he was without certain powers of discernment. He was aware that he had been tactless, and that the Chief Inspector was considered to have presumed. He allowed his voice to become a little warmer than it would have been over an ordinary business deal.

"I should think myself very fortunate if I could persuade you to give me your professional help in this matter. You see, there are aspects to which I do not really wish to invite the attention of the police. There are, in fact, points which they couldn't possibly handle."

Miss Silver said primly, "I could not undertake to keep anything from the police in a case of so much gravity."

"Quite so. Perhaps you will let me explain what is in my mind. I think you are too acute an observer not to have been struck by the stress which the murderer placed upon the danger of his being recognized. He said he wasn't taking any chances of it, and he was prepared to do murder rather than run any risk in that direction. Well, nobody wants to be recognized when he is committing an armed robbery, but a turned-up collar and a turned-down hat with a muffler over the lower part of the face would mess up any casual description. Now did Miss Paine describe him to you?"

"She did. But I am afraid there is not very much to be made of the description. She was a plain, downright person, and her mind was taken up with the shock she had received and the knowledge which she believed herself to have acquired. In these circumstances, her description did not go beyond the fact that the man wore a drab raincoat, that he was somewhere about thirty, and that he was of average height and complexion. The caretaker at the gallery does not seem able to add anything to this, though he appears to have had some conversation with him—and, significantly enough, upon the subject of Miss Paine's portrait, which I understand you have purchased. He recognized it, and most unfortunately the caretaker mentioned both her deafness and her proficiency in lip-reading."

"He recognized Miss Paine?"

"As the woman who had been looking in his direction when he made what he must have remembered as some highly compromising remarks. They could not have been overheard at the distance, but Miss Paine's lip-reading must have suggested a dangerous possibility. We do not know, and can only surmise, the lengths to which such a conclusion might have carried him. Inspector Abbott did go round to the gallery to see whether anything could be added to Miss Paine's description of the man she had watched."

Bellingdon said,

"Yes, I believe he did. As a matter of fact, I went round myself. Pegler is a nice old boy. I had met him, and I thought I'd like a word or two with him direct. He remembers seeing two men on the seat, and he didn't think they had anything to do with one another—says they came separately and left separately. That is all he does seem to have noticed about the one in the dark raincoat, but he remembers the other one stopping and talking about Miss Paine's portrait. By the way, Pegler says she came back afterwards and he told her how interested this man had been about her picture, and her being deaf, and the lip-reading. And he said she looked as if he had said something that upset her, and he hoped she didn't think he had taken a liberty."

Miss Silver said, "She had reason to be upset."

Bellingdon nodded.

"Well, to get back to this man and his description. I don't think Pegler is any help. He said he was quite a pleasant gentleman—and that was about all there was to it. Height? 'A bit taller than me, sir. At least that is what I should say.' Fair or dark? 'Nothing that you would notice either way.' Colour of his eyes? 'Well, I couldn't really say, sir.' And when you put all that together you've got something that would fit any man that wasn't extra tall or short, or that hadn't got red hair, or a beard, or a moustache, or something that stuck out so that you couldn't miss it."

Miss Silver agreed. Bellingdon went on.

"So we get back to the murderer. Why was he so much afraid of being identified that he must do murder? As the Chief Inspector has suggested, a motor-cyclist's cap and goggles would flummox anyone who wasn't an intimate. There you have it, Miss Silver—he wouldn't trust any disguise to shield him from the man he was going to rob. Perhaps it was his voice that would have given him away—voices are very individual. I don't know, but there must have been some reason why he preferred what he called a certainty and was perfectly prepared to shoot two people if there had been two in the car. There is another reason why I am forced to believe him to have been in close touch with my family circle. It was only in that circle that anyone knew when the bank would be handing over the necklace. I suppose you have heard about the necklace?"

She turned the soft mass of wool upon her lap. The

delicate fern pattern displayed its fronds for a moment and then fell lightly together again.

"Yes, Mr. Bellingdon, I have read about the necklace. An interesting and well-written account of a beautiful and valuable piece."

He gave a short grim laugh.

"A paste copy would be as beautiful, and no one would do murder for it. I say that to myself, and I've said it to my daughter, but all the time there's something in me that won't tolerate a fake."

Miss Silver looked up brightly.

"That is because it carries with it the suggestion of fraud. But if you call it a copy or let it stand on its own merits of design and craftsmanship, the stigma vanishes."

He shook his head.

"If I can't have a Rembrandt I don't want a copy. Not rational, but there are plenty of us all in the same boat. Which is why the price of the real thing keeps on going up, and why murder was done for my necklace in Cranberry Lane a couple of days ago. Well, we've run off the rails. I was saying there had got to be a contact with my family circle, so I had better tell you something more about it. To start with, I am a widower, and I have a daughter—twenty-four last birthday—married a couple of years ago, not exactly against my will, but certainly against my wish. Nothing much against him—nothing much to him. Rackety young fellow whose idea of amusing himself was to drive as near a hundred miles an hour as his car would let him, and when he wasn't doing that to spend as much money as possible in the shortest possible time. He finished up by crashing over a precipice in the Austrian Tyrol and leaving Moira a widow just about the time she was beginning to think she'd have done better to take my advice. Well, there she is—Moira Herne."

Miss Silver said, "Excuse me, Mr. Bellingdon—" She went over to the writing-table, took from a drawer a bright blue exercise-book and a neatly pointed pencil, and came back to her chair. Her knitting laid aside for the moment, she headed a page with the words The Bellingdon Necklace, placed Moira Herne's name on the left-hand side of the next line, and entered the particulars which Mr. Bellingdon had just imparted. When this had been done she said "Yes?" in an interrogative manner and waited for him to go on.

He said abruptly, "I have a service flat in town, but my home is at Merefields near Ledlington. Cranberry Lane is a short cut to it from the London road. It is a comfortable old-fashioned house, and I am lucky in having a good staff. The butler and cook have been with me for twenty years. They are husband and wife. The name is Hilton."

Miss Silver wrote it down.

"Then there's my secretary, Hubert Garratt. He has been in my employment for ten years, but I have actually known him for a great deal longer than that."

Miss Silver held her pencil suspended.

"He is not dead."

"The shot was not a fatal one?"

"Oh, yes, it was fatal all right. The person who was shot was not Hubert Garratt."

"The papers—"

"The papers had got hold of the wrong end of the stick. What information they had was correct, but it didn't go far enough—and don't bother about my mixing my metaphors, because I've never been able to worry about that. I was earning my living when I was fourteen, and the books I bothered with were the ones that were going to help me to earn it. But to come back to Hubert Garratt. I wrote and told the bank he'd be fetching the necklace at twelve noon on Tuesday. Now the people who knew that were myself and the bank, Hubert Garratt, my daughter, and two other people. Early on Tuesday morning I was told that Garratt was ill. Since the war he has a tendency to asthma. I went to see him, and found him quite disabled, and told him he wasn't to attempt to go for the necklace. I rang up the bank, spoke to the manager, and told him there was a change and I was sending Garratt's assistant, a young fellow called Arthur Hughes. The manager took the precaution of ringing off and then ringing me back, and I gave him Arthur's description and said he would show a letter from me naming him as Garratt's substitute. Well, that all went off without a hitch. Arthur left the bank with the necklace, but he was shot dead in Cranberry Lane."

Miss Silver confided these details to the blue exercise-book. Bellingdon watched her with an odd look upon his face. The pale blue knitting and the bright blue book, the pencil, the hair-net, the brooch which fastened the front of her olive-green cashmere, a rose carved out of black bog-oak with an Irish pearl at its heart, all combined to make as unlikely a picture of a private detective as he could well imagine. He thought he could transplant her to Merefields without there being the slightest risk of her being taken for one.

When she had finished writing she looked up.

"And the other two people who were aware that the necklace was being fetched—was Mr. Hughes one of them?"

"Well, no, he wasn't. As far as I know, he knew nothing about the plan until I called him in and told him he would have to go to the bank for me instead of Garratt."

"You say as far as you know, Mr. Bellingdon."

"Oh, that? It meant nothing. Garratt said he didn't mention it, and no one else would."

"And the other two people were?"

He made a mental note that she could be pertinacious.

"One of them is a guest in the house, and the other—there could be no possible connection."

Miss Silver gave a gentle cough.

"If I am to help you, Mr. Bellingdon, it would be better that I should have all the facts. As Lord Tennyson so wisely says, 'So trust me not at all or all in all.' "

"Does he? Well, it might do with some people, but I wouldn't like to say it would answer in every case. Anyhow there isn't any question about trusting here. The two people are my late wife's cousin, Elaine Bray—Miss Bray, who is kind enough to run Merefields for me—and Mrs. Scott who is a guest in the house."

Miss Silver remained in an attentive attitude. Without so much as a word or a look it was conveyed to Lucius Bellingdon that something further was expected. There are times when silence can be more particular than speech. Since the last thing he desired was any particularity in either of these two cases, he yielded the point with a trace of stubborn amusement.

"Miss Bray took charge of my daughter and of the management of the house when my wife died. She had been living with us for some years as my wife was not strong. I owe her a good deal. Mrs. Scott—" he tried, with what success he was not certain, to keep his voice and manner as indifferent as might be—"Mrs. Scott is, as I said, a guest and close personal friend."

Miss Silver wrote these things down. She also made a mental note that Mr. Bellingdon felt himself to be under an obligation to his late wife's cousin, and that it was something of a burden to him. In the case of Mrs. Scott she had no difficulty in discerning a warmer feeling and the fact that he did not desire this feeling to appear. She wrote in her book, and heard him say with a note of relief in his voice,

"Well, I think that is all. There is a gardener and his wife—she helps in the house—and there is a woman and a couple of girls who come in by the day from the village, but they could have had no knowledge of how or when I should be getting the diamonds out of the bank."

Miss Silver reflected that this was what was invariably said whenever an important leakage of information occurred. No matter how completely the event would prove him wrong, the person concerned invariably expressed entire confidence in those surrounding him and was prepared to dogmatize on the question of there being no possible way in which a leakage could have taken place. She picked up her knitting, drew on the blue wool, and said,

"Mr. Bellingdon, impossibilites do not occur. You will not ask me to believe that they do. This robbery and the resultant murder was no chance affair. It was very carefully planned, and every detail of the proposed transfer of the necklace was known to the people who planned it some nineteen hours before the crime took place. This is not in dispute. If the leakage did not occur in your own immediate circle, then it must have occurred at the bank. When you first notified them that you would be withdrawing the necklace, did you write, or did you telephone?"

"I wrote to the manager. You are thinking that a telephone conversation might have been overheard?"

"It had occurred to me."

He shook his head.

"There was no telephone communication until the Tuesday morning, when I rang up to say that Garratt was ill and that Arthur Hughes would be acting for him. The leakage had already occurred—at least on the previous day."

Miss Silver's needles clicked.

"That would not preclude a leakage from the bank. To whom did the manager either pass your letter or speak of the matter?"

"I took that up with him personally, and of course the police have done so too. He says nobody saw the letter except himself, and he locked it away carefully and only gave the necessary instructions when young Hughes arrived at the bank with my second letter next day. He is quite definite on these points."

Miss Silver observed a meditative silence. There was nothing to be gained by continuing to dot i's which had already been dotted, or to cross t's already sufficiently provided in that respect.

Lucius Bellingdon regarded her with a certain frowning intensity. It was the kind of look which was apt to make people nervous—it had, in fact, very seldom failed to do so. It failed now. Miss Silver went on knitting in a perfectly placid manner.

He leaned forward suddenly and said,

"When will you come down to Merefields?"

She did not appear to be at all taken aback.

"In what capacity, Mr. Bellingdon?"

"Well, I've got to find out who has been talking."

"You do not, I suppose, desire to advertise that fact. My usefulness would be very much impaired if it were known."

"My idea was that you should replace young Hughes as assistant secretary."

She appeared to consider this before saying, "I am not versed in typing or shorthand. Nor do I really feel that I could sustain the part."

He said,

"I get a great many begging letters and appeals of all sorts. I should think they might be quite in your line. Hughes was no good at them at all. They have to be weeded out. I don't read a tenth of them myself, the rest go straight into the waste-paper basket. Then there's a good deal of social correspondence. My daughter ought to do it, but she can't be bothered. I noticed that you write a very clear hand. Garratt will deal with anything that needs typing. What about it?"

The busy needles stopped. She laid down her hands upon the pale blue wool.

"Have you said anything about replacing Mr. Hughes?"

"Yes, I have. All I need do now is to ring up Miss Bray and tell her you have been recommended to me by a friend, and that I am bringing you down with me tomorrow."

10

Merefields lay in the spring sunshine with a sprinkle of daffodils in its shrubberies and a broad band of many coloured hyacinths where the drive spread into a wide sweep and half a dozen grey stone steps went up to the front door. The hyacinths looked across the gravel at the house, and from every room which faced that way you could look back at the hyacinths. Lucius Bellingdon pointed them out to Miss Silver with pride.

"Gardeners like cutting holes in the grass and putting in skimped-up mats of flowers. Donald was a bit obstinate when I said I wanted hyacinths all the way along opposite the house, and that sweet-smelling stuff my mother used to call cherry pie to come along after them."

Miss Silver smiled.

"But you got your way."

He nodded.

"Smell nice, don't they—but a bit heavy if you have them in the house. Well now, come along in and meet everyone. Lunch is at one and I'm ready for it, so I hope you are too."

They encountered Miss Bray in the hall. Bellingdon had expanded his original account of her on the way down.

"Ellen is what she was christened, but don't say I told you. She thinks Elaine sounds better. Personally I think it's silly, but what's the odds so long as it makes her happy? There's no reason why it should but it seems to, and I ought to be used to it by now."

She came towards them in a grey woollen dress with a dreary-looking black scarf trailing down below the waist on either side and a jet chain looped two or three times about her neck, which was long and thin. She had fair hair with a good deal of grey in it worn gathered into a loose untidy knot quite insufficiently controlled by an unusual number of hairpins. A further attempt to confine it with a piece of black velvet ribbon could not really be said to be successful. She peered at Miss Silver as if she were shortsighted, but her manner was perfectly amiable as she said,

"Oh, how do you do? I am afraid it is a great rush for you coming down here like this. Lucius did tell me your name, but I am afraid I have forgotten it. Names are so very difficult, don't you think? And so often they are very misleading. Now I find I so rarely think of my friends by their names. I always feel that there is something much more personal—something that cannot really be put into words—something which I have heard compared to the scent of a flower—"

Lucius Bellingdon said briskly,

"This is Miss Silver, Elaine, and I expect she would like to go to her room before lunch."

Miss Bray talked all the way up the beautiful staircase with its shallow steps and along a panelled corridor to a room which, she informed Miss Silver, was opposite to her own. It had a good view of the hyacinths and was most comfortably furnished with bright chintzes, a moss-green carpet, and what she was very pleased to see, a small electric fire. Previous experiences in the country had left her under no illusions as to the icy temperatures to which many habitual residents had apparently become enured. Her warmest clothing invariably accompanied her on a country visit, but it would be more comfortable not to require it. There was not only this convenient fire, but the sight of a radiator and the genial warmth of the temperature informed her that the house was centrally heated.

Miss Bray was assiduous in her attentions.

"The bathroom is next door. I cannot tell you how relieved I was when Lucius rang up and said that he had induced you to come down. Even in two days the letters and appeals have piled up in the most trying way. Poor Mr. Garratt is still far from well. I cannot think what can have brought on such a shocking attack. The begging letters are the worst, but Lucius does not think it right to tear them up unread. He tells me you are particularly well adapted to deal with them. It is work which I could not possibly undertake—it would upset me too much. I am afraid I am foolishly sensitive to anything sordid. The seamy side of life—it does not do for me to allow myself to come in contact with it. It haunts me. Now I'm sure *you* are very strong-minded!"

In her private capacity Miss Silver might have wished to

unpack and to tidy herself in privacy. In her professional capacity she could welcome any flow of words however tedious. People who talk all the time are seldom discreet. She owed no small part of her successes to the fact that she was outstandingly easy to talk to. Miss Bray found her a most sympathetic listener as she discoursed upon the difficulty of staffing a house like Merefields.

"Men really have no idea! Take the butler and the cook. Because they have been here for twenty years Lucius thinks they are perfect! And of course they think so too! I am sure I daren't say a word! And the girls from the village—of course quite untrained—one has to be after them every minute! And they don't like it! Only the other day Mrs. Hilton told me that Gloria Stubbs was thinking of giving in her notice, and when I wanted to know why, she said it might be better if I were to leave the training of the girls to her! It just shows, doesn't it!"

Miss Silver observed tactfully that the staffing and running of a big house must be very difficult indeed.

"And Moira is no help at all! I brought her up, you know, after my cousin died—at least she was sixteen, so I didn't really have the training of her, and she has been married since, which of course makes a difference, don't you think? But if I suggest her doing anything she only says that there are too many fingers in the pie already. She said that only yesterday, and I'm sure I can't think what she meant, because if the Ball is going to be put off—you know, I suppose, that Lucius was giving a fancy dress ball at The Luxe next month? That is why he was getting the necklace out of the bank—Moira wanted to see it. And I can't help feeling *intensely* thankful that it was stolen before it got here if it was going to be stolen at all. Lucius wasn't going to keep it here of course—it's too valuable. Moira wanted to see it, and then they were going to take it up to town and leave it at the jeweller's to be cleaned and taken care of until the day of the Ball. Of course it is terribly shocking about poor Arthur Hughes, but when I think it might have been Lucius and Moira I really can't be too thankful! I don't suppose Lucius will think it necessary to put off the Ball—there were such a lot of people coming. Moira thinks it would be absurd, but young people are so apt to be callous. I often think it would be so much more comfortable not to have such sensitive feelings, but on the other hand does one really want to be *insensitive?*"

Miss Silver opining that there was a happy mean and introducing a quotation from Lord Tennyson in support of this, they went down to lunch together on the best of terms.

Lucius Bellingdon and three other people were waiting for them—a girl in smoky blue who was Moira Herne, someone taller and older who was Mrs. Scott, and Mr. Hubert Garratt. Introduced by Bellingdon, Miss Silver found herself regarded with as complete a lack of concern as she could have desired.

Her own interest was, however, warmly engaged. Every person in this household had some part in the problem she was here to investigate. Because one of them had talked young Arthur Hughes lay dead. The leakage could have occurred through inadvertence, heedlessness, lack of self-control. It could have been the result of fear, of some burst of confidence, or of malice aforethought, but somehow through one of these people it must have come about. She could not neglect Mr. Bellingdon's secretary, Mr. Bellingdon's daughter, or Mr. Bellingdon's guest.

Moira Herne would have been remarked on anywhere for her ash-blonde colouring. As to her features, they were of the kind you really hardly notice. It was the gleaming hair with its soft full waves, the rather light eyes with a dark ring about the iris, and the fine white skin, which fixed and held the attention. The lashes and brows were slightly and artistically darkened to a golden brown. The mouth, which might have been too pale, had been deepened to a delightful rose, the pointed fingernails matched it to a shade. She allowed the eyes to rest upon Miss Silver in an indifferent stare and did not speak.

Mrs. Scott could hardly have exhibited a greater contrast in looks and manner. She was a tall, slim creature with smooth, dark hair, dark eyes, a skin warm with colour, a wide mouth, and teeth as white as hazel-nuts. She might have been anything between twenty-five and forty. Her voice as she said "How do you do?" had a quality of youth which it would probably never lose. She smiled, showing the white teeth, slipped into her place by Lucius Bellingdon, and began to talk to him about this and that. She had an easy charm of manner, a trick of saying things that made them sound interesting, a way of laughing with her eyes. It took Miss Silver rather less than a minute to discern that Lucius Bellingdon's feeling for her was something out of the ordinary.

Mr. Garratt was middle-aged and inclined to put on weight. He took the foot of the table opposite Mr. Bellingdon and sat there pale and depressed, eating little and talking less, with Moira Herne on one side of him and Miss Bray on the other. Miss Silver, between Miss Bray and her host, could hardly have been better placed. She need not talk, because Mr. Bellingdon was quite taken up with Mrs. Scott. She was therefore free to look and to listen.

The conversation might have been confined to that end of the table if it had not been for Elaine Bray. She appeared to be able to eat and talk at the same time, and was most solicitous about Mr. Garratt's loss of appetite.

"These eggs—now you really should! They are done in onion sauce—a Portuguese recipe, I believe. The cheese in it neutralizes the onion to a very great extent. Now how do you suppose you are going to get up your strength if you do not eat?"

Mr. Garratt said, "I don't know." He took about a dessertspoonful from the proffered dish and left it on his plate.

Moira Herne took a large helping and said in a drawling, husky voice that she adored onions. Her way of speaking was so much at variance with the ethereal fairness of her colouring as to heighten its effect. Miss Silver found herself wondering whether this was deliberate.

"Mrs. Hilton is a marvellous cook," said Annabel Scott. She smiled warmly and unconventionally at Hilton as she spoke, and turned back again to Lucius with a laughing "I shall put on pounds if I stay here too long!"

As the butler went back to the serving-table, Moira said in exactly the same voice and manner as before,

"Wilfrid is coming down for the weekend."

Miss Bray echoed the name in a fitful manner. Lucius said,

"That fellow Gaunt? He was here last week, wasn't he? I don't remember being struck with him."

Moira said, "I don't suppose you would be. I've been dancing with him quite a lot in town. He is a dream."

Elaine said, "My dear!" and Lucius enquired, "as a dancer?"

"Of course."

"Does he make it his life work?"

"He paints. He has two pictures in the Masters galleries."

Bellingdon's attention was caught.

"I bought a picture there the other day—a very good one."

Moira said "Oh—" And then, "Who was it by?"

"Not your friend Wilfrid, I'm afraid. A young man of the name of Moray—David Moray."

The large blue eyes gazed at him without expression. There was no expression in the husky voice as she said,

"Wilfrid hates him."

Lucius burst out laughing.

"Then that will be nice for them both! Because Moray is coming down for the week-end too. I asked him if he would like to see my pictures, and he said he would."

Moira just went on gazing.

"Wilfrid's picture is about a tombstone and as aspidistra. The tombstone is in a sort of blue mist, the aspidistra is in a pink pot, and there are some bones."

Annabel laughed and said, "Why, darling?"

"I don't know. He painted it like that. It doesn't really mean tombstones and aspidistras—it means things going on in your Unconscious."

"Darling, I should hate to have a pink aspidistra in my Unconscious!"

Moira shook her head.

"It was the pot that was pink."

It was at this point that Miss Bray came in on a worried note.

"Oh, my dear! Oh, Lucius! Do you really think—a party—just at this moment—is it really *suitable?*"

Moira's gaze shifted to her. She said without hurry,

"What do you call a party? Two men for the week-end? Not my idea of one, Ellen."

An unbecoming magenta flush spread over Miss Bray's face. To call her Ellen was Moira's way of punishing her. As a rule she avoided giving occasion for it, but at the moment her feelings of propriety were engaged. In the spirit of the proverb that you might as well be hanged for a sheep as for a lamb she added to her offence.

"I think we should be as quiet as possible—I think it will be expected of us. The house is full enough as it is." Her glance touched Annabel Scott, fell away, met Lucius Bellingdon's frown, and withdrew. "Of course"—the words came tumbling out—"the inquest was adjourned, and the funeral is over. I don't mean that we have to shut ourselves up, or that there is anything wrong about having a friend or two down quietly."

"Then what do you mean?" said Moira Herne. "Do you know?"

Miss Bray was twisting her long jet chain. She said in a nervous hurry,

"I was really thinking about the Ball. I don't know whether anything has been decided yet, but of course, with all those people coming—"

Moira said, "There is nothing to decide."

Miss Bray tried a second look at Lucius Bellingdon and found him frowning still. He said with some accentuation of his usually decided manner,

"There can be no question about the Ball. It will take place as arranged. The date is still a month away. No one could possibly expect us to call it off."

"No—no—of course not. I only thought we ought to know what is going to happen. I wasn't really suggesting—Naturally, as you say, a month is quite a long time."

He laughed.

"Did I? I don't remember. Anyhow there is nothing to worry about."

Hubert Garratt had taken no part in this interchange. He crumbled the slice of bread beside him and drank from a glass of water. The arrangements might have had nothing to do with him at all, yet the brunt of the work in connection with the Ball would fall to his share. As soon as lunch was over he disappeared.

The rest of the party adjourned to the drawing-room for coffee. Miss Silver found herself next to Mrs. Scott. She was about to remark on the view from the windows, where a smooth green lawn sloped gently to the windings of a stream, the banks all set with daffodils, when Moira Herne walked up to them coffee-cup in hand and said,

"I shall have to get another dress for the Ball. What a bore!"

Annabel laughed.

"Why should getting a new dress be a bore? And why do you have to get one anyway?"

Moira just stood there.

"The other dress was a copy of one Marie Antoinette really wore. I'm not going to wear it without the necklace —why should I? Anyway they say her things are unlucky."

Annabel Scott looked up at her appraisingly. It was rather as if she were looking at a picture or a statue.

"I don't know about unlucky, but definitely not in your line."

"I don't know what you mean."

The appraising look vanished. A wide flashing smile took its place.

"But darling—with your colouring! Why smother it with powder? Fancy having hair like yours and covering it up with a wig!"

Moira frowned.

"I didn't think about that. I wanted to wear the necklace. If it's gone, there doesn't seem to be much point about the rest of it. Now I don't know what to wear."

"Oh, you must be Undine! I didn't say anything before, because you'd got it all settled."

"Who was she? I've never heard of her."

Miss Silver was shocked. She was aware that the classic authors of her youth were now mere shadows from the past, but that La Motte Fouqué should have ceased to be even a shadow shook her. It appeared that Mrs. Scott at least knew something of his most famous creation.

"Undine was a water spirit. It's a German legend. She fell in love with an earthly knight and married him, but in the end he was false to her and she disappeared in a cloud of spray from a fountain. One of the Chopin ballades puts the story into music."

"You do know a lot, don't you?" said Moira Herne. And then, "What would she wear?"

Miss Silver considered that Mrs. Scott showed an amiable temper in her reply. Mrs. Herne's manner had been abrupt to the point of rudeness, but Annabel only laughed and said,

"Undine? Well, it might be rather enchanting, I think. Transparent green draperies like water flowing, and your hair brushed out into a sort of cloud like spray. Lucius, give me a pencil and paper and I'll show her."

There were both on an ornamental table in the window. She took them, drew rapidly, and held up the result to Moira. The sketch had caught a likeness, but it was a likeness with a twist on it. It was, in fact, Undine with her unearthly lightness and grace, her hair blown by some wind of glamour, her dress flowing with the lines of flowing water. Moira studied it attentively. In the end she enquired,

"Green chiffon?"

"Green and grey—very pale grey, to get the water effect. You could have crystal drops where the points of the dress come down. No, *not* diamonds—they mustn't be too bright."

She went across to the piano at the far end of the room and began to play the Undine ballade.

"Listen—this will give you the idea."

She had an exquisite touch. The rocking melody came on the air with real enchantment. When the storm of Kühleborn's anger broke she gave it only a few wild chords and dropped her hands from the keys.

"Lovely, isn't it?"

Moira Herne said in a grudging tone,

"It mightn't be bad, but no one will have the foggiest idea what it's meant for."

As Annabel Scott came back to her seat she was saying to herself, "She hasn't a spark of imagination. Why did I suggest Undine?"

11

Going through the hall, Lucius Bellingdon picked up a letter or two lying ready for the post. The one on the top attracted his attention. It was addressed to Miss Sally Foster, 13 Porlock Square. He stuck there, frowning at the number and the name of the square. In the end he called Moira and waited for her to come to him. She arrived without hurry, stared, and said,

"What are you doing with my letter?"

"I was going to post it—I'm going down into the village. Who is Sally Foster?"

Those curious light eyes of hers dwelt upon him without affection. She said,

"Why?"

He had been used to her for so many years that he was conscious of no fresh chill. There was no warmth in her, no kindness. You couldn't get blood from a stone. What he meant to get was an answer. He said,

"I know the address—that is all. I couldn't help seeing it. Who is this girl?"

"She was at school with me. Why do you want to know?"

"I have a reason. It's some time since you left school. Have you seen anything of her since?"

"She is Marigold Marchbank's secretary. One of the girls married Freddy Ambleton. I see quite a lot of them. Sally is a friend of theirs—I met her again like that."

"Do you know her well enough to ask her down here?"

She gave an odd laugh with a flavour of contempt,

"There's no harm in asking!"

He had continued to frown at the letter. Now he turned the same look on her.

"What is she like?"

"Very much the same as other people."

"About your age?"

She shrugged.

"More or less."

"And you know her fairly well. What were you writing to her about?"

"She asked me to make a four to go dancing. I said I couldn't."

He said, "Look here, I want you to ring her up and ask her down for the week-end."

She opened her eyes so widely that the dark line about the iris showed clear.

"But I don't want to."

His voice roughened.

"She needn't be in your way."

"Why do you want her?"

He said,

"Too long to go into. She comes from the same house as David Moray. I told you I'd asked him for the week-end—that is why I was struck by the address on your letter. She can help to entertain him, and to prevent your being bothered."

Moira considered the question in a leisurely manner. She didn't want Sally down at Merefields, but she didn't want this David Moray person either. She wanted Wilfrid, and she didn't really trust Wilfrid where Sally was concerned. On the other hand it might be a good plan to have a show-down. There would have to be one soon anyway. If

Wilfrid was in the same house with her and Sally he would have to show his hand. If David Moray was at all presentable he might come in usefully, either to distract Sally's attention or to flirt with herself and put Wilfrid on his mettle. Because the one thing she was really sure of in the whole situation was that, Sally or no Sally, Wilfrid had no intention of letting himself be cut out with Moira Herne. That was a development which he simply couldn't afford, and he knew it. Having reached this point, she said in a flat uninterested voice,

"Oh, well, I can ring her up if you want me to. Ellen will say it makes it more of a party, but I suppose you don't mind about that."

Lucius Bellingdon said, "Not a bit."

She was not prepared for his following her into the study and standing there looking out of the window with his back to her whilst she telephoned. Her voice came through to Sally without any more than its usual lack of expression.

"Is that you? . . . Moira Herne speaking. Look here, Wilfrid is coming down for the week-end, and another man. I expect you know him, because he seems to live in the same place as you do—David Moray. He is an artist. Probably too uncivilized, but Lucy has just bought one of his pictures, and he has asked him down, so I thought we had better make it a four, and then we could dance, or play something and it won't be too unutterably mouldy."

If it had been just Moira and Wilfrid, Sally would have found an excuse, but David was another matter. Moira had her own way with attractive men. It was an odd way but it appeared to get results. They became mesmerized and fell into vicious circles like moths about a lamp. Sally was unable to bear the thought of David as a moth. She mightn't be able to prevent the mesmerizing process, but at least she wouldn't be about thirty-five miles away enjoying the pleasures of the imagination. Sally's imagination could do wicked things when it really got going, and she didn't feel like giving it its head. Better be there on the spot and see for herself than have to listen to its insidious whisperings in Porlock Square. It was always possible that David might take against Moira. By all the rule she should. There was his Scottish common sense, and the detached and critical manner in which he regarded the female sex. He was wary, he was intolerant, and he thought well of his own judgement. He was, in fact, an odiously cocksure young man who wanted taking down quite a number of pegs. Only how could she bear to see anyone doing it? Especially Moira. The answer was that she couldn't. And that, illogically, was the reason why nothing would stop her from going to Merefields.

12

Miss Silver was able to make considerable progress with the pale blue baby shawl intended for a young friend and former client, Dorinda Leigh, now expecting her third child. Miss Bray, who was engaged in the domestic work of darning pillow-cases, bore her company and was most helpful and informative in her conversation. To many this perpetual trickle of talk might have seemed dull, but not to Miss Silver. She had a very genuine interest in the lives and the problems of other people, and when occupied upon a case nothing that she could learn about those concerned in it could be dismissed as trivial or worthless. As her needles moved rhythmically above the pale blue cloud in her lap and Miss Bray jerked at her linen thread, a picture of the Bellingdon household began to take shape.

"Of course he is a very clever man and he has been very successful, but I'm not sure that it didn't all come too suddenly for Lily. She wasn't ever what you would call strong, and when he began to go over to America on his business she fretted a lot—she was that kind, you know. There was some patent he had got for one of those new materials they keep making out of such very odd things. I really can't remember whether it was seaweed, or milk, or wood pulp, but he made a lot of money out of it and he had to go over to America about the patents. I remember his telling Lily they were going to be rich, and she cried about it afterwards and said she would rather have her husband."

Miss Silver had been turning the shawl. She looked up brightly.

"It was not possible for her to accompany him?"

Miss Bray shook her head in a mournful manner.

"Oh, no—she didn't like travelling. Not at all! And there is such a lot of travelling in a big place like the United States! He used to say she would get used to it, but I told him he hadn't the right to expect her to go. He didn't like my saying it of course, but if I didn't stand up for Lily, who was going to, I should like to know!"

"So she stayed at home?"

"And moped," said Miss Bray, digging into a darn in a haphazard way which Miss Silver found distressing. She was using far too thick a needle. The mended place would be sadly conspicuous. Miss Bray gazed at it disapprovingly, but it was evident that it was really Mr. Bellingdon who was being disapproved of. "Men are all the same," she continued. "He was free enough with the money, but you can't live on money, can you? What she wanted was company. That's why I came to live with them. And of course it's been very comfortable and all, but a big house is a lot of trouble, and I sometimes think—" Her voice trailed away.

Miss Silver wondered what she had been going to say. Whatever it was, it didn't get said. There was an interlude during which the shortcomings of the Hiltons were deplored.

"She may be a very good cook, and I don't say she isn't, but I am sure she is terribly extravagant. And I don't say that Hilton doesn't know his work, because he does, but I do say that Lucius ought to look into the accounts! I would be willing to do it myself though I am sure figures always make my head ache and it's so difficult to get them to come out right, don't you think so—but when I suggested it Lucius was really quite *rude!* I may be too sensitive—perhaps I am—but I think it's better than going round hurting people's feelings. But do you know what he said—and it wasn't only the words, but his voice and the way he looked at me. 'You let the Hiltons alone!' he said. 'And you let the accounts alone, and I'll let you alone!' And then he laughed and patted my shoulder and said, 'You wouldn't be a bit of good at either, and we'll all be a lot more comfortable if you'll leave well alone.' "

Miss Silver smiled.

"That sounds to me very much like the way in which a man talks to someone he is fond of—in fact very much like a brother. They do not think about being polite, they just feel that things like accounts are not really a woman's department. And if you do not feel very much at home with figures, I should think you would be grateful to be spared having to deal with them."

Something about Miss Silver's smile and the tone of her voice as she said this gave Miss Bray a pleasant sense of being sheltered from the rougher blasts of domestic life. She preened herself and admitted that she had always found arithmetic troublesome. They glided imperceptibly to other subjects and presently arrived at the question of the week-end party.

"Moira is really not at all domestic," Miss Bray lamented. "One does not expect a man to consider what sheets are at the wash—towels of course, and pillow-cases too. Not that the linen-cupboard is not well stocked, though we could certainly do with more sheets and I have been waiting for an opportunity of speaking to Lucius on the subject, but the laundry only delivers once a fortnight and rather irregularly at that—and the house so full—I'm sure every bed was occupied last week-end! So if Moira stopped to think, but of course she doesn't—" Miss Bray surveyed her completed darn and shook her head. "The linen gets no rest," she said.

Miss Silver pulled on her pale blue ball.

"Mrs. Herne invites a good many people?"

Miss Bray threw up her hands.

"They just come in and out, and I'm sure I don't know whether they are coming or going, or which of them are going to stay the night! Why, only last week-end just as I'd got all the rooms nicely arranged and the beds aired—and that's a thing I don't feel Mrs. Hilton sees to as she should, and you can't really trust the girls—Where was I? Oh, about the beds! You see, there are the five rooms in regular use, because that poor Mr. Hughes was sleeping in the house until he was murdered."

Miss Silver performed a simple calculation. Mr. Bellingdon, Mrs. Scott, Moira Herne, Miss Bray herself, and Arthur Hughes—that made five, and still left Hubert Garratt unaccounted for.

"Does Mr. Garratt not sleep in the house?"

"Oh, no, he doesn't. The East Lodge is empty, and he prefers being there. Mrs. Croft looks in to make his bed and tidy up on her way from the village, and he has all his meals here. It is quite a convenient arrangement, and he prefers it. But of course I should have said six beds are occupied, because as far as the linen is concerned he might as well be in the house. And on the top of the regular people last week-end there was Wilfrid Gaunt. He's a friend of Moira's, and always seems to me to be a most idle, frivolous young man, and I'm sure if I'd known he was coming down this week-end again I'd have left his sheets on the bed and not sent them to the wash. But that's Moira all over, she never thinks ahead. And Lucius had a couple in the Blue Room—some Americans called Rennick who are friends of his—very nice people, I'm sure. And of course Mrs. Scott was here, and my brother Arnold. And then at the last minute Moira just said casually that Clay Masterson would be staying the night, and I must say I was provoked!"

Miss Silver's memory was much too accurate and retentive for the name of Wilfrid Gaunt to have escaped her attention. He had been mentioned at lunch, and as Miss Bray spoke of him she was aware in retrospect of Paulina Paine talking of the portrait which Lucius Bellingdon had bought—"It is in this gallery, and it has been sold. A young cousin of mine, Wilfrid Gaunt, has two pictures there too." *A young cousin of mine, Wilfrid Gaunt*. Here was a link between Miss Paine, the gallery, and Merefields. She maintained her look of interest without accentuating it in any way, and when she spoke it was not of Wilfrid Gaunt. She said,

"And who is Clay Masterson?"

Miss Bray was unaccustomed to so much sympathetic attention, having passed most of her life in other people's houses without any very settled position or any qualifications for attracting interest or friendship. She found herself expanding in a very pleasurable manner.

"He has an aunt or cousin or something who lives on the other side of the village, and really there seems to be no reason at all why he should come and sleep here. As I said to Moira at the time, 'Even if something has gone wrong with his car, I suppose a healthy young man can walk a mile without finding it a hardship!' Not that it is a mile to the Gables, because it is well this side of the turning to Crowbury and we always count the mile from there, so I must say I didn't think he need stay the night, and I said so. But Moira insisted, even after I told her that the sheets wouldn't be aired, or the mattress or the blankets, because I should have to put him into the north room which we don't use unless we are obliged to."

"He is a friend of Mrs. Herne's?"

"They go out dancing together," said Miss Bray in a disapproving tone.

"He lives with this aunt?"

"Oh, no, he just comes and goes. He did very well in the war—at least Moira says he did. And he has a very good job in town, only I don't quite know what it is. I think Moira told me it had something to do with the antique business. I'm sure I don't know why such a lot of people go in for that nowadays—people who are quite well connected and high up in society. If it was nice new furniture or glass or china, they wouldn't touch it, but just because the things are old they think it's quite a smart thing to do. Why, there's Lady Hermione Scunthorpe—and she's a Duke's daughter—and several others I could mention, but it all seems very puzzling to me! This Mr. Masterson goes round looking for old things, and Moira says he is very good at it, so of course it wasn't at all convenient for him to have his car laid up."

Miss Silver had been getting on very well with her shawl. It quite filled her lap.

"You spoke of your brother being here. How very pleasant for you."

This did not appear to evoke any particular response. Miss Bray took one of her clumsy stitches and said,

"It was only for the week-end—he just stayed till the Monday evening. It would have been better if the house hadn't been so full."

"Your brother does not care for society?"

Miss Bray was regretting that she had mentioned Arnold. She flushed, the colour deepening towards her nose. Aware of this, she produced a handkerchief from her sleeve and chafed the afflicted feature with unfortunate results. Miss Silver thought it best to change the subject.

13

It was some time after tea that Lucius Bellingdon found himself showing Miss Silver his collection of pictures. He was a little uncertain as to just how this had come about. It had not really been his intention to show the pictures at all, at any rate not at this moment, and not to Miss Silver. Yet as the party at tea broke up he was aware of Miss Silver putting away her knitting in a flowered chintz bag with green plastic handles and looking up at him in a brightly intelligent manner.

"So kind of you, and I shall be most interested to see them," she was saying. And then, "I have some pictures that I am very fond of myself. Only reproductions of course, but in some cases I have been privileged to see the originals."

After which there was no doubt that he had in some way committed himself. They went up the stairs and through to the wing which he had restored in order to house his collection. There had been extensive damage by fire at the turn of the century, and the then owner had not been able to meet the expense of re-building.

"He'd let the insurance lapse. Silly thing to do, but I don't suppose he could find the money. Pity when an old family goes down hill like that, but no sense in hanging on to a place when you can't afford to keep it up. Takes the heart out of you trying to do something that can't be done."

Miss Silver said, "Yes indeed."

She listened with interest and respect to a disquisition on Dutch painting culminating in the proud display of a very small picture of a girl standing by an open window and putting tulips into a jar. She was a plain young woman, but the way the light came slanting through the window to touch the tulips and her smooth fair hair had an astonishing beauty. It had not occurred to her before that light could be painted, but it occurred to her now. Her comment to that effect certainly pleased Lucius Bellingdon. He went on talking, showed her a flower piece which she admired very much, and then all at once he was being addressed with some gravity.

"Mr. Bellingdon, may I take this opportunity of asking you to add to the information you have already given me?"

He showed some slight surprise, but no more than was natural.

"Why, certainly. What is it you want to know?"

"In the course of conversation Miss Bray mentioned that you had a house-party during this last week-end."

"Yes, there were people here—there generally are at the week-end."

"Quite so. But on this occasion, so shortly before the theft of the necklace and the murder of Mr. Hughes, I should be interested to hear anything that you can tell me about your guests."

He looked at her sharply.

"I don't see—"

"I think you must, Mr. Bellingdon. I do not know just when you decided to withdraw your necklace from the County Bank, but I imagine that all the details were already decided upon at the time of this week-end party. You informed me that you had communicated them to the manager in writing, and since Tuesday was the day for the withdrawal it seems probable that your letter would have been posted on the Saturday or Sunday. Therefore any leakage of information on the subject would be likely to have occurred during that time."

"It was posted on the Sunday."

His tone was one of displeasure. It was by no means Miss Silver's first experience of being invited to an investigation which subsequently proved very little to the taste of the person who had invited her. She looked steadily at Lucius Bellingdon and said,

"This is not pleasant for you, is it? Before we go any further I should like to say that I appreciate youı position. It is still for you to choose whether you really wish me to go on with the case. The police have it in hand, and there is no need for you to retain my services. It is still open to me to return to town and relieve you of the embarrassment of having introduced an enquiry agent into your private family circle. But what I must make quite clear to you is this. The course I have proposed is possible now, but it may not be possible tomorrow. It could, in fact, become impossible at any moment."

He was frowning deeply.

"What do you mean?"

"I mean that at present I feel myself at liberty to withdraw, but if I continue on the case I am not, and could not be, prepared to hush anything up. The case is one of murder. Anything that throws light upon the murderer's identity will be, and must be, at the disposal of the police. I am saying to you what I feel is my duty to say to any client. I cannot go into an investigation with the object of proving anyone guilty or anyone innocent. I can only go into it with the object of discovering the truth and serving the ends of justice."

He walked a little way from her, looked fixedly at a lowering seascape, and so remained for a slow minute or two. When he came back, she saw that he had made up his mind. He said,

"Well, I like to do business with someone who doesn't beat about the bush, and you don't do that. If there has been a leakage, I'm bound to trace it. It could have occurred through nothing worse than a tongue too loosely hung—I suppose you realize that."

She inclined her head.

"You wish me to remain here?"

He said "Yes—" in a considering tone. Then, more firmly, "Yes, I do. There is such a thing as any sort of certainty being better than not knowing where you are. If there's worm in a board I like to know it and have it out before it lets me through and I break my ankle—or my neck. And that being that, what do you want to know about last week-end?"

"Just who were the guests, and something about them."

"The question is, what did Elaine tell you? She can generally be trusted to talk."

Miss Silver coughed.

"I should prefer you to assume that Miss Bray did not say anything at all."

He gave a short laugh.

"That's a pretty tall order, but I'll do my best! To begin with you have to understand that there are very few week-ends when we don't have people here. Moira is young and she asks anyone she likes. I have people down on the sort of business that goes better when it isn't done in an office. Well, last week-end there was this young chap Wilfrid Gaunt who is coming down tonight—he's by way of fluttering round Moira. And another young chap called Masterson. And some people for me of the name of Rennick—Americans, a very nice couple. And Elaine's brother Arnold Bray. And that's the lot."

She asked him questions eliciting very much the same information as had been imparted by Miss Bray. Clay Masterson was a clever chap, keen to get on, but there wouldn't be a lot of money in running round the country looking for antiques—not at this time of the day.

"Everything worth having must have been pretty well combed out by now, and you have got to have all your wits about you not to be taken in. He's a friend of Moira's too. But she isn't serious about any of them. That's the worst of all this running about together—it's all very nice and easy, but it doesn't get a girl anywhere. What Moira wants is a home of her own, but all she does is to play around. It's "Darling" here and "Darling" there, but I wish I thought she cared a snap of her fingers for any of them."

"You would like your daughter to marry again?"

"I'd like to see her settled."

It was said with emphasis. Miss Silver did not pursue the subject. She turned instead to Mr. Arnold Bray.

"He is Miss Bray's brother?"

"He is. Didn't she mention him?"

"Only in passing."

He gave a short angry laugh.

"Well, one wouldn't feel tempted to dwell on Arnold! To be honest, he's a liability. I suppose most families have something of the sort knocking about. He comes when he's short of money, and he goes when he's got enough to make it worth his while. I can only stand him for just so long, and he trades on it. But if you are thinking of him for your murderer you'll have to think again. He simply hasn't got the guts."

Miss Silver asked a practical question.

"What does he do?"

Lucius Bellingdon was at his most overpowering as he replied,

"As little as he can help."

Observing the jut of his chin, the formidable curve of his nose, the characteristic air of command, it occurred to her that it might be possible that he had undervalued Arnold Bray in respect of what he had rather coarsely referred to as "guts." The expression offended her, but she did not allow herself to dwell upon that. What presented itself with some force was the fact that it would certainly require courage of some sort to obtrude oneself upon Mr. Bellingdon as an uninvited and unwanted guest, to say nothing of dunning him for money which he was under no obligation to supply.

Lucius said,

"If you asked him, I suppose he would describe himself as a commission agent. Goes round trying to get people to buy things they don't want and could get much better in a shop."

Miss Silver considered that Arnold Bray sounded very

much like the sort of person who might pass on any information he had the good fortune to pick up. With Elaine Bray aware that the necklace was to be fetched from the bank on Tuesday and her brother Arnold in the house for the week-end, she did not feel that the source of the leakage was very far to seek. She gave a slight preliminary cough and said,

"I do not wish to impute any wrong motive to Miss Bray, but she talks a good deal, and usually about the people round her and the things that are happening to them from day to day. Do you find it difficult to suppose that she may have mentioned your arrangements about the necklace to her brother, and that he may have repeated what she had told him? It could in either case have been done through inadvertence."

He was at his most abrupt as he said,

"That's out. She didn't know what my arrangements were. She knew I was getting the necklace. I suppose she knew that I was getting it on the Tuesday. She didn't know the time, or who would be fetching it."

"Who did know those things?"

"The bank manager because I wrote to him, Hubert Garratt who was supposed to be fetching the necklace, and later, but not until the Tuesday morning, Arthur Hughes, who had to take Hubert's place."

Miss Silver looked up at him.

"When you came to see me in town and I asked you how many people knew of your arrangements for withdrawing the necklace your reply included the bank manager, Mr. Garratt and Mr. Hughes, your daughter, and Miss Bray and Mrs. Scott."

He said with impatience,

"They knew I was getting it out of the bank. I told Moira that Hubert would fetch it on Tuesday."

"Did she regard it as a confidential communication, or as one which it would be natural to speak of amongst her friends and relations?"

He gave her a chagrined glance.

"Oh, well, I don't suppose she considered that it was a top-level secret. I suppose she may have spoken of it here in the house. I can't blame her if she did. One doesn't exactly go about expecting people to be murdered."

"When did you tell her?"

"I believe it was on the Sunday."

"Mr. Arnold Bray was still here?"

He shrugged his big shoulders.

"And Clay Masterson, and the Rennicks, and Wilfrid Gaunt."

"And Mrs. Scott?"

She saw an angry colour come up into his face, but he did not speak. After a moment she went on.

"Mrs. Herne could have mentioned the matter to any of these people. She could have mentioned it in the hearing of any of your staff. And any of these people could have mentioned it again. And all without evil intent. The ripples spread quickly in a pool. There were so many people in the house, some partially and some more accurately informed, and one of the latter a girl surrounded by her friends and with no particular reason to suppose that she would be doing wrong if she mentioned what was going to be a very important adjunct to her costume for the ball that you were giving. Is it difficult to see how this information could have passed rapidly from one to another until it reached someone who was prepared to turn it to his own advantage? At present we have only one clue to help us in searching for this person. It is the fact that the murderer could so little afford to be recognized that he was prepared to go to any length to avoid it. That is the point to which I find myself recurring. This man was someone who would not trust any disguise to protect him from being recognized by Mr. Garratt."

"By Hubert?" The words came slowly.

"It was Mr. Garratt who was to collect the necklace."

"I have given some attention to that point. It could mean that Mr. Hughes was equally dangerous, or that having made up his mind to shoot, the criminal's intention held in spite of the fact that it was no longer Mr. Garratt who would be the victim."

Lucius Bellingdon moved abruptly.

"I don't see that it gets us any forarder either way."

14

After leaving Lucius Bellingdon Miss Silver retired to her room, where an extremely comfortable easy chair offered an opportunity for rest and thought. For once her hands were unoccupied. Her knitting-bag lay on a stool beside her. She leaned back against the cushion, which admirably repeated the predominant colours in the very charming flowered chintz with which the chair was covered, and reviewed what she had gathered during the late interview. As she went over it in her mind, it was clear to her that anyone in the house could have known of and repeated the information which had made it possible for the necklace to be stolen. Mr. Bellingdon, having averred that Miss Bray did not know what were his arrangements about the necklace, went on to say that he supposed she knew that he was getting it out on the Tuesday, but stated that she did not know the time or who would be the messenger. Pressed as to who did know these things, he said the bank manager, Hubert Garratt, and at the last moment Arthur Hughes. But to further questioning he admitted that his daughter knew that the necklace was to be fetched on Tuesday. Miss Silver found herself perfectly convinced that what was known to Miss Bray and to Moira Herne would be no secret from the rest of the house-party. If it was generally known, it would be generally and freely discussed. In which case the Hiltons, Mrs. Stubbs, Mrs. Donald, the gardener's wife, and the dailies from the village could also have been in possession of the facts and could have passed them on just by way of gossip and without any criminal intent. She considered sedately that really men had very little idea of what went on in a house. It was the women who worked there, and especially those who went to and fro from their work to a neighbouring village, who had an unerring instinct for anything out of the way and an unflagging interest in retelling it. Lucius

Bellingdon might flatter himself that no one knew anything which he had not himself imparted, but she had no doubt that he was mistaken. As to his point about the time being unknown to anyone except himself and Hubert Garratt, Mr. Garratt might not have considered himself bound to secrecy. He might, for instance, have mentioned the matter to Mrs. Herne.

She had reached this point, when there came a gentle tapping on the door. Mrs. Scott made a graceful entrance.

"I do hope I am not disturbing you. I really did want to have a little talk if you can spare the time."

Her smile was charming. Her whole manner was charming. It said, "I want to be friends. I do hope you will let me." There was just a touch of diffidence which, like the quality of her voice, made her seem younger than she was.

Miss Silver responding, Annabel pulled up a second and rather smaller chair and sat down. All her movements were easy and pleasant to watch. She leaned forward now, an elbow on the arm of the chair, and said,

"I do hope you won't mind, but I know why you are here."

Whilst she was settling herself Miss Silver had reached for her knitting-bag. Taking out the almost completed shawl, she disposed its pale blue fluffiness upon her lap and began to knit. In reply to Annabel Scott's "I know why you are here" she looked at her with grave inquiry and said,

"Mr. Bellingdon has told you?"

There was a half shake of the head with its smooth dark hair. A half laugh was immediately checked, and Annabel was saying,

"Well, he did. But I knew already."

"Did you?"

Annabel smiled and nodded.

"Well, yes, I did. You see, I know Stacy Forrest*—in fact she's a kind of distant cousin. She did a miniature of me in the autumn. I wanted to give it to Lucius for Christmas, and he was quite terribly pleased with it. She does paint beautifully, doesn't she?"

Miss Silver acquiesced but did not enlarge upon the

**The Brading Collection.*

theme. She did not really imagine that Mrs. Scott had come here to talk about Stacy Forrest, who had been Stacy Mainwaring.

Annabel went on talking about her.

"Lucius is so critical, but he was delighted. She told me all about that affair of the Brading Collection and how marvellous you were, and when you came down here you were exactly the way she had described you, and of course I knew why you had come—I simply couldn't help it! So then I taxed Lucius with getting you down here professionally, and he had to own up. You won't be cross with him, will you?"

Miss Silver said, "No—" in a meditative tone, to which she presently added, "And how many people have you told about your discovery, Mrs. Scott?"

Annabel laughed.

"Now you're cross with me! I did so hope you wouldn't be, because I really want to talk to you. And I haven't, I really haven't, breathed a word to anyone. I promised Lucius I wouldn't. And of course you don't know me enough to trust me, but I don't break promises."

Miss Silver smiled. There was something very attractive about Annabel Scott, a warmth in the dark eyes, a natural charm. She pulled on her ball of pale blue wool and said,

"What did you want to talk to me about, Mrs. Scott?"

It was as if something had passed over a bright landscape, the glow and the brightness were less bright, less glowing. Annabel said,

"Well, I don't want to make too much of it, and I don't want to say anything to Lucius. And of course it may not have anything to do with it, but just in case it has I thought somebody ought to know." She paused, bit her lip, and then said in a hurry, "That Hughes boy was only twenty-two!"

Miss Silver said, "Yes," and waited for more.

Annabel went on.

"I didn't know him very well, I didn't even like him very much, but there he was, just a boy, and one minute he was all right, and the next someone had shot him dead for the sake of that wretched necklace!"

Miss Silver stopped knitting for a moment and made a quotation which she considered to be apposite.

" 'The lust of gain in the spirit of Cain,' as Lord Tennyson so aptly puts it."

If Annabel was taken aback she did not show it. She murmured, "Oh, yes," and Miss Silver turned the blue shawl and began to knit again. She said,

"Murder is indeed a terrible crime. If you know of anything which could throw any light upon the theft of the necklace and the death of Mr. Hughes you certainly should not keep it to yourself."

"That is what I thought. Of course, as I said, it may not have anything to do with Arthur Hughes being shot, but I can't seem to get it off my mind, so I thought if you would let me tell you about the snuffbox—"

"The snuffbox?"

"It's supposed to have belonged to Louis XVI—a really beautiful piece of enamel. Lucius was showing it to us last week-end. He bought it at a sale in Paris about a month ago, so it's still something new to show people, if you know what I mean."

"Yes, indeed."

"Well, he opened it to show the inside of the lid, and there it was, half full of snuff. Someone made a joke about the King's snuff, and Mr. Rennick was explaining that of course if it was, it wouldn't have any flavour left in it, and just as he was saying that Mrs. Rennick and I began to sneeze. Honestly, it was fierce! I can't imagine how anyone can touch the stuff, but of course everyone used it in those days. As a matter of fact, I believe lots of people do now. Too silly, isn't it?"

"A foolish habit."

"It must have made a horrid mess of all those silks and satins they used to wear, but if everybody did it, I suppose nobody minded. Anyhow the minute we began to sneeze Hubert Garratt absolutely covered his face with his handkerchief and made a bee line for the door, and Lucius shut up the snuffbox and said he ought to have remembered about Hubert getting asthma, and he hoped he hadn't been near enough for the snuff to have reached him. I was still sneezing, but someone asked would it do him any harm, and someone else—I think it was Clay Masterson—laughed and said, 'Well, he seems to think so, the way he bolted!' And Lucius put the box away and said it had better be cleaned out sometime." She paused, and added, "It doesn't seem very much when you tell it."

Miss Silver was looking at her in a brightly interrogative manner.

"That is not all?"

"No—" her voice had a reluctant sound—"not quite. Something made me look inside the box last night. It's in that big cabinet between the windows. I was alone in the drawing-room before the others came down, and I took it out and opened it—"

"Yes, Mrs. Scott?"

Annabel's bright colouring was one of her charms. The pure deep carnation was heightened momentarily. She said,

"Nearly all the snuff was gone."

Miss Silver said, "Dear me!"

Annabel nodded.

"That's what I thought. And I remembered something—" She paused with the half startled look of someone who has taken a step not fully realized or intended.

"Yes, Mrs. Scott?"

Annabel shook her head. Then, with a burst of confideuce, "Oh, I don't know—I must tell someone. Perhaps it isn't anything at all! It keeps coming niggling into my mind in a stupid kind of a whisper. You know the way things do—when you listen and try and make sense of them they aren't there any more, and when you say, 'Oh, well,' and get on with what you were doing, there they are again!"

Miss Silver said in her temperate voice,

"If you would like to tell me what is troubling you—"

Annabel sat up straight.

"Yes, I'm going to. I meant to all along, but you know how it is when it comes to taking the plunge."

She received an encouraging smile.

"It is something to do with the snuffbox?"

"Well, it is and it isn't. I mean, it looks as if it might be, but I don't know whether it is. I expect Lucius has told you all about Tuesday?"

Miss Silver released some strands of wool from her pale blue ball.

"It would be better if you were to assume that I know nothing except what was in the papers."

Annabel gave a quick laugh.

"Well, I don't know what was in the papers and what wasn't—it's all mixed up. But you know Lucius was getting the necklace out of the bank. Hubert Garratt was driving over—he was to be there at twelve. And then when it came to Tuesday morning, he hadn't come over to breakfast. Mrs. Croft who comes up from the village looks after the East Lodge. She goes in on her way to the house and as a rule Hubert is up and she can do his room, but when Lucius asked her if he was all right she said oh, no, he wasn't, he'd got a bad attack of his asthma. So Lucius went off to see him, and he really was bad. It didn't seem as if it was going to be possible for him to drive in to Ledlington and get the necklace. Lucius gave it as long as he could, and then he rang up the bank and said Arthur Hughes would go instead. But before that I took a thermos and coffee and went down to the East Lodge to see how Hubert was getting on. I didn't suppose he'd want to see me or anyone else, but it seemed so brutal just to leave him on his own, and I thought he might like the coffee. Well, actually, he was pretty bad, and he was quite grateful. I put his head straight and shook up the pillows and all that. He'd got everything into the most frightful mess—men do, don't they? And when he had had some of the coffee he staggered along to the bathroom for a wash. That's when I did the bed, and it was whilst I was doing it—" She stopped, leaned nearer, and dropped her voice. "It dropped off the pillows—he'd got them all piled up. I didn't know what it was at first, not until I picked up some of the grains and began to sneeze—" She broke off again, and then came out with, "You're not believing me—I can't see why you should. I couldn't believe it myself—not at first."

Miss Silver went on knitting.

"I have not said that I do not believe you, Mrs. Scott. Pray continue."

The dark eyes were not laughing now, they were wide and horrified.

"It was snuff—it really was—just the same as in the snuffbox! And it was there amongst his pillows! I picked up all the grains I could find and screwed them up in my handkerchief, and then I shook the pillows out of the window and beat them up and put them back on the bed. Well, it seems silly, but I hadn't any opportunity of comparing the grains I had got with the stuff in the snuffbox. There was all the business about Arthur Hughes being shot and the necklace stolen, and it really did go out of my head. Only, yesterday I had put on the same suit, and there was my handkerchief with the corner knotted up, and it all came back. So I changed early and got down before anyone else and looked inside the snuffbox. And most of the snuff was gone, but there was enough left for me to compare it with the grains in my handkerchief, and there wasn't any doubt about it at all, they were the same."

Miss Silver said, "Yes—" in a meditative voice.

Annabel Scott watched the rhythmic movement of her hands. Knitting-needles, pale blue wool, and a baby's shawl—they seemed such a long, long way from the thoughts that she had not wanted to think but which would not leave her alone. She said in a whispering voice,

"The snuffbox was nearly empty. Hubert went out of the room when it was open because he was nervous about the snuff. But there were grains of it amongst his pillows, and he had an attack of asthma. If he hadn't had it, he would have been the one to go and fetch the necklace from the bank, and he would have been the one who was shot. It's the sort of thing that sticks in your mind once you've thought about it. I can't get it out of mine."

Miss Silver said in her even voice,

"You have kept the handkerchief in which you knotted up the grains you found amongst Mr. Garratt's pillows?"

"Yes, I've got it."

"There are, of course, two possibilities, both of which imply a guilty knowledge of the plan to steal the necklace, either on the part of Mr. Garratt himself, or on the part of some other person. If it was he himself who possessed this knowledge, nothing would have been easier than for him to bring on his asthma by inhaling snuff. He would thus avoid being in charge of the necklace at the time of the theft. If, on the other hand, it was some other person who induced the atack, then that person's motive must have been either to protect Mr. Garratt or to involve Mr. Hughes, since it would not have been difficult to guess that he would be a probable substitute should Mr. Garratt be incapacitated."

Annabel gazed at her.

"It's all too horrid! Lucius has known Hubert for simply years. I can't believe he would do anything like that. And as to anyone wanting to get Arthur Hughes into trouble—" She stopped suddenly. "Miss Silver, you didn't mean anything worse than that! You didn't mean that you thought anyone might have planned to have Arthur shot!"

She had a feeling that she was being looked through and through as Miss Silver said,

"Will you tell me why you should have the thought of that?"

Annabel found herself without the ability to keep anything back. She said,

"Lucius told me about Miss Paine and the men she watched in that picture gallery. She told you one of them was looking in her direction, and that she could read what he was saying. I have a cousin who is deaf and can lip-read, so I know it can be done. Lucius said she told you this man said that the plan was to shoot the messenger who went for the necklace. If—if that was what was meant, then—then someone in this house—No it's too dreadful!"

Miss Silver said with gravity,

"The person who used the snuff may not have known that the plan to steal the necklace included the murder of the messenger. There could have been merely a knowledge that the necklace was to be stolen, and either a desire to protect Mr. Garratt or a wish to discredit Mr. Hughes. Do you know of anyone who could have had such a motive?"

Annabel said in rather a distracted way,

"I don't know. It's all too difficult. Arthur wasn't much liked. There wasn't anything you could put your finger on, but he just didn't fit in. Lucius didn't mean to keep him on. He was making a nuisance of himself about Moira for one thing."

"Did Mrs. Herne encourage him?"

Annabel made an odd but quite expressive gesture. Her hand came out palm upwards and empty. Yet there was a suggestion that she had something to offer.

"Oh, I don't know. She does something to these boys. It doesn't look like encouragement, but they go in off the deep end. Arthur Hughes had gone in off the deep end. I don't think Moira had any use for him, but he couldn't see it, and Lucius was getting annoyed. But all that is a long way off anyone wanting to get him into trouble."

"Had he an idea that he had been badly treated?"

"By Moira? I don't know. I daresay he had. You know, you are making me speak about her, and I didn't mean to. I ought not to, because I don't like her—I never have and I never shall."

"And why do you not like her, Mrs. Scott?"

Annabel's colour rose brightly.

"Because she doesn't care for anything or anyone except

herself—because she's got a lump of ice instead of a heart—because she makes Lucius unhappy! There—you've made me say it!"

Miss Silver said,

"Pray do not distress yourself."

Annabel looked back at her ruefully.

"I didn't mean to say it, you know. Right up to the last moment before I came and knocked on your door I had made up my mind that whatever happened I wouldn't breathe a word about Moira."

"Half confidences are not very helpful."

"No, they're not, are they? I suppose it's in for a penny in for a pound, and I don't say it won't be a relief to say what I really think, so here goes! She has been nothing but a trouble since she came into the family. When she married, I did think she would be off Lucius' hands. He didn't like Olly Herne. He was one of these ranting, bragging young men with a superiority complex if I'm to wrap it up, or plain swollen head if I'm leaving out the frills. He was a racing motorist, a perfect dare-devil in a car, and Moira fell for him. All Lucius could do was to tie up the money he settled on her. Well, he crashed over a precipice."

"During a race?"

"No, as a matter of fact he was off on his own. He and Moira had had a row, and he had left her planted and dashed off. It was rather frightful for her, because they had run out of money and she had to borrow to get home. The car was burnt out, so anything Olly had with him was lost. Moira turned up perfectly cool and said she didn't want to talk about any of it. Lucius thinks that in a way it was a relief. Anyhow she never speaks of him, and she hasn't got a photograph or anything. It might mean she cared more than we think, or it might mean that she just wanted to shut the door on Olly and not be bothered with him any more."

It was plain to Miss Silver that the latter view was the one to which Mrs. Scott inclined.

Annabel threw out her hands and said,

"There! I'm being thoroughly catty, and I've enjoyed it! You know, I wouldn't mind how many husbands she didn't care about, or how many young men she played fast and loose with, if she had just one spark of feeling for Lucius."

Miss Silver coughed mildly.

"Has Mr. Bellingdon any very deep feeling for her?"

Annabel looked startled.

"I don't suppose he has—in fact I know he hasn't. But he would have had if she had given him a chance, and she didn't. Of course the whole thing started wrong—his coming home and finding her there like that. I don't know how Lily dared. He must have been furious, and Lucius in a fury is something I shouldn't like to have happen to me!"

Miss Silver's busy needles stopped. She laid down her hands upon the pale blue shawl and said,

"My dear Mrs. Scott, you interest me extremely. Just why should Mr. Bellingdon have been furious?"

"Because Lily simply hadn't any right to go behind his back and adopt a baby whilst he was over in the States on business. And I really don't know how she dared!"

"Mrs. Herne is an adopted daughter?"

Annabel's eyes widened.

"You didn't know."

"I had no idea." She picked up her knitting again. "But surely—I did not think that an adoption could take place without the husband's consent."

"No, Lily couldn't do it legally, but she had taken the child and she made a great play about Lucius being away so much and how lonely her life was, and in the end he gave in. If Moira had been different, he would have got fond of her—I'm sure he would. But it wasn't a good start."

Miss Silver said, "No."

15

Sally Foster and David Moray arrived at Merefields next day in time for lunch. They travelled down together, David having discovered more or less by accident that Sally was to be a fellow guest.

"And why you didn't tell me before, I can't imagine."

Sally smiled brightly.

"We can't all have a lot of imagination. I daresay you do very well without it."

He frowned.

"As if an artist could get on at all without imagination! I would have you know that I've as much as I want and a bit over!"

She laughed.

"Isn't that nice, darling! No, consider that retracted—it just slipped out. I'm not to call you darling and you don't like it and it means nothing. And we're back where we were before I said it." He went on frowning.

"And still I don't know why you didn't tell me you were going to Merefields. I told you I was going there as soon as I knew, and you never said a word."

"Because I didn't know. Moira only asked me yesterday."

"Then why didn't you tell me yesterday?"

"Perhaps I wanted it to burst on you as a lovely surprise."

He said angrily, "We might actually have gone by different trains if I hadn't happened to come down the stairs just as you were telling Mrs. Mount that you were going into the country near Ledlington, and that you didn't want any letters forwarded because you would be back on Sunday night!"

Sally had a flash-back in which she saw herself standing in the hall explaining to Mrs. Mount, who was an old fuss and always had to be told everything, and who felt herself quite intolerably responsible since Paulina's death. She herself had been perfectly well aware of David coming down the stairs, and if she had taken pains to speak with extra clarity, there was always the excuse that Mrs. Mount was hard of hearing. Anyhow there had been no need for David to look like a thunderstorm and to take the first opportunity of scolding her up hill and down dale. It was quite idiotic of her to feel warmed and heartened by the scolding.

His voice cut in severely upon these reflections.

"It might have led to our each having a taxi from Ledlington. Did you think of that?"

Sally gazed at him, her eyes very bright, the lashes round them very dark. Nothing would have induced him to say so, but it is a fact that he was reminded of peat-water with the sun shining on it.

"The taxi? Oh, I *didn't!* Frightful of me, wasn't it? I expect I shall come to want some day. I just don't think of things like that. You've saved me from myself this time though. We'll share one!"

"If there isn't a bus," said David.

There wasn't a bus. The taxi ran out past the really old houses with their modern fronts, past the Victorian villas now divided into flats, past the bungalows called Kosi-Kot and Maryzone and Cassino out on to the open road, from which they presently turned into Cranberry Lane. There was nothing to show that this was the way Arthur Hughes had come a few days ago with a Queen's necklace in his pocket.

The first person they saw at Merefields was Lucius Bellingdon. He took them through to the drawing-room where Hilton was bringing in the tea.

"But they would like to take off their things! Miss Foster, I am *sure* you would like to go up to your room and take off your things!" Miss Bray was instant in hospitality. "Moira will take you up. She is a friend of yours, isn't she? Moira, I am sure Miss Foster would like to go to her room!"

Sally had seldom felt so little convinced of being regarded as a friend of Moira Herne's. The slow light eyes had slid over her without the faintest welcome. They rested now upon David Moray, and it was to David that she spoke.

"You are Lucy's latest discovery, aren't you? He's always finding them, and then—he finds them out."

The words turned to insolence, but just as they did so she began to smile. Sally remembered the trick of it from their schooldays—some outrageous remark, and then the smile which changed everything. It beckoned, it promised, and it was gone again, but you couldn't forget that it had been there.

Sally went upstairs with Moira and was shown her room. She was wondering why she had been asked to Merefields. Nothing could be more apparent than the fact that Moira didn't want her here. There had been a smile for David Moray, but none for Sally Foster. She was shown her room and abandoned.

Standing in front of the mirror, Sally discovered that it seemed to think that she was in a blazing temper. If she went down looking like this, everyone else would discover it too. You can subdue a brilliant colour with cream and powder, but how did you put out the angry fire in your eyes? Rather a pity to have to try, because it was all extremely becoming. And it wouldn't do, it simply wouldn't do. She had got to be the normal school friend who was no longer an intimate. There could be a cool allround friendliness, with just a hint of having outgrown what had been pleasant enough in its time—nothing more than that. If Moira Herne didn't know how to behave herself, Sally Foster did. Even if Moira made an absolutely dead set at David, it had nothing to do with Sally, and no one must think it had. She remembered with pleasure that Wilfrid would be there. If the worst came to the worst, she could always flirt with him.

16

Detective Inspector Abbott came out from Ledlington in the early afternoon next day and was closeted with Lucius Bellingdon. When they had talked for a time he interviewed members of the family party and of the household. It was not until the last of them was disposed of that he expressed a desire to see Miss Silver.

She came into the small writing-room which had been placed at his disposal, greeted him, and settled herself in an armless chair of the type which she preferred. Looking at her, Frank had the thought that she was a fixed point in a changing world. Wars came and went, political changes like vast landslides swept the habitable globe, monarchies dissolved and new tyrannies took their place, but here she was, not changed at all as far as he could see from the time when he had first encountered her, not changed indeed from a very much earlier time than that—wise and sedate, with her Edwardian hair-do, her old-fashioned clothes, her beaded slippers, and the large gold locket with her parents' initials entwined upon it in high relief. With her wisdom, her intelligence, her moralities, she was a continual delight to him. He looked across at her now, cocked an impudent eyebrow, and said,

"Well, ma'am, who did it?"

She extracted the blue shawl from her knitting-bag and took up the needles. She said,

"I have really no idea."

He laughed.

"No? You surprise me! Anyhow that makes us two hearts that beat as one. Or to be quite accurate, a number of hearts. The Yard haven't any idea either, nor have the Ledlington police, and nor have I. Do you know, I quite hoped that you would have had the murderer all taped and packaged and ready for me to take away."

Her glance reproved him.

"My dear Frank!"

"I know—I'm being frivolous, and frivolity doesn't mix with murder. But I've only had large doses of Inspector Crisp, all very brisk and efficient and quite furious at the Yard having been called in, but I've had to suffer the new Ledlington Superintendent, a most worthy and reliable officer and, I should say offhand, just about the most crashing bore in southern England. His name is Merrett and he deserves every letter of it, including the extra T! And having got that off my chest, let us get down to business. Have you got anything for me?"

She regarded him with indulgence.

"I think so. Nothing definite of course, but at least one curious thing has come to my notice."

She repeated what Annabel Scott had told her about the snuffbox and the grains of what was undoubtedly snuff which had been found amongst Hubert Garratt's pillows. He listened intently, and when she had finished he said,

"The inference being that Garratt's attack of asthma was deliberately induced either by himself—which would make him art and part in the plot to steal the necklace—or by someone else in the household who must have had a guilty motive. That certainly narrows things down a bit. You say the snuffbox was exhibited on the Sunday before the murder. Well, the snuff must have been used on the Monday night if Garratt had to be incapacitated from going to the bank on Tuesday morning. Which of the people now in the house were here on that Sunday, Monday, Tuesday?"

"All of them except Miss Foster and Mr. Moray."

"You pay your money and you take your choice! Which of them was interested in seeing to it that Hubert didn't go to the bank or—that Arthur Hughes did? The butler, the cook, the daily maids, the secretary, the attractive Mrs.

Scott, the garrulous aunt, the decorative daughter—which of them do you fancy?"

Miss Silver was knitting. She said in a noncommittal voice,

"There were also present until the Monday Mr. Clay Masterson, and Mr. Wilfrid Gaunt. They are friends of Mrs. Herne's. Mr. Masterson drives about the country picking up antiques. He has, I believe, a small business. Mr. Gaunt is an artist. He is also a cousin of Miss Paulina Paine's, and he is staying here now. It might perhaps be advisable to make some enquiries about these young men."

"And what about Arnold Bray? You've rather left him out, haven't you?"

"I was about to mention him, but I see that there was no need for me to do so."

"No, as it happens, there wasn't. The locals have had their eye on Bray from the word go. As a matter of fact he very nearly qualifies as being 'known to the police.' "

"Dear me!"

He nodded.

"He hasn't actually ever been run in, though he got as far as having his fingerprints taken a couple of years ago in connection with a case of blackmail. There had been anonymous letters of the 'pay up or I'll tell' order, and he was under suspicion, but there wasn't enough of a case and he slipped through the net. If he was in the house and any dirty work was going on, I should expect him to have a finger in it, but there's a strong consensus of opinion that he wouldn't be the man behind the gun. A petty small-town near crook and definitely allergic to firearms—that is how Arnold seems to strike those who know him—I won't say best."

Miss Silver pulled on her ball of wool.

"Mr. Bellingdon gave me very much the same description."

"Well, we can put Arnold through it. Sprinkling snuff on Garratt's pillows might be right up his street. We'll see what he has to say about it. Is there anyone else you fancy?"

She remained silent for a little. Then she said,

"There is Mr. Gaunt's connection with Miss Paine. I do not see how it can be more than a coincidence, and as a coincidence it is easily accounted for. Mrs. Herne is acquainted with Miss Sally Foster who has a flat in Miss Paine's house. She and David Moray, another tenant of

Miss Paine's, are here for the week-end—David Moray because Mr. Bellingdon has just bought his portrait of Miss Paine, which he considers to be a very fine picture. You see, all these people were loosely linked together before the robbery and murder took place. David Moray had not, I gather, met Mrs. Herne before, but the other two young people knew her quite well, so that what I mentioned as a coincidence is not really one at all. I was, I believe, merely thinking aloud when I used the expression."

He gave her a quizzical look tempered with affection.

"You pay me quite a compliment."

She went on as if he had not spoken.

"There is, however, a circumstance which I think you should know about, and which concerns Mrs. Herne. She is not really Mr. Bellingdon's daughter but an adopted child, and she was adopted without his knowledge or consent. I gather that there is no very strong tie of feeling between them."

She told him what Annabel Scott had said about Moira Herne's marriage and Oliver Herne's death, and continued,

"I have thought that perhaps some enquiries as to their friends and associates might be advisable. They may have been in contact with people who would have been interested in Mr. Bellingdon's wealth and his more valuable possessions, such as the Queen's Necklace. You will understand that I am not suggesting complicity on Mrs. Herne's part, but it is obvious that this crime was very carefully planned and could hardly have been carried out without professional backing. One of the men whom Miss Paine watched in the gallery had no part in the shooting or the actual robbery, but he was certainly indispensable to the success of the plot."

Frank nodded.

"He would be the fence. The other, the man who spoke, was of course the murderer, and it was he who must have been an intimate. Now, just let us sum up what we know about him, and we can start with that. He must *not* be recognized. Hubert Garratt would have recognized him, and so would Arthur Hughes. Therefore whoever fetches the necklace cannot be allowed to survive. For some reason he does not wish to shoot Hubert Garratt—or, let us say, he would prefer to shoot Arthur Hughes. Hence the snuff on Garratt's pillow. So we know that he is an intimate, that he cannot risk being recognized, and that he either doesn't want to shoot Garratt, or that he does want to shoot Hughes. In either case he is taking a tremendous risk and there must be a correspondingly strong motive to induce him to take it. The necklace is said to be worth thirty thousand pounds, but it would probably have to be broken up, and he'd be lucky if he got five thousand."

"Murder has been done for a great deal less than that, Frank."

"Of course it has. But—"

She put up her hand to stop him and said gravely,

"You conclude that Hubert Garratt was incapacitated in order that Arthur Hughes might take his place. Since talking to Mrs. Scott I have been considering that there might have been another and a far more likely substitute."

"My dear ma'am!"

She continued in the same tone.

"Arthur Hughes was a young man. He had not been very long in Mr. Bellingdon's employ, though he had been on social terms with the family both before he went up to college and after he came down. He was about to leave his appointment as secretary and take up another one. Mr. Bellingdon was annoyed at his attentions to Mrs. Herne. In these circumstances, do you consider that there was any justification for supposing that, with Mr. Garratt incapacitated, it would necessarily have been Arthur Hughes who would be deputed to fetch the necklace?"

"You mean the idea that someone might want Arthur Hughes out of the way won't hold water?"

"I mean something more than that. I mean that if Hubert Garratt were not able to fetch the necklace, the most natural person to do so would have been Mr. Bellingdon himself."

"Lucius Bellingdon!"

"I do not think the possibility could have been ignored. It may even have been desired and counted upon. A motive for the murder of Arthur Hughes eludes me, but it is not difficult to imagine that there might be strong and compelling motives for the murder of Lucius Bellingdon."

He was looking at her, his eyes cold and intent. He said,

"As what?"

"He is a very wealthy man. He controls large interests. His death would endow Mrs. Herne with a fortune. There are a number of young men vaguely connected with this affair whose interest in her is apparent. While Mr. Bellingdon lives he will continue to hold the purse-strings. He can disinherit Mrs. Herne. He wishes her to marry again, but he wishes her to marry suitably. He has a very marked partiality for Mrs. Scott. No one who has seen them together would be surprised if they were to announce an engagement."

He said, "You really mean all this?"

"My dear Frank!"

"With all the implications? I'm not insulting you by asking you whether you realize what they are."

"I believe I am fully aware of them."

"In fact you suggest that the theft of the necklace is no more than a cover up? That Arthur Hughes was shot merely because he was there and could have identified the criminal? And that the real purpose of the plot was the murder of Lucius Bellingdon?"

"I consider it to be a possibility."

"All right, let us go on considering it. It involves believing that Hughes was shot because he might have recognized the man who carried out the crime. And if the sole purpose of the crime was to kill Bellingdon, where was the need to run the risk of murdering Hughes? It would be known that he was the messenger in plenty of time to have called the whole thing off. Even if there was no accomplice in the household, or no opportunity of warning the man on the job—which is something I would find very difficult to believe—the man himself would have had the opportunity of sheering off. He must have been following Hughes for the best part of a mile and a half. He must have known that he wasn't following Bellingdon. Even at the last moment when he came abreast of him before driving him off the road and forcing him to stop there would be time for him to change the plan and draw back from murdering Hughes."

Miss Silver inclined her head.

"There would be time. But you have to consider that there was still the necklace. The prime object of the plot may have been the death of Mr. Bellingdon, but the apparent reason was the theft of the necklace. The details had all been worked out. It was to be handed over to the man whom Miss Paine saw in the gallery. It was probably to be out of the country before an alarm could be given. Thirty thousand pounds, or even a quarter of that sum, was not to be despised. In these circumstances a reckless and unscrupulous man would not shrink from murder. In fact, as we know, he did not shrink from it."

"And that, my dear ma'am, leaves us exactly where we were to start with."

She remained silent for a little. After which she said,

"We have been discussing a number of people connected with this household. I should be interested to know where each of them was, and what he or she was doing, at twelve o'clock last Tuesday when Arthur Hughes was shot in Cranberry Lane. I suppose enquiries of this kind have been made?"

He nodded.

"Oh, yes. The locals are very good at that kind of thing. You'll remember Crisp. Terrier at a rat-hole. Not a soul-mate of mine, but efficient as they come. Well, now, let's see—" He got out a notebook and flicked over the pages. "We'll start at the top. Mr. Lucius Bellingdon says he didn't leave the house and grounds until the news of the murder reached him. He was actually in the garden talking to Donald the gardener from twelve o'clock until the half hour, and Mrs. Scott was with him. Alibi for both of them, reinforced by Donald. They were planning a water garden. Mr. Garratt states that he was incapacitated by asthma. He was visited shortly before ten by Mr. Bellingdon, who confirms his condition, and by Mrs. Scott a little later. She says he was still pretty bad, and that she stayed there getting him to take some coffee and generally tidying up for about twenty minutes, when she joined Mr. Bellingdon in the garden. Since Garratt was still in bed and incapacitated shortly before twelve he could hardly have been following Hughes from the bank at twelve o'clock and murdering him in Cranberry Lane as soon as the coast was clear. Moreover he hasn't got a car and wouldn't have had time to steal one. In fact another beautiful alibi."

Miss Silver inclined her head, but did not speak. Frank went on.

"Hilton and Mrs. Hilton and the rest of the staff are all accounted for, and I don't think we need seriously consider Miss Bray. Not, I think, the stuff of which the efficient criminal is made, and as a matter of fact I gather that she was, as usual, very busy getting in the way of the staff. So we come to Mrs. Herne."

Miss Silver said, "Yes?"

"Well, nobody seems to like Mrs. Herne very much.

Crips didn't say so, but I got the impression that her local reputation wasn't too good. She was in a motor smash when a man was killed, and she went to a dance the same night. She wasn't actually to blame, but people didn't like it. All the same she couldn't have shot Arthur Hughes, because she caught the ten-forty-five to London, where she was met by Mr. Wilfrid Gaunt, after which they dropped in at a newsreel and had lunch together at the Luxe."

"Dear me."

Frank cocked an eyebrow.

"It strikes you that way? Perhaps. But it's an unbreakable alibi for both of them, unless they were in it together. There is no actual proof that he met her beyond the fact that they both say he did, and the same applies to the newsreel. But when it comes to the lunch at the Luxe, the head waiter backs them up. He knows them by sight, and they were there having lunch at a quarter past one. Of course, if the first part of the story was a lie upon which they were agreed, either of them could have shot Arthur Hughes, handed over the necklace to the anonymous gentleman in the dark raincoat—who was probably one of our leading fences—and joined the other in time for a well earned lunch. It would require some neat dovetailing, but it could certainly have been done. I don't say it was done, but it could have been. So there we are. Let us turn to Arnold Bray, who hasn't got an alibi at all in the sense of being able to prove that he wasn't in Cranberry Lane at twelve o'clock. What he says is that he borrowed a bike from his landlady and was on his way to Ledstow, when a tyre went flat and he had to walk. He says he wasn't feeling well and he couldn't make it, so he got through the hedge into a field and sat down to rest. Then, he says, he went to sleep, and by the time he woke up it was getting on for one o'clock, so he walked the bike back to Ledlington. The only part of the story for which there is any corroboration is that he did borrow the bike, and he did bring it back with a flat tyre at something after one. He could have been picking up a car either by theft or as a loan and mudering Arthur Hughes, but I shouldn't think it was at all likely. As far as stealing one goes, no car was reported as missing between eleven and one and the whole thing was much too serious a job for the acquisition of a car to have been left to chance. Of course someone who was in the plot might have lent him one, but from what I hear of Bray I just can't see anyone risking it. He's the type that goes to bits in an emergency, and personally I think he's out of it. Which brings us to Clay Masterson."

Miss Silver gazed at him with interest.

"My dear ma'am, the part would fit him like a glove! He's everybody's first suspect, and there isn't a single shred of evidence against him. Rather a tough young man with rather a rackety reputation. Owns a car, and has a perfectly legitimate excuse for driving about the countryside since, as you have already mentioned, he has a small antique business. He says he was on his way up the London road on Tuesday to attend a sale at Wimbledon. It was just a small affair, but he had been tipped off that there was some good stuff there which the big dealers hadn't got wind of. He says the things he was interested in were due to come up any time after one o'clock, and that's when he got there. Well, there was the sale just as he says, and he got there a little after one, and he bought six chairs, one with a broken leg and the others fairly rickety, but he says they're Chippendale and they'll be as good as new by the time he's done with them. He also got a very dirty Persian carpet which he says is worth a lot but it went for a song. All perfectly above board and bona fide, but he would have had time to shoot Arthur Hughes on the way up and hand the necklace over before he arrived at the sale. Perhaps he didn't, but on the other hand perhaps he did. He's a very slick young man, and I have a horrid feeling that we may never know. And that, so far as I can see, is the entire field. You haven't got a hunch about any of them, have you?"

Miss Silver said in a reserved voice, "Not at the moment, Frank."

17

A small shabby woman was sitting in the bus which runs out of Ledlington and passes the entrance to Cranberry Lane. She had the name of the turning written down on a rubbed piece of paper, and she had showed it to the conductor as well as taking a frequent look at it herself, so she hoped there would be no mistake about putting her down. Being Saturday and the traffic all in the opposite direction, she was alone in the bus, which was scheduled to run out to Poynings and Little Poynton and return with a full load for the late house at the cinema. She would have been happier if there had been other passengers, because she could have asked them to be sure she didn't miss her turning. She had always found people so kind about that sort of thing. You had only to say that you were not used to travelling, and it was wonderful how kind they were. There would, of course, be no need to tell anyone why she had come to Ledlington, or why she was getting off at Cranberry Lane. Not that there was any secret about it, but it might start her off crying again, and that wouldn't do. It wouldn't matter so much if she were to cry later on. It was all so very recent, and nobody would be surprised if she could not quite control her feelings, but it wouldn't do to cry before she got to Merefields—oh, no, it wouldn't do at all. She took a final look at the paper in her hand and then put it away in an old black handbag.

She was all in black from head to foot, but none of it was new. She had bought the coat and skirt when Arthur's father and mother were killed in that terrible railway accident twenty years ago, and the blouse and hat when her old Aunt Mary died. People didn't wear mourning so much now, but she had always kept her black and put it away carefully in camphor, not those horrid moth-balls, so that it came out quite fresh and nice when it was wanted.

She had worn it to Arthur's funeral yesterday morning. It was at Golders Green and everything very nice, but it did seem to her they had rather hurried it on. That would be his father's relations. They had been very good to Arthur of course—paid all his school bills and sent him to college, and put him in the way of being in a good social position and getting this post as Mr. Bellingdon's secretary. Ever so pleased he was about it, poor boy, and no one could tell it would turn out the way it had. The tears came up in her eyes and she got out her handkerchief and dabbed at them.

She hadn't seen so much of Arthur the last few years, but when he did come he was always just the same, full of talk about his friends, and his games, and his girls. Always one for the girls, Arthur was. Not in any horrid way—she was sure about that—but he liked them pretty and he liked them smart and a credit to him when he took them out. It came a bit expensive of course, but she had always tried to help him. Those Hughes relations who had paid for his schooling and his college fees, they weren't as well off as they had been, and once he got a job they expected him to keep himself. Sounded as if they were a little bit mean, she thought. But there, it wasn't right to judge, and they were paying for the funeral. No, it was Mr. Bellingdon who was doing that, and very kind and generous of him, but only right, because Arthur had been doing his errand when he was shot. She had to put her handkerchief to her eyes again as she thought about Arthur being shot. She was glad now that there were no other passengers. She wouldn't have liked to sit in a bus and cry before strangers however kind they were—and people were very kind when they thought you were in trouble.

Before there was time to put her handkerchief away the bus had come to a standstill, and there was the conductor putting his head in and saying, "Cranberry Lane." It quite startled her, but it stopped the flow of tears, which was a good thing.

Half a mile up the lane and she would come to the village, and right in the middle of the village she would see the entrance to Merefields.

"You can't miss it," the conductor told her as she got down. "The gate stands open and there's a couple of pillars with pineapples on them."

She thanked him and began to walk up the lane, wishing that her legs felt stronger and that she didn't keep thinking about Arthur being shot.

The thought kept coming back. It had happened in this lane, somewhere between the high road and the village. Perhaps it was just round this corner—perhaps it was round the next . . . She mustn't think about where it happened. She must only think about going to see Arthur's girl and doing her best to comfort her. She must have been terribly upset not to be able to come to the funeral. She had thought she would see her there, and she had tried to screw up her courage to ask Mr. Bellingdon how she was, but when it came to the point she couldn't manage it. He had spoken to her very kindly after it was all over, but when it came to asking him about his daughter she couldn't do it. For one thing, Arthur always spoke of her as Moira, but he said she had been married and he hadn't told her what her married name was. She didn't like to say Moira, and she didn't like to say your daughter, so she didn't say anything at all. Mr. Bellingdon hadn't given his consent to there being anything between them—she knew that—so it wouldn't have done for her to put herself forward.

She could see the first house in the village now. She went on until she came to the open gate between the two tall pillars. Merefields looked to be a big place. There were some lovely trees. The house was quite a long way from the entrance. She would be glad to sit down and rest.

She came out upon the gravel sweep and saw the house on one side of it, and the great bank of coloured hyacinths on the other. Lovely they were, and a beautiful scent out here in the air but too heavy to have in the house. She couldn't sit in a room with more than one or two of them, not for very long.

Minnie Jones crossed the gravel, went up the half dozen steps to the front door, and pulled upon the wrought-iron bell. When Hilton opened the door, there she was, very small and black, with her hands clasped upon the handle of her shabby bag. She made a tentative step forward as the door swung in and said in a wavering voice,

"I have come to see Mr. Bellingdon's daughter. I'm afraid I don't know her married name."

Hilton wasn't quite sure of his ground. Anyone who came calling would know the name of the lady they were calling on—it stood to reason they would. If that little person didn't know Mrs. Herne's name, it meant that she wasn't a caller. Of course she might be collecting from something—there were all sorts that did that. If you asked him, she didn't look fit for it, and that was a fact. And she didn't look like a beggar either. Something about her that made you feel she was all right—nice quiet manner—pretty way of speaking.

Before he could say anything she was looking at him with anxious blue eyes and saying,

"She is here, isn't she?"

He found himself admitting it.

"Then I'm sure she will see me. My name is Jones—Miss Jones, and I am Arthur Hughes's aunt, his mother's sister. You must have known him of course."

Her eyes brimmed up with tears. Astonishing how blue they were in that little faded face. He hadn't like Arthur Hughes very much. La-di-da ways and a bit too much taking himself for granted. But when all was said and done it was one thing to read about shootings in the papers, and quite another to have them happen just round the corner from your own front door, and to someone who was living in the house. He said what a shocking thing it was and showed her into the morning-room.

She was glad enough to sit down. It wasn't a long walk, but it doesn't take much to tire you when your heart is heavy. Her friend Florrie Williams that she lived with hadn't wanted her to come—said it was too much for her right on top of the shock she had had and the funeral and all. But she hadn't felt that she could rest until she had been down to see Arthur's girl and give her the letters. He had trusted them to her and told her to keep them safe, and now that he was gone the proper person to have them was the girl who had written them. She couldn't rest until she had done her errand, and she had told Florrie so. She leaned back in her chair and closed her eyes.

It was a little time before the door opened and Moira Herne came in. When you have heard a lot about someone, there is always a moment in a first actual meeting when it seems as if the person whom you have only met in thought is one person, and the one who confronts you in the flesh is another. Minnie Jones had this feeling very strongly as she got out of her chair and came forward to meet Moira Herne. There was the Moira whom poor Arthur had talked about by the hour, the Moira whom he had loved and who had loved him and who must be brokenhearted at his death, and there was this girl who was coming into the room. She wore dark blue slacks and a tight scarlet jumper, and she didn't look as if she had a heart to break. Minnie had a quick stab of conscience for that. You couldn't judge people by how they looked. A heart didn't show unless you wore it on your sleeve, and why should you do that?

She put out her hand, but since there was no answering movement she let it drop again as she said,

"I am Arthur's aunt, my dear. His mother was my sister Gwen. I expect he has told you about me, and I have heard a great deal about you."

There was a blue and green rug on the morning-room floor. It would be a little over six foot wide. Minnie had the thought that it was like a stream of green and blue water flowing between them, she on the one side of it and Moira on the other. Into this thought and mingling with it, came the remembrance of the parable in the Bible about the rich man and Lazarus. Lazarus was in Abraham's bosom and Dives was in a place of punishment, and between them there was a great gulf fixed. The thought was vague enough—it neither labelled Moira nor herself. But that the gulf was there between them was something she didn't have to think about. It was there. From the other side of it Moira said,

"What do you want?"

And from her side of the gulf Minnie answered her.

"I wanted to comfort you."

It was already in the past tense, because she knew now that Moira didn't want her comfort.

Moira stood there and stared. She said,

"Why?"

"For Arthur's death."

"I don't know what you mean. I don't know why you've come."

Minnie straightened herself as she would have done if she had been suddenly called upon to lift a weight. It was too heavy for her, but she had to lift it. She said in a small steady voice,

"I brought you some things which I thought you would like to have. I thought it would comfort you to have them."

"I don't know what you mean."

"He talked to me about you. He said you were in love with each other. He said you were going to be married."

"I'm afraid he was telling the tale."

All the way that she had come Minnie had thought about what she was going to say to the girl whom Arthur had loved and who had lost him. Now that she was here and everything was quite different from what she had thought it was going to be, she still had to say what she had planned to say. Her mind and her thought were set and she could not change them. She said,

"There were the letters—your letters. I thought perhaps you would like to have them back."

That light fixed look of Moira's changed. It had been cold enough, now it became wary. She said,

"So that's it, is it? My letters? What do you want for them?"

Minnie Jones was not able to understand what was being said to her. It was like hearing something in a foreign language—there is a sound and there are words, but you don't know what they mean. She didn't know what Moira meant.

She had left her black handbag on the arm of the chair. She turned round to get it now. She began to open it.

"He kept them. I thought you would like to have them."

Moira crossed the blue and green rug and came to stand beside her.

"Have you got them with you—all of them? Let me have them—they're mine!"

The bag was a capacious one. It held the packet of letters easily enough. There were not so very many of them. The affair had been a brief madness—a quick blaze up like burning straw, a rush of hot air, and then nothing but ash. No, there were not so many of the letters, but there ought to be more than this. She said so without compromise.

"There ought to be more. Where are the rest?"

"I don't know."

"He said he had burned them—he promised he would. Where are they?"

She had been flicking over the letters in the packet. There were two missing—the really damning ones. And the photographs. She must have been bad to let him take them—quite quite mad. If Lucy set eyes on them it would be all up with her. It was the sort of thing he was strict about, and not one penny more would she get from him. She knew that well enough. She had to have those letters back, and the photographs, no matter what it cost her. She said sharply,

"There are two more letters, and three photographs—snapshots. He destroyed the films, but he had taken prints from them and he wouldn't give them up. Where are they?"

Minnie gazed at her.

"He had a very beautiful photograph of you in evening dress."

"These were not in evening dress."

They had not, as a matter of fact, been in any kind of dress at all. She really must have been mad. She said abruptly,

"You've got them of course. And if you've got them, you know damn well that I've got to have them! Stop holding out on me and come to the point! How much do you want? And you'd better be moderate, because I'm broke, and if you push me too hard, I shall just hand you over to the police. So get a move on!"

The whole fatigue of these days since Arthur's death seemed to be pressing down on Minnie Jones. You can take one day at a time and do your best with it, but this wasn't one day, it was five days—Tuesday, Wednesday, Thursday, Friday, Saturday—and it was too much. She didn't seem able to think properly. She heard Moira say,

"You can be sent to prison for blackmail."

Once long ago when she and Gwen were girls they had been chased by a bull. Down in the country it was, and Gwen had a dress with poppies on it and a red hat, and the bull had chased them. Gwen ran, but Minnie couldn't run. She couldn't think, she couldn't move. And then Gwen came running back. She had unfastened her brooch and she had it in her hand, and when Minnie didn't move she ran the pin of the brooch right into her arm, and the next thing Minnie knew they were running together, and they got out of the field before the bull could catch them. It was an odd thing to remember all this long time afterwards, when Gwen had been dead for twenty years, but Moira saying that about prison and blackmail was like the pin of the brooch running into her arm and rousing her up to run away from the bull. Prison—blackmail—the words pricked sharply home. She said,

"Oh!" And then, "You oughtn't to say a thing like that—it's not right!"

"The letters and the photographs—where are they? Did you bring them with you?"

She remembered then. There was the packet of letters and there was an envelope, stuck down. She didn't know what was in it because she hadn't opened it. It was marked *"Private. Keep safe. M.H."* and she had put it in her bag just in case. And because Arthur had marked it *"Keep safe"* she had put it in the inside pocket, which had really been made to take a piece of looking-glass, only the glass had been broken years ago. The envelope was there now. If it had Moira's letters in it and the photographs which she didn't want anyone to see, of course she would give them to her. But before she did that she must open the envelope and make sure of what was in it, because Arthur had marked it *"Private, keep safe."* She had the bag in her two hands, her fingers clenched hard. She moved back now until she came to a table that had books on it and coloured primroses in a glass bowl. She set down the bag on the top of the books and opened it and got out the envelope. She didn't like opening it, because it was marked private, but she had to be sure of what was in it. Her fingers fumbled with the flap of the envelope. It was gummed down very securely.

When Moira reached for it, she moved back quickly and put the table between them. Something in her haste must have strengthened her fingers, because the envelope tore. A snapshot dropped out. It went fluttering down, to lie upon the carpet and be seen for what it was. She saw it quite clearly, and so did Moira Herne. The blood came up into Minnie's face and then went ebbing away until it was all quite gone.

Moira picked up the snapshot and held out her hand. Minnie Jones put the envelope into it and shut the bag. She didn't say anything, and Moira didn't say anything. There was a little fire burning on the hearth. Moira went over and knelt there, burning the snapshots, burning the envelope and everything in it, burning the letters.

Minnie Jones went out of the room, and across the hall, and out of the front door. She began to walk down the drive.

18

The drive went on for a little way before it turned and was out of sight of the house. All the time she was crossing the gravel sweep and walking down the open stretch of the drive Minnie Jones felt as if the house was watching her. In her own mind and in her thoughts she had been beaten and stripped and turned away. If it had happened to her body it would not have hurt her more. When she got round the corner of the drive and there were trees between her and all those staring windows it was a little better. There was some shelter, some protection, but this very fact brought with it the fuller realization of what had happened. She shrank from it, but she could not shut it out. She had seen the photograph, and she couldn't shut it out. She had gone to take comfort to the girl whom Arthur loved and who must be breaking her heart for him, and her comfort wasn't needed, because it wasn't love that had been between them, it was wickedness. This girl had led Arthur into wickedness. She had been married, she wasn't just an ignorant girl. She would know what she was doing, and she had led Arthur astray. The pain and sorrow and shame of it came down on her like a black cloud, so that she no longer knew where she was going. It was not until her feet were stumbling on rougher ground that a sense of her surroundings came back to her and she found that she had left the drive and wandered in amongst the trees and shrubs which bordered it.

She was standing with a hand stretched out before her and resting upon the bough of a small tree. It had its first leaves about it like a green cloud. She stood there holding onto it and not knowing what to do next, because her legs were shaking and there was a weakness in them and in her whole body. If she could sit down and rest for a little, perhaps some of her strength would come back and she would be able to walk down Cranberry Lane and get on to the Ledlington bus. She mustn't miss it—oh, no, she mustn't miss it—or her train. Florrie would be dreadfully worried if she missed her train. Florrie hadn't wanted her to come.

At this point her thinking became very much confused. The bough seemed to be slipping out of her hand—everything seemed to be slipping. She had a dim sense that she was falling. And then that was gone too—everything was gone.

Miss Silver had walked down to the village to post a letter to her niece Ethel Burkett. Having received the news that Ethel's sister Gladys whose irresponsible conduct had been giving her family a good deal of anxiety had now returned to her home and husband, she had hastened to relieve Ethel's mind.

"Andrew Robinson," she wrote, "is a man for whom I feel a great deal of respect. He does not pretend that Gladys's conduct has not gravely displeased him, but he is prepared to overlook it and say no more about the matter. He believes her friend Mrs. Farmer to be a thoroughly bad influence, and is glad to be able to tell me that she will shortly be leaving Blackheath on a visit to her married daughter in South Africa. I can only hope that she too will have learned a lesson, and that her mischief-making proclivities will not be employed to impair the harmony of her daughter's home."

The letter posted, and the evening being clear and still,

Miss Silver diverged from the drive and contemplated with pleasure the green park land with which Merefields was surrounded. There were many fine clumps of trees coming into leaf, the ground undulated in a manner very agreeable to the eye, and a stretch of ornamental water brightened the scene.

Amid these surroundings she strolled for a time, her thoughts dwelling with gratitude and relief upon the outcome of what had threatened to become a painful family problem. Returning through the shrubbery in the direction of the drive, she was following a narrow path set on either side with trees and bushes in their spring greenery, when her eye was attracted by something not at all in keeping with this rural beauty. It was, in fact, something of an extremely disquieting nature. What she saw was a woman's hand in a black thread glove and a woman's arm in a black cloth sleeve. The hand and arm lay upon the ground, and they lay very still. There was no more than that to be seen, because there was a froth of white bird cherry in the way. It was not in Miss Silver to hesitate before what might prove to be an unpleasant situation. She stepped off the path, pushed aside a blossoming bough, and saw Minnie Jones lying where she had fallen on the damp earth.

She lay on her side, that one hand and arm stretched out as if when it was too late she had groped for something to break her fall. Her rather long black skirt was quite neatly disposed. Her shabby black hat had tilted and almost covered her face. She lay dreadfully still. Miss Silver went down on her knees, reached for the hand, and found it lax and warm. The warmth came through the black thread glove. She stripped it off and felt for the pulse in the wrist. She felt for it, but at first she could not find it. She had to shift her grasp more than once before she could feel the faint, slow beat. It was very faint indeed. Miss Silver took off the hat, took off her own scarf and laid it under the head, and considered what she had better do next. The woman was not young. The now exposed features were drawn and colourless. It was evident that assistance must be sought, but in order to summon it she must leave the poor thing alone, and this she really did not like to do.

She had just made up her mind that to hurry to the house was the only possible course for her to follow, when the hand which she was holding stirred faintly and a pair of blue eyes blinked up at her from the pale face. It was obvious that at first they did not see her. They had the look with which a very young infant gazes at what it cannot understand. They shut, and opened again, and this time they saw. The hand which lay in hers closed and clung, Miss Silver said in her kindest voice,

"You will be all right now."

The eyes shut again. A few moments passed before they opened. Minnie Jones said,

"I fell—"

"Did you hurt yourself?"

The reply came in a faint wondering tone.

"I—don't—think so—" Then after a pause, "It was—a long way. I was—so tired—"

It was some time before Miss Silver felt it prudent to ask a question.

"Were you on your way to the house?"

The head was feebly shaken.

"No—I was coming away—" The eyes filled with tears. "I can't go back there—I can't—"

Miss Silver said very gently indeed, "Why can you not go back?"

When Minnie Jones began to think about it afterwards she was both surprised and shocked. That she should tell a stranger about coming to see Moira Herne and being treated in the way in which she had been treated was a thing that she would never be able to understand. But at the time it seemed the most natural thing in the world. She had come from unkindness, and she had met with kindness. She had been cold, and lost, and dreadfully alone. Her very heart had been cold. The kindness warmed her, and she wasn't alone any more. She said,

"I came to see Arthur's girl. I'm his aunt—Minnie Jones. He told me about her. He said they were going to be married, only her father hadn't given his consent. She has been married before. But it was the money, you see—there was such a lot of money. Young people oughtn't to think so much about money, but they do. Arthur said they would have to have her father's consent. And he left her letters with me, to keep them safe because he hadn't anywhere to lock them up, and it wouldn't do for anyone to see them." She struggled to raise herself a little and to feel for her handkerchief. When Miss Silver had found it for her she went on. "Arthur talked about her a lot. He was very proud of her being fond of him, and he said her father would come round. I thought she would be at the funeral, but she wasn't. Mr. Bellingdon came, but not

Moira. And I thought it would be because she was too upset, so I came down this afternoon to see her and to bring her the letters. I go out sewing in the mornings, so I couldn't get away by an earlier train. My friend didn't want me to come, but I thought, 'She's Arthur's girl, and we can be sorry together and comfort each other.' " The tears ran down her face, and she said, "I didn't know what she was like."

"You saw her?"

"Yes, I saw her. I oughtn't to have come. She thought I wanted money for the letters, and she talked about the police. She didn't love Arthur. She only thought about getting her letters back, and the photographs."

"There were photographs?"

Minnie closed her eyes as if it would help her to shut out what she had seen. She said, "Yes," in a whispering voice. And then, "They were in a separate envelope—stuck down. Arthur had written *'Private'* on it, and *'Keep Safely.'* I wasn't going to look at anything, but I thought I ought to open the envelope—I wish I hadn't. One of the photographs fell out on to the floor between us—we couldn't help seeing it. All I wanted to do after that was to get away. She was wicked, and she had made Arthur wicked too."

Miss Silver sat there. She would have to return to the house, but it did not seem possible to take this poor thing back there. It was after six o'clock. She would have to get Annabel Scott to help her. If Minnie Jones was well enough to travel, Annabel could drive her to Ledlington and see her on to a train, but she could not believe that it would be right for her to travel alone. She said, "Are you far from your home?" and was relieved to learn that Miss Jones resided in one of the nearer London suburbs. She said tentatively,

"You spoke of a friend—"

Minnie was sitting up now. She responded with more strength in her voice.

"Oh, yes—Mrs. Williams—she lives with me. And she will be ever so worried if I miss my train. Oh dear, I shall never catch it! It was the six-twenty."

Miss Silver looked at her watch.

"I am afraid it has gone, but there will be another in a little under an hour. That will give you time to have some refreshment, and if there is any way of letting your friend know perhaps she could meet you at the other end."

A little colour came back into Minnie's face.

"Oh, that would be nice!"

"Are you on the telephone?"

Minnie shook her head.

"Oh, no. But Mr. Pegler would take a message. He's Florrie's brother-in-law and ever so kind."

Miss Silver never forgot a name. This was an uncommon one, and she had heard it before. She repeated it with a question in her voice.

"Mr. Pegler?"

Minnie nodded.

"He lives just round the corner. The people in the house are relations. It's a grocery business, so they have the telephone, and if they're out he answers it. And Saturday evenings they go to the pictures, and Mr. Pegler comes round to Florrie and me, only tonight he said he thought he'd stay at home because of me coming back tired and wanting to rest. He's ever so considerate."

A grocery business—the Masters gallery—there might be a link between them, or there might not. Pegler was certainly an uncommon name. Miss Silver remarked upon this fact.

"That is a name one does not often hear. I believe I have only once come across it before. A friend mentioned it to me then in connection with a picture gallery."

Minnie brightened.

"The Masters gallery. That would be our Mr. Pegler—he's worked for them for years."

Miss Silver proceeded with caution.

"My friend was a deaf lady—a Miss Paine. She had learned to do lip-reading, and she told me Mr. Pegler was very much interested, as he had a little grand-daughter who was deaf."

Minnie had begun to look a great deal more like herself. She said in quite an animated voice,

"Oh, yes— little Doris. She's a sweet little thing. Miss Paine told him all about how to get her taught, and he was ever so grateful. You know, she was run over the other day, poor thing. Mr. Pegler was quite upset about it, and about having the police in at the gallery asking him about the lip-reading. Seems a funny sort of thing for them to want to know about, and of course he couldn't tell them anything. He couldn't make it out at all, he said. Miss Paine came in to see the pictures on account of her portrait being there, and when she'd gone away there was a gentleman came from the other end of the gallery, and he got asking Mr. Pegler all sorts of questions about Miss Paine and her portrait. And when Mr. Pegler told him about how deaf she was but that no one would know it on account of her doing this lip-reading, well, he said you would hardly credit how interested the gentleman was. And what was so funny was that the police were just as interested as the gentleman. It was after poor Miss Paine had had the accident, and they wanted to know about the lip-reading, and about the gentleman that was interested in it. But of course Mr. Pegler couldn't tell them anything more about that—" She paused, and added, "Not then."

All the time that she had been speaking the scene in the morning-room at Merefields had been getting fainter in her mind, the way a dream gets fainter when you wake up and get out of bed and wash, and dress, and do your hair. Miss Silver, observing this, was beginning to feel a good deal happier about her travelling alone. She felt able to give more of her attention to the fact that Mr. Pegler's name had cropped up in rather a surprising manner, and less to the question of whether Miss Jones was likely to be overtaken by a second attack of faintness. She was still a little divided in her mind when Minnie concluded with the words "Not then." If they meant anything at all, they meant that although Mr. Pegler had found himself unable to give the police any information about the gentleman in the gallery, he had subsequently become possessed of some such information. It seemed imperative to discover what this might be. Whatever thoughts she may have had about Miss Jones's train and the advisability of allowing her to continue to sit upon the ground, which at this time of year could hardly fail to be damp, were dismissed. She repeated Minnie's last words with a strong note of enquiry.

"Not then, Miss Jones? Do you mean—"

Minnie Jones nodded.

"I don't suppose I should have known anything about it, only I was with him. I had been round to the shop for some potatoes—we had run right out—and Mr. Pegler walked back with me. He's always so kind like that. Well, just as we came to the corner on the High Street, there was a man standing—right under the street-lamp. Two men there were really, waiting to go across the road and talking to each other. We didn't have to cross, and after we'd gone by Mr. Pegler said, 'See that gentleman, Min? That's the one I told you about that was looking at that Miss Paine's portrait and was so interested when I told him about her lip-reading. The police wanted to know about him, though I'm sure I don't know why—you remember?' So I said I did, and he said, 'Funny seeing him again.' And it was, wasn't it?"

"Miss Jones, what did he look like?"

Minnie stopped to think. Then she said in a hesitating voice,

"Well, I don't know. He was pretty much like anyone else, if you know what I mean. He'd a drab coat on and one of those soft hats, and—well, he was pretty much like anyone else."

"But Mr. Pegler recognized him?"

"Oh, yes, he *did*. He's got a wonderful eye for a face—never forgets one, he says. Now, if it had been the other gentleman, I don't say I wouldn't have remembered him myself, but Mr. Pegler's one—" she shook her head—"I don't suppose I'd know him if I saw him again this minute."

Miss Silver was not interested in the other gentleman. She said,

"Was Mr. Pegler going to tell the police that he had seen this gentleman again?"

"Oh, no, he wouldn't do that. It was just the lip-reading they were interested in, not anything else."

Miss Silver let that pass. It would be for the police to pick up this thread, and they could be safely left to do so. Changing the subject, she imparted her immediate plans to Miss Jones.

"If you would rather not come back to the house—"

Minnie became alarmingly pale.

"Oh, no—I couldn't do that—"

"Then will you just sit here quietly whilst I go and fetch someone who will drive you to the station. I will accompany you and see you off, and I will ring up Mr. Pegler and ask him to meet you. Do you feel quite able for that?"

Minnie Jones said, "Oh, *yes*," and then, "how kind you are."

19

When Miss Silver had left her to go up to the house Minnie Jones did what she could to tidy herself. She regretted the piece of looking-glass which had once had a place in her bag, but which had met the fate which waits on pocket-mirrors quite a number of years ago. A vague impression that it was unlucky to break a looking-glass had always prevented her from replacing anything so likely to get broken again, but she had a comb in her bag, and she could make sure that her hair was neat without looking at it. She dusted her hat with her handkerchief and put it on again. The ground was not damp enough to have stained her coat, for which she was grateful. There were some specks of what looked like bark and a withered leaf or two adhering to the black stuff. When she had brushed them off she considered that she had done as much as she could.

She felt weak, but not ill. Miss Silver had been so very kind, and she was going to be driven to the station. She would not have to go back to the house, and she would not have to see Moira Herne again. She wouldn't have to see her, and she must try—oh, yes, she must try very hard not to think about her.

The trouble about that kind of resolution is that it is apt to defeat its own ends. If you have to make a strong effort not to think about someone, it means that they are there, stuck fast in your mind like a thorn that has run in so far that you can't see it. You only know that it is there because it hurts.

Minnie had got to her feet. She moved now, taking the small path which led back to the drive.

She did not have to wait very long. Miss Silver had been fortunate in finding Annabel Scott alone. A very few words were enough to explain the predicament and enlist her help. Annabel ran up to her room for a coat, and coming back with the least possible delay, suggested that they should walk round to the garage together and avoid comment by starting from there. As the car turned into the drive she laughed and said,

"We shan't have very much time to make ourselves beautiful before dinner! Lucius always pretends that he despises make-up, so he ought to be pleased. Actually, he likes it all right if it's done well. The art of concealing that there's any art to conceal!"

They picked up Minnie Jones and ran out along Cranberry Lane on to the high road. Minnie, on the back seat with Miss Silver, found herself definitely assuaged. Mrs. Scott was being ever so kind. She had pressed her hand and said, "We were all so sorry about Arthur," and it was said the way you say things when you really mean them. Miss Silver slipped a hand inside her arm and said she thought there would be time for her to have a cup of tea and something to eat at the station. A cup of tea would be lovely. Everyone was being so kind.

It was when they were coming down the incline to the station yard that something happened. Miss Silver said, "Here we are," and Minnie leaned forward to look out of the window. The down train had just come in, and passengers who had arrived by it were emerging. Minnie would not have expected to know any of them, but a good deal to her surprise she was aware of a face that she had seen before. She said, "Oh!" and when Miss Silver asked her whether there was anything the matter something seemed to push the words right out of her mouth. She didn't know why, but that was the way it seemed. She said,

"That gentleman coming out now—that's the one that was with the gentleman Mr. Pegler recognized."

Annabel was backing into a parking-place. Minnie Jones continued to point. The man who had come out of the station continued to walk up the incline. Miss Silver said firmly,

"Do you mean that this is the gentleman who talked with Mr. Pegler in the gallery?"

Minnie didn't mean anything of the sort. She hastened to make it perfectly clear that she didn't.

"Oh, no, this was the other one we saw last night in the Emden Road. I said I'd know him again—you remember I did."

Annabel, taking her hands from the wheel, looked where they were looking.

"Someone you know?" she said, "what—not that man!"

Minnie nodded.

"Oh, yes, that's him. I said I'd know him."

Annabel began to say something and stopped. Miss Silver touched her on the shoulder.

"Mrs. Scott, do you know who it is?"

The answer had a laughing inflection.

"Rather better than I want to."

Miss Silver spoke low and insistently.

"Who is it?"

And Annabel Scott said,

"It's Arnold Bray."

20

Sally Foster was engaged in wondering why she had been such a blithering fool as to come down to Merefields. If she hadn't been very nicely brought up she would have used a worse word. Early association with a great-aunt whom she had really loved with all her heart was still a handicap when it came to availing herself of a free modern idiom. Well, here she was at Merefields—here they all were, Wilfrid, David, Moira, and herself, with Clay Masterson breezing in when he felt like it. Like Wilfrid and David, he had no time for anyone but Moira. Nobody had time for Sally Foster, nobody wanted her. Nobody would have turned their head or taken the slightest notice if she had dropped down dead at their feet or just melted into the surrounding air.

The question as to why she had been asked had resolved itself when Lucius Bellingdon displayed a passionate interest in her last interview with Paulina Paine. He wanted to know all about it, and she really hadn't got anything to tell him. Paulina had come in on the Monday evening just as she and David were going out, and she had stopped them and talked to David about his cousins the Charles Morays. She asked David for their telephone number, and they had gone up to Sally's room, all three of them, and David had put through the call. What Paulina wanted was Miss Maud

Silver's address, and David had taken it down for her. And that was simply and absolutely All.

After Lucius had done a bit of cross-examination and had become convinced that it really was all, he had only too obviously lost interest and gone back to concentrating upon Annabel Scott, with occasional time off for interviews with Miss Silver and, or, the police.

Naturally, by this time there wasn't much about Miss Silver's position that Sally didn't know. What she had not been able to guess for herself she had wormed out of David Moray. And it had got her exactly nowhere at all. The week-end was still a total loss. Sally gritted her teeth and meditated getting someone to send her a telegram, or to ring her up and say she was urgently wanted in town. She had got as far as sitting down to write to Jessica Meredith, when she remembered that Jessica was being bridesmaid at a cousin's wedding in Wales. On this she decided that she had better dress for dinner. A glance in the mirror brought it home to her that she must do what she could about her face. Sometimes the harder you tried the less effect it seemed to have. Of course nobody could pretend that yellow walnut made a becoming frame for a looking-glass. All the furniture in this room was constructed of yellow walnut, and the walls were covered with a yellow paper which had bunches of daffodils on it. It was a north room, and in theory all this yellow was supposed to make it look as if it faced south. In practice, Sally decided that all it did was to make her look yellow too. The really awful thing was that she had brought a new dress down with her and the very minute she put it on she knew that it wasn't going to do. Not here, not now. Because it was almost exactly like the wallpaper, only the yellow bunches on an ivory ground were primroses instead of daffodils. She had loved it in the shop, and she had loved it when she put in on at home. It had thrown up the chestnut in her hair and made her eyes look warm, it had flattered her skin. It didn't do any of these things now.

She snatched up her hand-glass, went to the window, pushed back the amber curtains as far as they would go, and faced the light. The yellow room receded and her spirits rose. The dress really *was* pretty, and she definitely didn't look as if she was getting jaundice. She finished herself off and went downstairs feeling better.

She was going to need all the moral support that she could get, because when she got into the drawing-room

Moira was there with Wilfrid and Clay Masterson, and none of them took the least notice of her. They were grouped round the fireplace, and as the temperature had in the last hour decided on one of those melodramatic drops which make the English spring so delightful, the hearth had its attractions. The fact that nobody made room for her set a spark to Sally's temper. She walked up to them, was stared at by Moira, and greeted by Wilfrid with an insulting "Darling, you look cold."

Sally said, "I am cold."

"Darling, so am I. And I was here first!"

Wilfrid was naturally capable of anything. She had always known that, and as far as he was concerned her feelings were armoured. She got between him and Clay Masterson and felt pleased with herself. No one had introduced them, but Moira never did introduce anyone. All her set were supposed to know each other. Sally wasn't really in her set.

Clay said, "What were we talking about?" in the kind of voice which means that someone has butted in and spoiled whatever it was you were going to say. In the circumstances, it was perhaps not surprising that she did not find herself attracted to him, but she supposed that some people might have found him attractive. He had rather the air of expecting it himself. Of medium height, not handsome and not plain—Sally found herself summing him up as very sure of himself. She supposed that would go down with some people. With Moira for instance. Moira was a trampler. If you gave her an inch, she would take an ell and despise you from the depths of whatever did duty for a heart, and she liked someone who would stand up to her and give as good as he got. Clay was saying,

"It was a marvellous piece of luck! And the fool hadn't the slightest idea of what he'd got. Said he'd done the place up proper when he got married somewhere about fifty years ago—bought a nice upholstered suite and shoved the old stuff away in the attic! And there it was—oak dresser, very good lines, and a lovely corner-cupboard. Handles all gone of course."

Wilfrid laughed.

"Well, take care you haven't been had!" he said. "That's quite a good confidence trick, you know—reproductions well weathered and knocked about a bit and shoved away in an attic or an outhouse."

Clay Masterson said,

"I wasn't born yesterday."

And then the door opened to let in Annabel Scott with David Moray, and Hubert Garratt silent and depressed. They too came over to the fire, Annabel with her smiling charm, David the tallest of the men, his fair hair always a little rough no matter how much it was brushed. Sally's heart gave an angry jerk. He was a thoroughly tiresome creature. He wasn't in the least the sort of man she had ever meant to fall in love with. She wasn't in love with him. She hadn't any intention of being in love with anyone for years and years and years. It was a pleasant thing to play with, but go in head over ears and get drowned in it—no thank you!

They were talking and laughing now. Annabel's entrance had made the conversation general. Sally spoke and laughed, and saw that David did neither. He just stood there on the outer edge of the group and looked at Moira Herne. Her glimmering hair was like an auriole. She was wearing something that was the colour of splintered ice. Her hands were ringless and her neck was bare. Her eyes were like pale jewels, water-bright.

He went on looking whilst Lucius Bellingdon came in. He was followed by Miss Bray in a hurry. She must have been in a hurry when she dressed too, for her old-fashioned black lace was done up crooked and her hair was wispy. Behind her came Miss Silver, quiet and composed, in the neat dark blue crêpe-de Chine which her niece Ethel Burkett had persuaded her to buy during their holiday at Clifton-on-Sea. The price had shocked her at the time, but the dress had proved to be a Standby. It was suitable, it was ladylike.

Moira Herne turned her gaze upon Miss Bray and said,

"Late again, Ellen? What about the example to the young? I expect Mrs. Hilton will give notice. She will if it's something that's going to spoil. It must be damnable to be a cook and have people late for meals. I should want to throw the soup at them." Her voice drawled a little. It had no inflexions.

Miss Bray flushed in an unbecoming manner. She began an indistinguishable murmur in which most of the words were lost, but it was broken in upon by David Moray, who took this moment to cross over to Moira Herne and to say without any preliminaries, "I would like to paint you."

Moira did not appear to be displeased. The pale bright

eyes were turned upon him. Since he was so tall, she had to look up, which enhanced the effect.

"You want to paint my portrait? What would you want for doing it—a frightful lot? What about it, Lucy? You would have to pay for it. I'm broke."

David was looking at her between narrowed lids. Without waiting for Lucius Bellingdon to speak he said in quite a casual way,

"No, not a portrait. A head. Medusa."

She stared.

"Medusa? What do you mean? Was she somebody?" She looked round the group. "Does anyone know who she was? Because I don't. I never could be bothered with things like history. After all, it's *now* you have to live. I can't see any sense in cluttering your mind up with who people were or what they did hundreds of years ago."

Annabel Scott laughed her attractive laugh.

"Medusa goes back a long way farther than that!"

"Does she? Why does he think I'm like her?"

Annabel said, "I don't know. She was a priestess in the temple of Pallas Athene. She took a lover there, and the goddess punished her by turning her into a gorgon."

Moira said, "Oh—" and Annabel went on sweetly.

"They had clashing wings and they were horrible to look at, but Medusa kept her beautiful face, only snakes grew out of her hair, and her eyes turned people to stone."

Moira appeared to consider this information. Then she stared at David.

"Were you going to paint snakes in my hair?"

"Oh, no."

"Or clashing wings?"

"No—just the head."

She said without any change in her voice or expression,

"It might be rather fun. You could start tomorrow."

The door opened. Hilton appeared on the threshold. He looked like a man whose wife had just been speaking her mind. He said, "Dinner is served."

As they went in, Lucius Bellingdon said to Annabel Scott,

"Just what did all that mean?"

"That he wants to paint her."

His eyebrows rose.

"As Medusa?"

"So he says—but without the snakes."

"Then why Medusa?"

"Darling, if you don't know, I can't tell you."

At the moment he could only be aware that Annabel had called him darling. All these young things called everyone darling and it meant nothing at all, but it was the first time Annabel had said it to him.

They had reached the dining-room before he had himself enough in hand to say,

"We'll see what he makes of it. That young man can paint."

21

After dinner they rolled back the rugs in the drawing-room and danced. Annabel played for them until Lucius Bellingdon produced a gramophone and a pile of records and made her come and dance too. She danced as delightfully as she played.

Sally found herself with Wilfrid as a partner, but he had not asked her until Moira had gone off with Clay Masterson. She thought, "Well, anyhow he won't be proposing to me any more, and that's something." Aloud she said,

"You're holding me too tight."

"Darling, why so captious? I'm holding you the way I've always done, and you haven't minded it before."

"Perhaps I just suffered in silence."

He shook his head.

"Not like you, darling—the tongue has always moved freely. Haven't you noticed it yourself?"

She laughed lightly.

"Perhaps I have."

He said in a complacent voice, "Our steps go well together."

"Which is what you say to every girl you dance with, isn't it?"

"Darling, it's part of my charm. And you should never dissect charm—the soul of it eludes you. Let us change the subject. Do you know that I am going to be your landlord?"

"You!"

He nodded.

"It's a prosaic thought, but facts are so often prosaic. Paulina left me the house, so you see I can now evict David and move in on the top floor myself. It will cheer you like anything to be able to see me every day, and I shall demand a definite touch of respect as well as the prompt payment of the rent. David can have my room if he likes, but I don't recommend it. Mrs. Hunnable is a shocking cook."

Sally experienced a pleasant sparkling anger. It warmed the colour in her cheeks. She said,

"You can't turn David out!"

"Watch me, darling, and you'll see that I can. Unconscious of his doom, the poor young artist plays—which is partly a quotation and partly my very own. When he gets back on Monday there will be a short well phrased note waiting for him. By the way, do you know whether he pays by the week, or the month, or the quarter?"

The eyes which Sally raised to his had a dancing light.

"He pays by the quarter. And I'm afraid you can't turn him out. He isn't a Scot for nothing, and he got Paulina to sign an agreement." She paused, and added, "So did I."

Wilfrid gazed reproachfully at her.

"An unwomanly action. And the Scotch are all the same—a practical, money-grubbing lot. No one with the soul of an artist would bother with anything so sordid as an agreement. I shall have to see if I can't find a loophole. We will now leave the distressing subject and give an exhibition performance which will make all the others green with envy. 'On with the dance, let joy be unconfined'!"

Their steps did go well together, but as far as an exhibition performance went it was Clay and Moira who would have stolen the show. Whatever else Moira was or was not, she could dance, and Clay Masterson was her match. They hardly seemed to speak—just drifted on the music as if it was a wind that carried them, her head a little tilted, her face blank, her light hair floating. Once, when he bent and said something, her lips parted and her eyes half closed.

Rather to Sally's surprise, David asked her for the next dance, and that without a glance in the direction of Moira Herne. Any pleasure this may have given her, however, subsided when she found that all he wanted was to talk about Moira.

"She's a marvellous subject, and I should think she'd be a good model. She really can keep still. Have you noticed that? Most people, especially women, can't keep still at all. If they are not moving their feet or fidgeting with their hands, or feeling to see if their hair is all right, they are flicking their eyelashes up and down or doing things with their lips. Do you suppose it's just restlessness, or do they think it's attractive and the way to make people look at them?"

Sally allowed a small gurgling laugh to escape her. She loved David when he was earnest and didactic.

She said,

"Darling, I wouldn't know. If I move it's because I want to, or because a hair has got loose and is tickling me."

"David frowned.

"I told you not to call me darling! You only do it to make me lose my temper, and I won't have it! We were talking about Moira. You mayn't have noticed it, but she never fidgets."

Sally gave him her wide, warm smile.

"Medusa wouldn't. And I should think she would be the perfect model. But it was the other people who got turned into stone wasn't it—not Medusa herself?"

His quick frown merged into a considering look. He said with an eager note in his voice,

"I got the idea as soon as I saw her, and I've been watching her."

Sally said briefly, "That would have been difficult to miss."

He went on as if she had not spoken.

"I got a sketch or two of her this afternoon. Now I want her to sit. I've got to get that cold look—you know what I mean."

Sally nodded.

"She has always had it. I told you I was at school with her."

She wanted to say a great deal more than that, but of course she couldn't. Moira had always been poison. He would have to find it out for himself.

He said,

"You see, Medusa, she's human. At least she was, but she's lost the human touch and whatever she looks at loses it too. She drains it out till there's no warmth or feeling left. Just poison and bright ice—that's what I've got to try and paint, not snakes in the hair."

Sally heard herself say, "Can you do it?"

"Oh, I think so. I've got a feeling about it. If it lasts, I can do it. If it doesn't—" He frowned and broke off. "It's quite strong. I expect it will last."

Sally did not admire herself for what she said next, but she said it all the same.

"How pleased Moira is going to be."

He looked at her very directly under those frowning brows and said,

"I don't care whether she's pleased or not. I want to paint her."

22

It was no more than nine o'clock when Hubert Garratt got up and made his way to the door. As far as Miss Silver could tell he had not spoken to anyone either during dinner or since they had come into the drawing-room and the young people had begun to dance. When addressed, his replies had been monosyllabic and as nearly as possible inaudible. As the dancers required most of the floor space, he was more or less forced into the group of those who were looking on. They had their little coterie around the hearth—Miss Bray with some rather aimless crochet work, Miss Silver with her knitting, Mr. Garratt barricaded behind *The Times.* He now folded the paper neatly and left it lying across the arm of the chair. Looking after him, Miss Silver observed that he did not appear to be at all well, and went on to enquire whether he was always as silent. Miss Bray's reply was a little confused. She had dropped a stitch and was not being very successful in her attempts to pick it up again.

"Hubert? I don't think I noticed. He isn't a person you notice very much. Did you say you thought he looked ill?"

"He does not look well. This affair has been a great shock to him."

Miss Bray had retrieved her stitch. The threads all round it were strained and the pattern would be spoiled, but she did not seem to mind. She said with a sort of bright vagueness, "Oh, yes, *indeed,*" and began to talk about something else.

At the far end of the room, where curtains of green brocade screened the two long windows which overlooked the park, Lucius Bellingdon stood with Annabel Scott. They had been dancing, but had come to a standstill here. With a brief "It's hot" he sent the curtains sliding to right and left and opened a window in the recess behind them. The air came in softly and was grateful. The moon was up and nearly full. By day the prospect would be bright with colour—green of the grass and a hundred other shades of green in swelling bud and breaking leaf—now all muted, all half seen as something in a dream. From the room behind them a panel of light slanted between the curtains and met the moonlight. As they stood there, Annabel moved a step nearer and said,

"Arnold is back."

He took some time to answer. When he did so, it was to say,

"What makes you think he's back?"

"I saw him."

"Where?"

"Coming out of the station in Ledlington."

"When?"

"A couple of hours ago."

"What were you doing in Ledlington a couple of hours ago?"

"I was taking Minnie Jones to catch her train."

"Minnie Jones!"

"Yes. She is Arthur's aunt."

"I know that. What was she doing here?"

"You'll have to ask Miss Silver about that. I gather she found the poor thing fainting in the park. She is quite terribly discreet, and she wouldn't have told me that if she hadn't been obliged to. But there was I with a car and an obliging disposition, and there was Minnie with no car and a train to catch, so Miss Silver forthcame, which she wouldn't have done if there had been any other way of getting Minnie to the station."

He was frowning in the manner which most people found intimidating.

"What on earth made her come here?"

"Minnie Jones? Your guess is as good as mine. Mine would be that she came to see Moira."

The intimidating quality was in his voice as he said,

"What makes you say that?"

"I'm not saying it—I just told you it would be my guess."

"Your reason for a guess like that?"

She gave him a fleeting look. There was anger in him. She wasn't afraid of his anger—she would never be afraid of it. She said,

"Guessing and reason don't go together." And then, "Don't you really know that there was something between her and Arthur?"

He gave a half contemptuous laugh.

"There was something on his side—any fool could see that. But on hers—I certainly never thought—"

The things that Annabel could have said remained unspoken. They burned in her, but she kept them back. What she did say was,

"Why has Arnold come back?"

"I don't know."

"How much did you give him this time?"

He shrugged.

"Twenty pounds."

"Do you suppose he's spent it?"

"Well, he said he only wanted it to tide him over."

After a moment she said,

"Minnie Jones recognized him."

"She hadn't ever seen him before!"

"Oh, yes, she had. She had seen him in London with"—her voice indicated quotation marks—" 'the gentleman who talked with Mr. Pegler in the gallery.' "

Lucius Bellingdon asked sharply,

"Who said that?"

"Miss Silver. Minnie saw Arnold coming out of the station, and she said, 'That's the one who was with the gentleman Mr. Pegler recognized.' Miss Silver asked her if it was Arnold who talked to Mr. Pegler in the gallery, and Minnie said, 'Oh, no, it was the other one.' You had better hear the whole thing from Miss Silver herself. Neither she nor Minnie knew Arnold by name until I told them who he was, but Minnie and Mr. Pegler had seen him with the man whom you and the police have been looking for. Miss Silver is a perfect clam, but when we were driving back together and she found that you had told me about Miss Paine and that lip-reading business she did let out as much as that. Of course it's the sort of thing that might mean a lot, or it might mean nothing at all. Nobody could be surprised to hear that Arnold had any number of shady acquaintances. This gallery man might just be a casual contact. Or he might not. The point is that Arnold knows him, and I should think it was up to the police to find out what else he knows."

The door in the drawing-room behind them opened. Hilton stood there looking in. As he skirted the room in their direction, Lucius moved to meet him. He came up close and said in a lowered voice,

"It's the London Inspector, sir. He says he is sorry to disturb you, but if you could spare him a few minutes—"

23

Sally was dancing with Wilfrid Gaunt. He was finding it amusing to propose to her under Moira's eye, and to speculate as to how far its resemblance to Medusa's would be increased if she were to guess what was happening. Sally was not amused, because the last thing she wanted was the kind of devastating scene of which Moira was capable, and the last thing Wilfrid wanted was to be taken at his word. If she had had the satisfaction of feeling that there was someone in love with her, even if David wasn't, it would have been a solace. But Wilfrid wasn't in love with anybody but himself. Her eyes were very bright as she said,

"Really, Wilfrid, it would serve you right if I were to say yes!"

"Darling, you're not going to?"

"I said it would serve you right if I did, and so it would!"

He shook his head.

"It would be no good anyone marrying me if she couldn't keep her temper."

Some of the things which Sally had been thinking came boiling up to the surface. She said in a spirited undertone,

"Well, Moira wouldn't keep her temper."

He sighed.

"Darling, how right you are."

Moira was dancing with Clay Masterson. He held her very close, and they did not speak. David Moray, straightening up from changing a record, watched them with frowning intensity. In the comfortable neighbourhood of the fire Miss Silver knitted and listened to Miss Bray's interminable account of Moira's wedding.

"Six bridesmaids in green, and the dresses were quite terribly expensive. But I would have preferred some other colour, only of course I wasn't consulted. Bridesmaids are really very difficult, don't you think? There was one very lumpy girl and she looked terrible. But she was the daughter of a man with a lot of influence about motor racing, and Oliver would insist on Moira having her. Moira and he had quite a dreadful quarrel about it, but he got his own way in the end—Oliver did, you know, even with Moira. I didn't like him, but I thought perhaps it would be good for her if she married him, because he could make her do what he said. She didn't like it, but she used to have to give way, and I think that was a good plan—don't you?"

Miss Silver said in a restrained tone,

"That would depend on what he wanted her to do, would it not?"

It was at this point that Annabel Scott came over to them and stood warming herself. Half turning from the fire, she said,

"Oh, Lucius asked me to say would you mind coming to him in the study."

The message did not surprise Miss Silver—Hilton's entrance had not surprised her. She gathered up her knitting and made her way to the study, where she greeted Frank Abbott with the formality which she always observed in the presence of strangers.

Lucius Bellingdon stood with his back to the hearth looking grim. He said curtly,

"Sit down, please. I hear you rang up the Inspector and asked him to come here tonight."

Miss Silver took the chair which he indicated. Her manner widened the distance between them. She said,

"Something had occurred which I felt should be imparted to the police without delay. If there had been time to consult you, I should have done so. I think Mrs. Scott will have given you an account of what happened."

"Miss Jones's visit—yes."

She produced one of her sudden smiles.

"Then you will know that we came very near to being late for dinner. I did not feel that you would wish this to become a matter for comment."

"No—I shouldn't. Will you now tell me and Inspector Abbott just what made you risk being late?"

She told the story in her carefully accurate manner. Moira Herne was mentioned only in passing.

"Miss Jones had been up to the house, where I believe she saw Mrs. Herne. On her way down the drive she felt faint and lost consciousness. It was fortunate that I came upon her, as she had stumbled in among the bushes at the edge of the drive and she might not have been found for some time."

Having introduced what she had to say with this economy of words, she described how Minnie had recognized a man who was coming out of the station at Ledlington, and how Annabel Scott had identified him as Mr. Arnold Bray.

When she had finished Frank Abbott said,

"Let's get all this as clear as we can. Miss Jones is a friend of Mr. Pegler, the caretaker at the Masters gallery. I think you saw him, Mr. Bellingdon."

Lucius Bellingdon said, "Yes."

"Well, I saw him too. He is the only link we've got with the man who, according to Miss Paine, was one of the people who planned the theft of your necklace and the murder of your secretary. Up to now Pegler has been a complete wash-out. He saw this man, and he talked to him and told him all about Miss Paine, and how good she was at lip-reading. And it's not much of a guess to suppose that he put the wind up him to a considerable extent, with the result that Miss Paine met with an accident—and I can't help thinking that Mr. Pegler is lucky not to have met with one too. But after all that, the only description that Pegler could give was one which would have fitted almost anyone. And now Miss Jones says she recognized the man in the street—and after dark at that!"

Miss Silver sat with her hands folded on her knitting-bag.

"This man was standing under a street-lamp with Mr. Bray. They were waiting to cross the road. Miss Jones says that the light was good, and that Mr. Pegler never forgets a face. I believe it to be quite possible to have a good visual memory without possessing any faculty of description."

Lucius Bellingdon said,

"What day was this?"

"Yesterday evening about eight o'clock."

"Then you'd better get hold of Arnold Bray and ask him who he was with last night, Inspector."

"Yes, we'll do that."

Lucius gave a short, hard laugh.

"You may get something out of him if you scare him enough. What no one is going to get me to believe is that Arnold had any hand in stealing the necklace or shooting Arthur Hughes!"

24

Arnold Bray was duly interviewed. He had a room in a poor lodging-house and everything shabby about him. If he was engaged in criminal enterprises, he certainly had not succeeded in making them pay. He had a soft voice, a nervous manner, and a strong family resemblance to his sister. Frank Abbott, who had accompanied Inspector Crisp on this domiciliary visit, found himself sharing Lucius Bellingdon's inability to accept him as the murderer of Arthur Hughes.

"Mr. Bray, you were in Putney last night, in the High Street."

Crisp's bark produced a noticeable access of nervousness.

"Any reason why I shouldn't have been?"

"We would like to know what you were doing there."

"I had a bit of business to attend to."

"Mind saying what it was?"

"Yes, I do. It was private." His eyes flickered away from Crisp's hard stare.

"You were seen in the High Street with a man whom we should like to interview."

"Who saw me?"

"That's neither here nor there, Mr. Bray. You were seen, and the man you were with was seen. What name do you know him by?"

He certainly was very nervous indeed.

"Look here, what's all this about? I was in Putney on private business of my own. If you want to know, I was looking about for a second-hand bicycle. Someone told me a friend of his had got one he wanted to sell, and I thought I would have a look at it. He must have given me the wrong address or something, because when I got there I couldn't find the place and nobody seemed to know anything about it—you know how it is. If I was talking to anyone, it would be when I was was trying to find out about this chap's address."

If he was making it up as he went along, it wasn't a bad effort. He obviously thought so himself, because his manner became more confident. Frank Abbott said in an easygoing way,

"What was his name, this chap you were looking for?"

Arnold Bray said,

"Robertson—Jack Robertson."

"And the address?"

"Well, that's where the whole thing slipped up. The man who told me about it said this chap with the bike was lodging with some people in the Emden Road. He didn't remember the name, and wasn't too sure of the number but he thought it was 79 or 97—anyway something with a seven and a nine in it. So that's what I was doing—asking whether anyone knew this Jack Robertson."

Crisp went on staring at him.

"Very much of a wild goose chase, wasn't it? What was the name of the chap who told you about Robertson and this bike he was supposed to be selling?"

Arnold Bray looked almost smug.

"I'm afraid I don't know, Inspector. It was just a chap I got talking to in the local."

Crisp went on asking questions, but they got him nowhere. The moment when Arnold Bray could have been scared into a breakdown was over. Taken by surprise, and undoubtedly shaken, he had managed to produce a story which it was difficult to disprove. They mightn't believe it, but it was the sort of thing that could easily have happened. It was, in fact, the sort of thing that did happen, and nothing in the interview had brought them, or was likely to bring them, a single step nearer to the man whom Paulina Paine had watched in the Masters gallery.

As they walked away, Frank Abbott said,

"He was rattled all right."

Crisp barked.

"He's the kind who always would be rattled if a police officer spoke to him."

"Yet you say he has never been in trouble?"

Crisp frowned.

"He's been on the edge of it to my certain knowledge. Hangs about there, I'd say. Some day he'll go over the edge—then we'll get him."

After a minute or two Frank Abbott said,

"What about putting a tail on him? If he's in with this man we want he's likely enough to communicate with him—ring up, or go and see him. I've an idea we did rattle him more than a little. If he's in this show at all, it's as a subordinate, and if he's the sort I take him for and we've scared him, then he's liable to run to his boss about it. I think it's worth trying."

Frank Abbott was right about Arnold Bray being scared. When the two police officers had gone he sat down and put his head in his hands. He had got off this time, but they might come sneaking back—the police had a nasty way of doing that. He must try and remember exactly what he had told them. If there was the slightest slip anywhere, they would think that he had made the whole thing up.

He went over it slowly bit by bit. Someone in the local who had mentioned a bike that was going cheap in Putney. Nothing they could check up on there. And the chap who had the bike to sell . . . Yes, Robertson. He had hit on the name because of seeing it on a tradesman's van in Putney. It was the kind of name anyone might have, with a respectable Scotch sound about it. But he had tacked a Christian name on to it. Now what had he got to do that for? Just for a moment he wasn't sure what the name was. It might have been Jack, or Joe, or Bill, or Jim, or anything.

He sat there and sweated, until all at once it came to

him that it was Jack, because what was in his mind was the old tag about "as sure as my name is Jack Robinson," and at the last minute he had given it a twist and made it Robertson. So that was all right. But he'd have to pass the word that they'd been seen on Friday night. No more Putney for either of them if there was anyone there who could spot them like that and pass the word to the police. And if they weren't going to meet again in a hurry, then there would have to be some arrangement about the money.

After a bit he went down to the call-box in the station yard. He had to stand and watch whilst a red-faced woman talked at length. A call-box was supposed to be sound-proof, but things were not always what they were supposed to be. If the door didn't quite fit, you might just as well be out in the street.

As he waited for the red-faced woman to finish her conversation he was pleased to observe that he could not hear a word she was saying. When she came out and he took her place it was with a certain sense of confidence that he got through the preliminaries, dropped in the required coins, and pressed button "A."

The voice that answered was a stranger's. In response to his "Can I speak to the gentleman who is lodging with you?" it said, "I'll see," and faded out.

Waiting there, his nerves got the better of him again. The telephone-box became a trap, shutting him in for everyone to stare at. Why had he got himself into this damned affair at all? It had looked like easy money. Nothing to do but pass on a little information—and look where it had landed him! If he had known, he would never have touched it. It might have been better if he had come clean and told the police what they wanted to know. No, no, he couldn't do that, but the thought was in his mind. Thirty miles away he heard a man's step crossing a room and the crackle of the receiver as it was lifted from the table where it had been laid. The voice he was waiting for said, "Hallo!" He heard his own voice shake.

"It's Arnold."

"What do you want?"

"We were seen together on Friday night in the High Street. I thought I had better let you know."

"Who saw us?"

"I don't know."

"Who told you we'd been seen?"

"The police. They said I'd been seen talking to someone they wanted to interview."

There was the beginning of a laugh at the other end.

"Then it was Pegler—I thought I saw him. But he doesn't know you—I wonder how—Oh, well, I'd better avoid the neighbourhood. I had a chance of rather a good deal, and it ought to have been safe enough after dark. A bit of damned bad luck the old boy happening along. Where are you speaking from?"

"The call-box outside the station."

"Anybody been tailing you?"

Arnold felt a rush of panic.

"No—no—of course not."

The other man said, "I wonder—" And then, "What did you tell the police?"

"Nothing—nothing. I swear I didn't. I said I'd been looking for a man who had a bike to sell and I couldn't find the address—if I was seen talking to anyone, it would be whilst I was making enquiries."

"Did they believe you?"

"Why shouldn't they?"

"Why should they? On the other hand, they can't prove anything. When they asked you who you were talking to, what did you tell them?"

"I said I didn't know what they meant—I wasn't talking to anyone in particular, only asking about this man who had the bike to sell."

"Well, that's not too bad. Now you just listen to me! You carry on the way we settled it. Get off this line and stay off it. Don't write, or ring up, or ask any questions. Just stay put in the bosom of the family, and if you get a chance to do what we planned, get on with it!"

"I don't know that I can stay put."

"You've got to! You're no use to me anywhere else!"

"Suppose he won't have me there—"

"Get Ellen to turn the water-tap—she's quite good at it. And now get off!"

Arnold Bray said, "Wait—"

"What is it?"

"The money—"

"What about it?"

"I want my share."

The voice said lightly, "Oh, you'll get it," and the receiver went back with a click.

Arnold Bray hung up at his end. The receiver came wet from his sweating palm. The paths of crime had become very alarming to tread.

25

"He's not feeling at all well," said Elaine.

Lucius Bellingdon threw her a look tinged with a certain grim humour.

"We have a National Health Service," he said.

"Oh, Lucius—"

"Surgery twice daily. And I forget whether you have to pay anything for a prescription at the moment or not, but he ought to have enough left out of what I gave him to pay for that."

Miss Bray got out a crumpled pocket-handkerchief and pressed it to her eyes.

"He wants care," she said. "He has never been strong, and there are only the two of us left. I remember my poor mother used to say she had always been afraid that she wouldn't rear him. He only weighed five pounds when he was born, and the doctor said—"

Lucius Bellingdon broke in upon these reminiscences.

"Well, whatever it was, he was wrong, and getting on for fifty years out of date. What is the matter with Arnold anyhow?"

ming eyes and repeated her previous remark.

"He needs care." Then, with rapid inconsequence, "I could put him in poor Arthur's room. His things have all been cleared out of it, and it wouldn't take long to air the bed—a couple of hot water bottles and a fire. And you really needn't see him except at meals."

She had the kind of clinging pertinacity which is more exasperating than heated opposition. Lily had been like that too. He said,

"Oh, he'll be well enough to come down to meals, will he?"

The tears began to run down Elaine's face. When she

cried like that she brought Lily back to him with painful clarity. Lily had always cried when he wouldn't do something she wanted him to do. She hadn't wanted him to go out to the States, and she had cried almost without ceasing until the moment of his departure. And when he came back and he found that she had taken upon herself to acquire a strange baby in his absence, she had cried again and gone on crying until he had given way and said that Moira could be kept. It was all very much as if she had been a puppy or a kitten, but because Lily had done the thing behind his back, and because he had given way against his will and his judgment, a cold deep resentment had put paid to what remained of their relationship. He did not like to be reminded of these things. When Elaine cried he was reminded of them. There was no real likeness to Lily, it was just that they cried in the same way. Against all reason it made him feel that he was being a brute. He bent a portentous frown upon Lily's cousin and said,

"For any sake stop crying! If Arnold really isn't well he can come here for a bit, but it's no use either of you thinking he can make a habit of it."

The flow of tears stopped abruptly. There were sniffings, there were dabbings, there was a gush of sentiment.

"So kind—I'm sure I don't know what we should all do without you. He will be so grateful. I'm sure if you were our own relation instead of just dear Lily's husband we couldn't be more grateful. In fact very few people's relations are so generous and so kind."

He removed himself, and she was presently talking to Arnold Bray ringing up from the station call-box. In reply to his "Is it all right?" she gave twittering assurances that it was.

"Only I think perhaps you had better keep out of his way as much as you can. He thinks you ought to have made the money go farther . . . Oh, you've got some of it left? I must tell him that. I wish I had known . . . Oh, you don't want me to? Really, Arnold, I can't see why, when it would please him . . . Oh, I see. But I don't think there's much chance of your getting any more . . . Oh, Arnold, I don't think you ought to say that! I wouldn't call him mean—I wouldn't really. If he hadn't been careful about money, I don't suppose he'd have had such a lot of it. Anyhow he says you can come, and I'm putting you in Arthur's room . . . Why? Because we're really full. These weekend people seem to be staying on. David Moray is going to do a portrait of Moira, and Sally Foster has got a holiday—at least it's not really a holiday, but the woman she works for rang her up and said she was going over to Paris for a week and Sally could have the time off. I don't suppose she'd have said anything about it, only she was taking the call in the hall and Lucius heard her say, "Then you won't be wanting me for a week," and he asked her to stay on. So you see, I don't know how many of the rooms will go on being full, or for how long. And it's all very well, but one has to consider things like sheets and towels, because there's nothing wears them out like constant use—only men never think of things like that, and Lucius is worse than most of them through being a widower for so long."

It was at this point that Arnold Bray stopped trying to get a word in edgeways and rang off.

26

It being Sunday morning, Miss Silver attended the village church. She was gratified by the company of Mr. Bellingdon and Mrs. Scott, and discovered Annabel to be the possessor of a particularly sweet singing voice. She had an affection for these small village churches with their air of having grown up with the place and their mementoes of its past history. This one contained quite an elaborate memorial of the Merefield family, now extinct, in the form of a wall sculpture of Sir Lucas de Merefield and his wife Philippa. They kneeled facing each other in stone, he in armour, and she in robe and wimple with five daughters behind her puppet-small, and five boys behind him, all with bent heads and folded hands. It seemed strange that so prolific a family should have died out, but Miss Silver had remarked the same phenomenon in her own time—the overlarge family of one generation becoming diminished or even extinguished in the next. Of course, in the case of the Merefields a great many generations had passed since Lucas and Philippa had produced their family of ten. She remembered to have heard that the last Merefield, another

Philippa, had died in extreme old age at about the time of the first world war. Dismissing these thoughts as unsuitable to the occasion, she turned her mind to higher things.

A middle-aged woman in a hat which resembled Miss Silver's own wrestled with a voluntary beyond her skill. Glimpses of her profile crimsoned with exertion were afforded by a curtain which must always have been skimpy and had recently lost a hook. The music stopped, Annabel Scott relaxed, and an old man with a kind voice began the Order of Morning Prayer:

"When the wicked man turneth away from his wickedness that he hath committed and doeth that which is lawful and right, he shall save his soul alive."

It came into Miss Silver's mind that there is always a place for returning and repentance.

The rest of the party did not go to church. Sally had meant to, but when it came to the point it was beyond her. There was something about the way Moira looked at her and said, "I suppose you'll go to church," that made her say, "Oh, no"—just like that. She hadn't meant to say it, but once it was said she wasn't going to go back on it. And in the end she might as well have gone, because Moira disappeared and David disappeared, and Wilfrid trailed about after her behaving more like a gadfly than you would think any human creature could. She told him so, and felt that she couldn't have pleased him more.

Nothing happened for the rest of the day except acres of exasperation and dullness. She hadn't been pleased with herself to start with, and by the evening she never wanted to see herself again. David remained absent, Moira remained absent. Miss Bray looked as if she had been crying. Her brother Arnold arrived just before lunch on a bicycle with a suit-case. From the brief contact which Sally had had with him it seemed unlikely that he would have an enlivening effect upon his surroundings. One Miss Bray was enough for any house, and Arnold was quite distressingly like his sister—the same fair indeterminate colouring, the same trickle of talk which seemed to have neither starting-point nor stopping-place. There were differences of course. To do Elaine justice, she didn't look shifty, and Arnold did. Fortunately, he retired to his room almost at once, and Elaine said he was resting.

Sally was at a loose end. Miss Silver conversed with Elaine. Lucius and Annabel had gone out in his car and had driven away into the blue. Wilfrid continued to cling, and she could have murdered him. If he had been silent it wouldn't have been so bad. But Wilfrid was never silent.

"Let us mingle our tears, darling. You are cut out, and so am I—you with David, and I with Moira. All my hopes of twenty thousand a year or whatever it's likely to be gone down the drain! Let us weep on one another's shoulders."

Sally was imprudent enough to answer him.

"You may want to weep, but I don't know why you should think that I do."

"Ah, that is my sensitive nature. The slightest pang of the beloved object and I feel it as my own."

"I thought it was Moira who was the beloved object."

"Darling, I never said so. The pang one feels on losing twenty thousand a year is of a different and a more earthy nature. Have I ever disguised from you that I have an earthy side?"

"No, you haven't. It would be too difficult."

He blew her a languid kiss.

"You don't know what I can do if I try."

Sally said in a tone of rage,

"I shall have a telephone call and catch the first train tomorrow! I can't think why I said I would stay on!"

"Darling, you wanted to keep an eye on David—it's quite simple. By the way, I suppose you know he has gone up to town to get his painting tackle."

It hadn't occurred to her. She said,

"Has he?"

Wilfrid nodded.

"So as to start painting Medusa bright and early tomorrow morning. I gather Moira's idea is to have the sittings in the North Lodge, all nice and private. It's been empty for donkey's years, but it used to be let to a man called Hodges who was quite a good artist, and Lucius let him build on a studio with a north light. So you see, there's some cheese in the mousetrap." A malicious glance flicked over her.

Sally said another thing which she hadn't meant to say.

"Is it a mousetrap?"

The words just came and there they were.

Wilfrid raised his eyebrows.

"Darling, be your age!"

Sally gave him a look and ran out of the room.

Another thing that she oughtn't to have done. She had

lived for twenty-two years with Sally Foster. They had their ups and downs, but on the whole they had got on very well. Now, for the first time in her life, she hadn't a good word to say for her. No proper pride, no stiff upper lip. Not even a decent try at keeping her end up. She just couldn't have given herself away more lavishly had she set out to do it. And to Wilfrid! And the last, worst dreg of the whole thing was that she didn't really care. If David was going to have a wretched sordid affair with Moira, what she ought to be feeling was "Well, that's their look-out and a good riddance to both of them!"

She couldn't do it, she didn't even want to do it. Moira was poison and David was going to get hurt. Poison hurt you—it could hurt you dreadfully. She couldn't bear David to be hurt. She stared out of the window of her room and saw that it was getting dark. There were low black clouds, very low and very black. She tied a handkerchief over her head. She wanted to get out of the house into the air, and if it poured with rain and soaked her she didn't mind, and if there was a thunderstorm or a cloudburst she didn't mind. All she cared about was getting out of the house without anyone seeing her. She went out by a side door, achieved a path through a shrubbery, and experienced a slight lift of the spirits. There is something about escaping which has this effect.

She emerged from the shrubbery on to a drive. It wasn't the drive you went down to get to the village. Well, so much the better—she might have met anyone there. Something said, "This is the drive which goes to the North Lodge." She countered with "I don't know it's the north drive, do I?" And the thing that talked came back with a "Well, you hope it is."

The drive, wherever it led to, showed signs of being less in use than the other one. The trees on either side of it leaned together, and the shrubberies were overgrown. Before the war there had been five gardeners at Merefields. Now there was Donald, an old man who pottered in the greenhouses, and two lads who were waiting to be called up for their military service. The drive grew narrower and the bushes thicker, and then there was the gate in front of her, and to the right of it, almost hidden by shrubs and trees, was the lodge. What she didn't know was that it was the North Lodge. Only she was sure that it was. She pushed a little creaking gate and went up a path that was slimy with moss to a hodded door. There was a window on either side of it and the blinds were down. There was a step that felt slimy too. If the place had stood empty for donkey's years as Wilfrid had said, it probably hadn't been cleaned since before the war. It was dark here under the trees and getting darker. She put out a hand and touched a rusty knocker.

And then quite suddenly there was a brilliant flash and the thunder and the rain broke together. She stood in close to the door while a curtain of water fell between her and the way she had come. The hood over the door wasn't going to keep her from being soaked to the skin. She pressed herself as close to the door as she could and felt it give. It swung in, and everything was dark in the house. If it was empty, there wouldn't be anyone there to make a light. If it was the North Lodge it had been empty for years. There was another flash of lightning, very bright. It showed her a narrow passage with a door on either side and one at the far end. There was some scuffed linoleum on the floor. All the doors were shut. She stepped into the passage and it was dark again.

If this was the North Lodge it was empty, and if it was empty, why was the door left open like this? She thought about calling out to see if there was anyone there, and it wasn't a thought she liked. It was still in her mind, when there was a third flash and the door at the end of the passage began to open.

27

The thunder crashed overhead. What the flash had disclosed was a moving door. Doors don't move unless someone is moving them. This door was opening and someone was coming through. The lightning flared again. For a moment the place was as bright as day. She saw David Moray coming towards her, and he may have been frowning at the lightning or he may have been frowning at her, but he was certainly frowning. The frown went with her, into the dark that followed the flash, and she thought that it was for her. She wondered why David should look as if he hated her. He came down the passage and spoke through the noise of the storm.

"What are you doing here?"

He had his hands on her shoulders and was bending down to her ear, or she would not have heard him. The rain banged on the roof over their heads. They stood there together, and there was anger between them. Sally said, stiffening the words with her anger so that they would reach him,

"There's a cloudburst—I suppose you haven't noticed it."

The lightning lit them up again. The passage swam in the blue fire. He reached over her shoulder and pushed the door. Then he had her by the arm and was taking her down the passage. She caught bits of what he was saying. Something about not being deaf, and then,

"Come and look at this damned place. I don't know what to do about it."

They went through to the room from which he had come. It was the kitchen. There was just enough light to distinguish the wooden table and a chair or two, and the range. There was a dresser against the farther wall and linoleum on the floor. The next flash of lightning was not as vivid as the others had been, and the thunder was farther off. The kitchen led into a kind of lean-to scullery. Outside the back door there was a narrow flagged passage with the rain splashing down into it, and on the other side of the passage a large dark structure which she guessed to be the studio erected by the late Hodges. It was as nearly dark as makes no difference in the scullery, and the noise was deafening. David had her by the arm. When she realized that she was expected to walk out into the rain she stopped walking and lifted her voice against the weather.

"No, David!"

His voice did better than hers, for she heard his "What?" quite distinctly.

"I'm—not—going—out—into—that—rain."

He must have caught some of that, because he bent right down to her ear and shouted.

"It's only a step! Come along!"

And with that his arm came round her waist and she was being swung right off her feet and jumped across the passage into the open doorway on the other side.

He was laughing when he set her down.

"There! We're all right now and out of the wet!"

"I'm drenched."

"You can't be—you weren't out in it long enough. But I don't know why you hadn't the sense to bring a coat."

"I didn't know there was going to be a storm."

He turned a considering eye upon her.

"How did you get here anyway? You didn't know I was going to be here."

"Of course I didn't know!"

The fury of the rain had lessened, or else the roof of this place didn't help it to make as much noise. Surprisingly, they could hear themselves speak. The indignation in Sally's voice didn't seem to register. He said,

"No, you couldn't have known, because I didn't know myself. It just seemed a good idea to bring my stuff straight here, so I dropped off my bus at the corner and came along. But now I'm not sure that it's going to do."

Sally said, "Why?"

They couldn't really see each other, though it wasn't as dark as it had been in the lodge. They were just shadows against the screen of the two big windows which looked north—a shadow David and a shadow Sally. She didn't need a light to tell that the shadow David was frowning again. He said,

"Well, I don't know. The place is all right—very good light—"

She couldn't resist an interruption.

"Darling, it's practically pitch dark."

He resumed with vigour.

"I'm not talking about now. I came and saw it this morning—naturally."

"Of course—you would! Did Moira come with you?"

"Why shouldn't she?"

"No reason at all. You are going to paint her here, aren't you?"

His voice lost some of its vigour.

"Well—I don't know—"

"You don't know if you're going to paint her?"

He said angrily, "Of course I'm going to paint her! What I'm not sure about is doing it here. It's—it's a bit out of the way."

It occurred to Sally with pleasure that he was not unaware of the mousetrap of Wilfrid's metaphor. He might want the cheese, but his Scottish caution was aroused. She said in her sweetest voice,

"But darling, isn't that just what you want—no interruptions—nobody coming in and out to see how you're getting on—just you and Medusa? What more could you possibly want?"

Her wrist was caught in a bruising grip. He said, "Stop it!" and Sally said, "Stop what?"

"The way you are going on! As if I wanted to be alone with the damned girl! I don't! I want to paint that picture! I'm going to paint it, and it's going to be good—it's going to be damned good! And you are going to come and see fair play!"

"I'm going to *what?*"

"You're going to come to the sittings and see that she doesn't get up to any of her tricks."

Sally laughed.

"Darling, chaperones are extinct! Anyhow I don't feel as if I should like the part. And *how* Moira would love me!"

The pressure on her wrist increased.

"Do you want her to love you?"

She said in a taunting voice, "Don't you?"

He let go of her with such a furious gesture that she cried out.

"What's the matter?"

"You nearly broke my wrist—that's all."

He said, "You shouldn't say things like that. You know perfectly well—you know perfectly well—"

His voice stopped. It was as if they had come abruptly upon the edge of something there in this darkened place. Another step, another word, and they might be over the edge. If Sally could have got her breath she would have asked what it was that she was supposed to know, but she couldn't get her breath, or at least not enough to carry the words.

David went past her to the door and said,

"We'd better be getting along."

Sally stood where she was. There were bright candles in her mind—big shining ones as bright as stars. She found a handful of everyday words.

"I don't want to get wet."

David found a handful too.

"It has stopped raining."

She came to stand beside him and look out. The eaves of the lodge dripped into the passage and the flags ran like a brook, but there really wasn't any more rain. David swung her across as he had done when they had come, and then turned back to stand in the wet and lock the studio door. He said briefly, "I'll fetch my things in the morning. The house will be better." And then they came through into the kitchen and he opened the kitchen door.

The passage beyond was dark. Just for a moment a flicker of light showed that the door on the right was ajar. The flicker came from the room behind the door. Someone could have used a lighter, or struck a match, or switched on an electric torch. Sally put out a hand and clutched at David's arm, and before anything else could happen someone laughed where the flicker had been. No one who had heard that laugh before could possibly mistake it. It belonged to Moira Herne, and at the thought of Moira finding her here with David in the dark Sally was shaken with a fierce anger. She had known Moira long enough to know exactly what she would say and what sort of story she would make of it. It served her right for ever coming down to Merefields, but there is no consolation in knowing that you have asked for trouble and tumbled right into the middle of it. At the moment the one bright spot was that David was having the sense to hold his tongue. It would have been quite dreadfully like him to call out to Moira and let them in for whatever was coming. Mercifully, he just stood there and neither said nor did anything at all.

Sally pushed the kitchen door to screen them, and she pulled on David's arm to get him to come back across the kitchen and through the scullery and out by the back door. If they could get round the lodge and back into the drive they could get clear away. She might have known that it wouldn't be any good. David was going to be the sort of husband who demands loudly why he is being pinched or his foot trodden on, when you are trying to give him a hint. He now said in what he doubtless supposed to be a whisper,

"Why are you pulling me?"

Sally said, "Ssh!" and the door on the right of the passage swung in. They could not see anything, but they could hear. And first, along there at the end of the passage, there was the swing of the door and someone coming through, and the someone was Moira Herne. No one could mistake that voice. It was Moira, and she stopped in the open doorway and spoke to someone behind her in the dark front room. It must have been quite dark there, because the blinds were down as Sally had seen them when she came up the path. And Moira said,

"You're sure it will come tomorrow—absolutely sure? Because I won't go on until it does—I can tell you that."

There was the murmur of a man's voice, but nothing to tell who the man might be.

Moira stood where she was and said,

"Well, I'm just telling you—that's all. As to David, I've told you you needn't worry. I can fix it all right. I'll just tell him this place isn't suitable. Come along, or I'll be late!"

She went out of the front door, and there was another footstep that followed her. It was a man's step. They didn't see him, they didn't hear him speak. They heard Moira go out, they heard him follow her, and they heard the front door shut.

Sally and David walked up the drive in silence, as they had stood in silence on the flagged path to the lodge and heard Moira and the man who was with her turn the other way and go down to the gate and out into the lane beyond. There must have been a car waiting there, for after a minute or two they could hear the purr of the engine and the sound of it dying away.

They did not move for quite a while after that. Moira might have been just seeing the man off and coming back herself. They stood in the dripping garden and waited to see whether she would come. It was strange to stand so close together and have nothing to say.

When quite a long time had passed David said, "She's gone with him—she won't come now," and they went out of the little creaking gate and shut it behind them, and so on and up the drive. It wasn't until they could see the lights of the house that Sally said.

"You never finished what you were saying back there in the lodge, David."

"Didn't I?"

"No, you didn't. You said I hadn't any business to say what I was saying."

He said in his frowning voice, "I haven't the slightest idea what you were saying."

Sally laughed.

"Darling, you know perfectly well. And you should stick to telling the truth, because you don't tell at all a convincing lie. I said how Moira would love me if I came and chaperoned her sittings. And you said, 'Do you want her to love you?' and I said, 'Don't you?' And then you nearly broke my wrist and said something about my *knowing*. Well, now I should like to be told what it is I'm supposed to know."

There was one of those silences. Sally wasn't going to break it, and David wasn't going to break it, so where did you go from there?

Sally came up close and slipped a hand inside his arm. It didn't get any encouragement, but at least it didn't get pushed away. So far so good, but at any moment there might be an explosion. There was a tingling feeling from her fingertips up to her shoulders. She rubbed her cheek against the rough stuff of his sleeve and said,

"David, tell me—"

She heard him take a deep angry breath. The arm which she had been holding was jerked away from her touch. Her own arm was taken and gripped.

"You know perfectly well what I started to say, and I'm not saying it! And you know why! When I'm in a position to say it, it will be said, but it won't be said before!"

Sally wanted to laugh, she wanted to cry, and she wanted quite dreadfully to slap his face just as hard as she could. The trouble about slapping is that to be at all satisfactory it has to be spontaneous, because the minute you begin to think about it the civilized bit of you gets up and won't let you do it. Well, if you've got to be civilized you might as well take the smooth with the rough. She gave a nice little modern laugh, and said,

"Darling, how fierce you are! And of course you don't know it, but you're hurting me. You know, we really shall have to hurry, or we shan't have time to change, and Elaine will be in a fuss."

28

Miss Bray was certainly in a fuss, but it wasn't about them. Lucius Bellingdon had rung up to say that his car had broken down at Emberley, which was fifteen miles away, and he and Annabel were therefore going to be late.

"And he said not to wait supper, because they would have something there, and of course I said it would be quite all right whenever they came, because with everyone out on Sunday evening we always do have cold. Most inconvenient, but there it is. But he just said, 'We're dining here,' and rang off. What I can't understand is why the car should have broken down."

Wilfrid said in his light malicious voice,

"My dear Miss Bray, what did you expect it to do? It's the oldest dodge in the world. All the best cars are trained to oblige."

Elaine looked at him, first puzzled and then cross.

"I'm sure I don't know what you mean. But they are bound to be frightfully late, and if Lucius says not to wait, we had better go in."

Moira walked in just as they were sitting down. She had been home long enough to change into a pale green housecoat and to make up her face. When she heard that Lucius and Annabel had been stuck at Emberley she lifted her eyebrows and remarked that they were probably bearing up. After which she slid into her place, addressed David as "My sweet," and said that cold food was foul, and too early-Victorian to be expected to eat it on Sunday evening, but as there wasn't anything else, he could give her some chicken-salad. As he complied he was considering that she must certainly have taken a lift in the car which they had heard driving away.

Aware of his silent gaze, she met it with her own light stare and said,

"Well, what is it? I'll give you a penny for your thoughts—tuppence if they're worth it."

They were waiting on themselves. He brought round her plate of salad and set it down.

"I don't think they are. I was just wondering how long it took you to dress."

She said, "Ages." And then, in exactly the same voice, "Oh, by the way, the North Lodge is a wash-out as far as my sittings go. We'll have them up here at the house. There's quite a good sort of attic place—"

Elaine raised a protesting voice.

"Oh, Moira, no—not the attic!"

"And why not?"

"My dear, it's so dusty—and things spread about all over the floor!"

Moira dismissed the topic with a casual "It'll do." She turned to David, who had gone back to his seat on the other side of the table. "Did you get your stuff all right?"

It was a curious little passage. Sally wondered about it. First Moira had been all over the idea of having the sittings at the North Lodge, and now she was calling them off. And she was calling them off because the man whom she met at the lodge had told her to call them off. As to his reason, it could be one of two, or it could be both of them together. He might want to keep the North Lodge for his own private meetings with Moira, or he might be cutting up rough at the idea of her meeting anyone else there. Whichever it was, Moira could hardly have appeared more indifferent than she did.

Lucius and Annabel were very late. To all enquiries he merely said that they had dined, and that they had had to leave the car in Emberley and hire one to come home. But to Miss Silver in the study he was more communicative. A touch on her arm indicated that he wished to see her there, and after a discreet interval she had followed him.

She found him with his back to her, looking out of the window. At the sound of the closing door he turned and came towards her. Her attention was at once engaged by the way he looked. There was a hardness and severity which exceeded anything which she had seen in him. The effect was formidable indeed. Without any preliminaries he said,

"The car was tampered with."

Miss Silver gave no indication of surprise. She said in a very composed manner,

"Let us sit down, Mr. Bellingdon."

It was like having tepid water splashed in his face. The check affronted him, but he was sufficiently master of himself to set a chair for her and to take one himself. When she was seated she looked at him thoughtfully and said,

"You have reason to believe that the mishap to your car was not accidental?"

"I know it wasn't. There is a steep hill just out of Emberley. A wheel came off there. Fortunately, we had almost reached the bottom. If it had happened a little sooner, we should probably have both been killed. The hill takes two bad corners, and there is a sheer drop into a quarry. If we hadn't been past the danger points we should have had it. As it was, we crashed into a bank and pretty well wrecked the car."

"Mr. Bellingdon, are you sure that the wheel had been tampered with?"

He said, "Perfectly—if you mean am I sure in my own mind. I couldn't prove it."

"How would it have been done?"

"Anyone with a spanner could loosen the nuts. I suppose you've seen a wheel changed—well, it's as easy as that. Anyone who wanted me to have an accident could have done it. Parker could have done it." He gave a short laugh. "He has driven for me and looked after my car for fifteen years, but he could have had a sudden urge to kill me. It would have to be a particularly strong one, because whatever he feels about me, I should have said he worshipped the car, and it was bound to be pretty badly damaged. There's negligence of course, but I've never known him negligent yet. And there's no chance of its having happened in a strange garage, because we haven't been near one, and if we had, Parker has a deep-rooted distrust of mechanics and he'd have checked everything over."

Though much of this was Greek to Miss Silver, she continued to look intelligent. After a brief pause Lucius Bellingdon said harshly,

"Well, where do we go from there? Anyone could have done it, but I don't believe it was Parker. There's no way of proving anything, but I think someone has made an attempt upon my life—" He paused, and added on a harder note, "and Annabel's."

"You have indeed had a providential escape."

He got up, drove his hands into his pockets, and went over to the writing-table. After standing there for a moment he turned and said.

"It doesn't seem to surprise you that there has been an attempt on my life?"

"No, Mr. Bellingdon."

"Why?"

She regarded him with composure.

"I have feared that such an attempt might be made."

His "Why?" was repeated as sharply as before.

"Because I have not been able to feel any assurance that one such attempt has not already been made."

"What do you mean?"

"Has it never occurred to you that the person who induced Mr. Garratt's fit of asthma may quite reasonably have supposed that, your secretary being incapacitated, you would fetch the necklace yourself?"

He bent a hard frowning gaze upon her.

"It was Arthur Hughes who was shot."

"I have never been able to believe that his death was intended."

"Then why shoot him?"

"The necklace was in any case a tempting prize, and the person who took it could not risk being recognized. But I have always thought it possible that the theft of the necklace was originally intended to cover a darker and more ambitious crime."

His laugh conveyed no idea of mirth.

"What's the good of wrapping it up? You might just as well say straight out that someone wanted to kill me. I take it that is what you meant?"

"Yes, Mr. Bellingdon, that is what I meant."

"Then don't let us beat about the bush any longer. The theft of the necklace was a blind. I was to be murdered. Perhaps you can tell me why."

She observed him mildly.

"Yes, the motive is of the first importance. Setting on one side those cases where a sudden impulse may produce a fatal result, and considering only those which involve premeditation, there are, generally speaking, three main motives for what the law calls wilful murder—love, hatred, and the desire for gain. I use the word love in the sense in which the murderer would doubtless use it, and not in my own understanding of it. I should, perhaps, have employed the term jealousy instead, since what is involved is what the French would call the *crime passionnel*."

A momentary gleam of humour passed across his face.

"Well, I think you may count that one out. And I can't think of anyone who hates me enough to kill me—not offhand—" He broke off with an effect of suddenness.

After waiting to see if he would proceed she said,

"The third motive remains. You have great worldy possessions."

There was a silence. He turned back to the table and stood there, straightening the pen-tray, lifting a stick of sealing-wax, a pencil. After a little he turned back again.

"You may just as well say what you mean."

She said it.

"Mr. Bellingdon, who would profit by your death?"

He said without any change of expression.

"To a limited extent quite a number of people." Then, as if the sound of his own voice had touched something off, look and manner betrayed a mounting intensity of feeling. "What are you suggesting? You'll have to come out with it. I've never had any patience with hints, and you've gone too far to draw back. If you suspect anyone, you must come out with your suspicions. If you have an accusation to make, you must make it."

Miss Silver maintained her quiet manner.

"Mr. Bellingdon, I have asked you who would profit by your death. You have not answered my question. You have asked me to be plain with you, and I am prepared to do as you ask. If, as I suppose, Mrs. Herne would benefit very largely under your will, I think you may have to consider whether she may not be the object of some design—"

He broke in as if he could no longer control himself.

"What do you mean by some design? You wrap everything up! Are you accusing Moira of trying to kill me?"

Miss Silver coughed in a reproving manner.

"That was not my intention. If Mrs. Herne were your heiress, that might provide a motive for a man who believed that she would be willing to share her inheritance with him."

With a quick impatient gesture he said,

"A prospective son-in-law is usually prepared to wait for the decent course of nature. I don't know which of Moira's young men you imagine would risk a hanging to anticipate it. People do these things in melodrama, not in real life."

She said soberly,

"Can you pick up a newspaper without finding material for a melodrama? The passions of greed and lust are essentially crude. They do not change."

He said in a more moderate tone,

"The whole thing is preposterous. To start with, your hypothetical murderer would have to be pretty sure of Moira before he risked his neck by bumping me off. As far as I can see, there isn't anyone in that position. Men come round her and she amuses herself with them, but there's never been the slightest sign of anything serious since her husband's death—not on her side at any rate."

She did not answer him. She could have told him that he

was arguing against his own fear, his own inward doubt, but she remained silent. It was only after an uneasy pause, when he said on a sharpened note, "Well, haven't you anything to say?" that she spoke.

"Mr. Bellingdon, we are dealing with facts, not fancies. May I remind you of some of them? There was a plan to steal your necklace. The plan provided for the death of the person in charge of it. Mr. Garratt, who was to have been that person, was incapacitated, I believe deliberately. The most likely person to have taken his place was yourself. The person who did take his place was murdered. The whole plan could only have been devised and carried out by someone who was in close touch with your household. So much for the first crime. There has now been an attempt at a second. In this case not only you yourself were clearly aimed at, but Mrs. Scott was involved. Can you neglect the possibility that there may be further attempts, and that she may be involved in those?"

He made an abrupt movement.

"No, I can't. She must go away."

"Do you think that she will go?"

Lucius Bellingdon said, "No."

"Your car has been tampered with and you have had a narrow escape. I gather that the accident which occurred was rendered especially dangerous by the fact that it took place on this particularly steep hill."

"Yes."

"Then the question would seem to arise as to whether it would have been possible for the person who tampered with your car to count on your driving down such a hill."

"Yes, that question might arise."

"May I ask whether you had planned to go the way you did, and whether anyone knew that you had made such a plan?"

"Yes, it was known. I spoke of it in the drawing-room before lunch. I think you were not present."

"Will you tell who were present?"

He said in an even voice,

"I think all the rest of the party." He ran over the names in an undertone, "Elaine—Hubert—Arnold Bray—Sally Foster and that young Moray—Moira—Wilfrid Gaunt—Annabel—"

She said,

"You see, there is the same pattern. Anyone could have

tampered with the car, but only certain people knew that you would be driving down this dangerous hill."

He walked past her to the window, flung the curtains rattling back, and pushed the casement wide. The wind had dropped and the sky was clear. The smell of the damp earth came in, and a faint herby tang from the rosemary bush against the wall. When he was a boy he had had an ungovernable temper. He had learned to govern it, to harness it to his purposes, to make it do his bidding. It was there at his call. Not for years had it come so near to breaking loose. He stood there mastering it. When he turned and came back to his table he had the look of a man who has the upper hand of himself. His voice was grave and resolute as he said,

"Miss Silver, I offered you a professional engagement, and you accepted it. You have formed certain opinions—you are within your rights in expressing them. I invited you to come down here, and I told you that you would have a free hand. On my part, I have to decide whether I desire the arrangement between us to continue. In the event of my doing so, what have you to offer me in the way of advice?"

Miss Silver's look was as grave as his own. She said,

"I believe you to be in considerable danger. It is not possible to say just how pressing the danger may be. From the fact that this attempt on you has followed so closely upon the murder of Mr. Hughes, and from the ruthless manner in which that murder was carried out, I am inclined to consider it to be very pressing indeed. In these circumstances, I would strongly urge you to protect yourself by letting it be known that you have made important alterations in your will."

He gave her a sharp glance.

"Who told you that I was thinking of doing so?"

She smiled faintly.

"No one, Mr. Bellingdon. It occurred to me as advisable."

After a short silence he said,

"And if I were to let it be known that I intended to alter my will?"

"I should consider that very inadvisable indeed."

"Yes? On what grounds?"

"I do not really have to tell you that." Her tone was indulgent.

He said, "No," and then, "I've a good mind to do it all

the same. In which case it would be now or never for the hypothetical gentleman whom you suspect of wanting to murder me. If there's anything in this very unpleasant theory of yours, he'll either have to get on with the job before I alter my will or give it up."

"I believe that you would be taking a very great risk."

"Well, do you know, I'd rather take it and get it over. I'm an impatient man and I don't like sitting and waiting for things to happen. If there is another attempt, it may provide us with some sort of evidence. This one isn't going to do much in that line, you know. The garage is a converted coach-house. Parker lives over it. He's a bachelor, and he has his Sundays off—spends them with relations in Ledlington. The place would be open all day. Moira has a car there, and so has Annabel."

She made no reply. After a moment he spoke again.

"Well, what about it? I've told you my plan. Will you stay and see it through?"

"Do you wish me to do so?"

Oddly enough, he did. She had come nearer to making him lose his temper than anyone had done for years, but he wanted her to stay.

Having said so, he received her acceptance with an unexplained feeling of relief. She had risen to her feet and was going towards the door, when he overtook her. He had an impulse to speak—to voice his anxieties about Annabel, to ask her what could be done to keep her safe, when she anticipated him. At the very threshold she turned and spoke.

"You are in a good deal of concern about Mrs. Scott."

He said, "Don't you think I have reason to be?"

"Yes, I think so."

"I have begged her to go. She won't hear of it. That is my one objection to this plan of mine—if I speak of altering my will, it may be thought—it *will* be thought—" Speaking with unusual emotion, he was now unable to proceed.

Miss Silver said, "Yes."

There was a silence between them. She put out her hand to the door, but she did not open it. Instead she turned again and said,

"A little while ago I angered you by referring to Mrs. Herne's interest under your will. You have asked me to be plain. You have just admitted that the announcement of a prospective change in your dispositions might bring about another attempt upon your life, and that this attempt might endanger Mrs. Scott. This would implicate either Mrs. Herne herself or someone directly and overwhelmingly interested in her inheritance."

"Miss Silver—"

"Pray allow me to continue. You said that she has many admirers but no serious commitment to any of them, and that there could be no one sufficiently sure of her interest to risk so much upon it. I agree that anyone who took that risk would have to feel very sure of his claim on her. In fact, I think that only a legal claim would provide a strong enough inducement."

He repeated her words,

"A legal claim—"

She said with the utmost gravity,

"Mr. Bellingdon, are you perfectly persuaded in your own mind that Mrs. Herne's husband is dead?"

They stood looking at one another. She saw surprise, anger, and something else succeed each other in his aspect. She was not entirely sure of what the third expression might be. She did not think that fear would be in keeping with his character, but it might perhaps be caution. He said,

"There has never been the slightest doubt on the subject. Oliver Herne took his car out and crashed on a mountain road. He was alone, and the car was burnt out. The body was considerably disfigured, but there was no reason to doubt that it was his. It was identified by Moira and his mechanic. His signet-ring and his cigarette-case were recovered. There has never been the slightest reason to suppose that the evidence was insufficient or unreliable. I should like to ask why you have made this astonishing suggestion."

She said,

"I think you know why I have made it. You said yourself that the hypothetical murderer whom we were discussing would have to be very sure of his claim upon Mrs. Herne if the realization of that claim was to be the motive for his attempt on your life. From what I have been told about Mr. Herne by yourself as well as by others I have formed the impression that he was a reckless young man, living for excitement and not too scrupulous as to how he came by it. Such a character would fit into the pattern of recent events, and a husband's claim upon Mrs. Herne's inheritance might provide the temptation."

He gave an angry laugh.

"I'm afraid you have too much imagination!" he said. "Moira's marriage was turning out just as I told her it would turn out. He was spending her money, and they were quarrelling all the time. Any feeling she may have had for him was quite gone and they were on the brink of a divorce. I can assure you that as far as Oliver Herne is concerned I can rest easy and so can he. He won't come back from the grave to trouble us."

29

The parcel arrived by the first post on Monday morning. Miss Silver saw it as she passed through the hall. She had come down early because she wished to use the telephone without being overheard. There were several instruments to choose from. She decided upon the one in Mr. Bellingdon's study, trusting to her very keen hearing to inform her if there should be any intrusion upon the line.

It being after eight o'clock, Detective Inspector Frank Abbott was out of bed and half way through his shaving. At the sound of Miss Silver's voice he relaxed from the stricter official manner.

"Reverend preceptress! I had a horrible idea that it might be the Chief wanting to know what I thought I was doing down here, and whether the Commissioner plus the Public and the Press would be satisfied that I was earning my keep, or words to that effect. What can I do for you?"

Miss Silver told him, exercising the strictest discretion. No names were mentioned, and a further safeguard was provided by the use of the French language. As in the case of Chaucer's immortal Prioress, this was not the French of Paris, but it had the merit of leaving Frank in no doubt as to what was required of him.

"And there should be no delay."

On these words she rang off.

It was as she was returning from the study that she saw the parcel. It had only just been delivered, and Hilton was in the act of putting it down on the hall table. It was about the size of a shoe-box and of a very untidy appearance, the wrapping-paper being stained and frayed, and the string consisting of odd pieces untidily knotted together.

Lucius Bellingdon brought it into the dining-room with him and set it down on a window-seat. Annabel, coming in behind him, remarked on it.

"Lucius, what an extraordinary-looking box!"

He nodded without speaking and began to open his letters.

Elaine said in a fretful voice that she hoped it wasn't plants. Nurseries packed them so damp, and they stained anything you put them down on.

Lucius looked up briefly.

"I haven't been sending for any plants," he said.

Moira came drifting in, stared at the parcel, and went to pour herself a cup of coffee. The others came in one by one—David, Wilfrid, Sally, Arnold Bray, and Hubert Garratt, so that they were all there when Lucius pushed the remainder of his letters over to his secretary and picked up the parcel. He cut the string, dropped the disreputable wrapping upon the window-seat, and came over to the table with a battered cardboard box in his hand. The lifted lid disclosed a mass of rather damp newspaper.

Moira turned round with her coffee-cup in her hand and Miss Bray stopped in the middle of a dissertation upon how difficult it was to get the downstairs rooms done before breakfast. Miss Silver thought afterwards that it was curious how everyone stopped what they were doing and watched whilst Lucius took off a pad of crushed newspaper and dropped it on the floor. There was more paper underneath, all crushed together, all looking as if it had been left out in the rain. He said, "What on earth—" And then there was something that felt hard amongst the squashed-up newsprint and he fished it out and began to peel the last soft wrappings away. Miss Silver saw his face change. Everyone heard him exclaim, and in a moment everyone knew why.

There isn't anything quite so squalid as dirty paper, but the paper dropped away. The morning light from three long windows dazzled upon something as bright as itself. Brighter, because this was light concentrated and splintered into rainbows. What dangled from Lucius Bellingdon's big brown hand was a looped chain of diamonds curiously and beautifully wrought with bows and tassels which caught the brightness and did wonderful things with it. He looked down at it with a curious set expression.

In the momentary hush that followed Miss Silver glanced about her. Annabel Scott's colour had risen. Her eyes were wide. Elaine Bray's mouth had fallen open. She put up a hand to her hair and tidied a straggling lock. David Moray was frowning, his brows drawn together and his face hard. Sally Foster lay back in her chair. She looked frightened, and all her colour was gone. Wilfrid Gaunt had a startled air. He had been saying something to Sally and smiling as he said it. The smile was not quite gone. Arnold Bray had dropped his napkin and was stooping to pick it up. Hubert Garratt, like Sally, was leaning back. He looked very ill.

The person who moved first was Moira Herne. There was only just time for that general gasp of astonishment, for Miss Silver's almost instantaneous impression, before she was on her feet, her light hair floating and her hands stretched out.

"Oh, it's my necklace! Oh, Lucy!"

Even in a moment like this it was intensely disagreeable to Miss Silver to hear Mr. Bellingdon addressed in this manner. It was a habit which should never have been allowed to grow up. At the same time she realized the necessity for making a conscientious effort not to allow it to prejudice her against Moira Herne.

Mr. Bellingdon raised his eyebrows and said in his coolest voice,

"Your necklace, Moira?"

There was a little flush on her white skin.

"You said I could have it—for the Ball. You gave it to me."

He repeated her words in such a manner as to reverse the meaning.

"Nonsense! I said you could have it for the Ball." After a momentary pause he continued. "Since you have given up the idea of appearing as Marie Antoinette, you won't require it now. As a matter of fact—the associations—I shouldn't have thought you would have cared about wearing it."

Her hands had remained stretched out as if reaching for it—long white hands with scarlet nails. They dropped back now, but slowly. She said,

"It's mine—you gave it to me."

Lucius Bellingdon pushed it down into his breast pocket and said,

"I did nothing of the sort! Anyhow the police will want to examine it. And all this wrapping stuff must be kept—they'll want to see it. As to the necklace, I shall get rid of it as soon as possible. And now suppose we have breakfast."

Everyone began to move, to talk, and to help themselves to tea, to coffee, to the cereals and other food on the side table. Only Moira, having risen from her seat, did not come back to it again. She went out of the room, turning on the threshold as if she had something more to say. But whatever it was it didn't get said. She looked at Lucius Bellingdon, who had his back to her, and then she went out and shut the door behind her very softly.

It would have seemed more natural if she had banged it, and Miss Silver for one would have been happier. There had been so much violence in the look, so much control in that soft shutting of the door—so much unnatural control. David Moray drew a long breath and turned to Sally on his left.

"Medusa with a vengeance!" he said.

She looked back at him, and he saw how pale she was.

"What's the matter?"

"Nothing."

He said abruptly, "I'll get you some coffee," and pushed back his chair.

Neither of them quite knew what they said or why they were saying it. Miss Silver's look came back to them, came back to Arnold Bray. He had been a long time picking up his napkin. His hand shook, and instead of being flushed from stooping he was pale. The arrival of the parcel had certainly started something. This would not, of course, have been Miss Silver's way of putting it, but it was undoubtedly the conclusion at which she arrived. It was, to be sure, a surprising event, and undoubtedly many of the people were surprised. Whether this was the case with all of them, she could not be certain.

The person she felt sure about was Moira Herne. There had been pleasure and excitement, there had been the evidence of an avid desire in her reaction, but she did not think that there had been any surprise. The usual blankness of her expression had been violently broken up, at first pleasurably, and then in disappointment and anger quite painful to witness.

And why had Hubert Garratt that sick expression? As the thought went through her mind, he got up and went to the serving-table. Watching him, she saw his hand shake on the teapot, the milk jug. He poured himself a cup of tea and came back holding it with a kind of determined steadiness, but when he lifted it to his lips he bent his head half way to meet it and his hand was shaking again.

The most normal person in the room was Miss Bray. She exclaimed just as one would have expected her to exclaim, asked a number of questions which no one could possibly answer, and produced a gratified stream of conjecture and speculation with which nobody but Wilfrid attempted to cope.

"Now really, you know, I do call this a very extraordinary thing. It was of course extraordinary that the necklace should have been stolen, but it does seem a great deal more extraordinary that it should have been sent back. Now do you suppose that the person who took it had a sudden change of heart? You do hear of such things, don't you? I remember a long time ago reading about a case like that—in a magazine or a book. I forget what the man had stolen, but he heard the clock strike twelve one night, and it suddenly came over him how wrong he had been and he made up his mind to send it back. Perhaps that is what has happened now."

Sally took a sip of the coffee which David had brought her. She thought, "It has come back because Moira said it was to come back. She knows who took it, and she knows who murdered Arthur Hughes. Don't have anything to do with her, David—don't, don't, *don't!*" She shut her eyes, because everything in the room had begun to tilt and slide. She took another scalding sip of coffee and pushed the cup away. David's hand came down hard upon her knee. Her own went groping to meet it and was held.

Wilfrid Gaunt was saying something about the necklace being too hot to hold, and Elaine Bray went on and on and on about valuable jewellery being only an anxiety, and why did people want to have it anyway when you could get such beautiful paste? It may be said that everyone was glad when breakfast was over.

Lucius Bellingdon rang up the police. When he had done that he told Hilton to find Mrs. Herne and ask her to come to him in the study. She arrived, the old indifferent look back upon her face and the old drawl back in her voice.

"You wanted me?"

The words set up an echo in his mind. He had never wanted her. They had started wrong. It was Lily who had done this to both of them. Lily—weak, obstinate, harmless—she had done enough harm without meaning to.

The mornings were cold. There was a little fire on the hearth. Moira had lighted a cigarette. She wore grey slacks and an emerald pull-over. She stood with one foot up on the kerb and blew a smoke-ring. It broke, and the haze was between them. He said,

"Come and sit down."

"I'd rather stand."

He slewed round his writing-chair so as to face her.

"Just as you like. I want to talk to you before the police come."

She drew at her cigarette.

"The police?"

"Naturally. I have to report the fact that I believe my car to have been tampered with. There is also the return of the necklace."

"Your car—I thought you had a smash—"

"I did. I should like the police to find out why."

Her eyebrows rose.

"Getting a bit jumpy, aren't you?"

"You can put it that way."

After a brief pause he went on speaking.

"That scene you made in the dining-room was a mistake."

"Was it?"

"I think so. You wanted to put it on record that I had given you the necklace. Exactly the reverse has happened. Everyone who was there will be in a position to say that I contradicted you when you said so. I contradicted you flat, and reminded you that it was merely to have been lent to you for the Ball. I went on to say that I intended to get rid of it as soon as possible."

She stood there looking down into the fire, smoking her cigarette, her hand steady, her face colourless. Perhaps it was the brilliant emerald of the pull-over which gave the blanched skin its harder, older look. Perhaps not. She had nothing to say. Lucius Bellingdon went on.

"I have been meaning to speak to you for some time

now. I don't think it will be any surprise to you to hear that I am thinking of making certain changes. I am, in fact, going to be married."

She said with an accentuation of her drawl, "So Annabel has brought it off. It's been fairly obvious that that was what she was after."

He went on as if she had not spoken.

"My marriage will necessitate a good many other alterations."

"Alterations?"

"To my will, amongst other things. I shall have to make a new one."

"Is that supposed to affect me?"

"It does affect you—that is to say, it will. All the changes will affect you. I think it is only fair to tell you so."

He paused briefly, but she neither looked at him nor spoke. The hand with the cigarette went up to her lips and came down again. The lips parted, a cloud of smoke was expelled. The lips closed again. He went on.

"I don't think the present arrangements have been a great success. I believe we shall all be happier when changes have been made. I shall make Elaine an allowance, and if she likes to set up house with Arnold she can. Since it will be an allowance and not a settlement, he won't be able to sponge upon her to any marked extent."

"And are you going to make me an allowance too?"

"No, I don't think so. You have your settlement."

"You don't suppose I can live on that!"

"I think that you will have to."

She sketched a gesture with the cigarette.

"Well, I can't."

When he made no reply, she looked at him for the first time. If he had had any illusions as to their relationship that look would have killed them. It would have killed him if it had had the power. He met it with a hardening of his determination.

"You will have to. Are you in debt?"

"What do you suppose?"

He said, "You had better make out a list of what you owe and let me have it. I will see that you start clear, but from now on you will have to stand on your own feet."

She was looking down now at her own hand. A curl of smoke went up from the cigarette which it held. She said,

"It can't be done."

He had a moment of compunction, of desire to be quit of the strain between them. He said,

"I realize that this has come on you a bit suddenly. You have expected everything to go on just as it has for years. I don't want to make it too hard for you. I will add to your settlement by an allowance of five hundred a year on the understanding that you keep free of debt."

"And suppose I don't?"

"The allowance will go to paying what you owe until you are clear again." He tried for an easier tone. "Come, you know, it's not such a bad offer."

He got a glancing look of which he made nothing.

"That's what you say. Is that all? Because if it is, I'll go."

He said, "Yes, that's all."

She flicked her cigarette into the fire and went.

30

The police arrived—Inspector Crisp, Inspector Abbott. After seeing Mr. Bellingdon in his study and viewing the necklace they collected all the wrappings and the crushed paper in which it had been packed in order to examine them for fingerprints and other possible clues, and proceeded to interview Parker and other members of the household on the subject of the car.

Parker could hardly have been less co-operative. He had taken the ten-thirty bus into Ledlington on Sunday morning, and he had taken the ten-thirty-five bus back to the corner on Sunday night. If there had been any tampering with the car, it hadn't been done when he was about. No, it stood to reason the garage wasn't locked. What would be the sense of locking it with everyone in the house wanting to get in and out and take their cars of a Sunday? Mrs. Herne, she had hers out regular. Mrs. Scott, she might have hers out or she mightn't, and if she didn't Mr. Bellingdon would be wanting one of his. A fine business it would be if everything was locked up and no one could get at it.

Inspector Crisp was short with him, and got short answers back. Parker's cars were the core of his heart, and he was prepared to stick up to the police or anyone else who suggested that he might have neglected them. As for the rest of the household, Arnold Bray said he had arrived on a bicycle and had put it away in one of the old loose-boxes opposite the garage. When? Oh, sometime before lunch. Couldn't he be a little more particular as to the time? No, he didn't think he could. He didn't look at his watch, he just wandered round to the stables and put the bicycle away.

"Didn't you notice if any of the cars were out, Mr. Bray?"

"Oh, no. I just put my bicycle into the loose-box and came up to the house."

"Did you see anyone?"

"Oh, no."

Moira Herne said that she had taken out her car in the morning. She had run David Moray in to Ledlington to the station, and then she had joined a party of friends. She had got back about six and gone for a walk in the grounds.

"Did you see anyone when you were at the garage in the morning?"

She gave Inspector Crisp her bright, pale stare.

"Only Hubert."

Crisp knew what he would have liked to do with her. Slapping—that was what she wanted, and it hadn't been done. Under that look of hers his class-consciousness flared. He knew her sort—brought up in the lap of luxury and never done an honest day's work in her life. He restrained himself, but his tone was sharp as he said,

"You mean Mr. Hubert Garratt?"

"Yes, I said so—Hubert."

"What was Mr. Garratt doing?"

"Coming out of the garage."

"Coming out as you went in?"

"That's what I said."

They were all together in the study, Inspector Abbott at one end of the writing-table taking notes. Hubert Garratt had a chair with his back to the light. He looked ill. When Crisp turned to him he said,

"I was having a look at my car. I thought of taking it out, and I was checking the oil."

"Did you go out?"

"No—I didn't feel well enough."

Crisp went on with his questions, and they got him exactly nowhere.

Most of the party had been in or near the garage. Each of them had had some perfectly natural reason for being there. Any one of them could have loosened the nuts on the wheel of Mr. Bellingdon's car. But Moira Herne had not been there at lunch when he had talked of going out on the road which led down over Emberley Hill. Nothing to say whether she already knew that Mr. Bellingdon intended to go that way.

When the questioning was over and the party was dispersing, Annabel Scott lingered. Inspector Crisp was busy with the box in which the necklace had come. She found the London Inspector at her elbow.

"Mrs. Scott—whose choice was the drive to Emberley?"

She looked at him, a little surprised.

"I think it was mine. I wanted to see some friends—the Coldwells. They live about ten miles out on the other side."

"Had you mentioned this to anyone?"

She said, "I expect so," and got a quick "Please think whether you did."

He was watching her face. Definitely easy to look at. Lovely eyes and an air of charm. Something more than good looks too—intelligence. She was saying,

"Yes, I must have spoken of it. Muriel Coldwell is one of my oldest friends. She rang up on Saturday evening and said couldn't we come over."

Her colour had deepened. He said,

"Mrs. Coldwell rang up, and you came away from the telephone and spoke of her invitation?"

"I told Mr. Bellingdon about it."

"And afterwards you spoke of it—to whom?"

They were standing together near the door. They kept their voices low. Over by the writing-table Lucius Bellingdon and Crisp were making a parcel of the wrappings. Annabel said,

"To Miss Bray—I know I did that."

"Who else was there at the time?"

Her eyes had a distressed look.

"I think—nearly everyone—"

He dropped his voice lower still.

"Was Mrs. Herne there?"

There was an effect of withdrawal. He wondered whether she was going to answer him.

In the end she said, "Yes, I think so," and went out of the room.

31

It was a little later that Miss Silver, who had been looking for Sally Foster, came upon her in what had once been a schoolroom. Lucius Bellingdon had taken it over as it was when he bought the house. But Moira Herne had never done her lessons here. She had gone to an expensive school selected by Lily Bellingdon, and the Victorian atmosphere had remained intact. Two of the walls were lined with books. There was a Turkey carpet on the floor, and a large pale green globe on a mahogany stand. There were old comfortable chairs and a practical table. Sally had come here for refuge. You can't stay in your bedroom when the maids have to get in and do it. She wanted to get away from the others, and very particularly she wanted to get away from Moira Herne. She didn't know what to do, and she had to think.

She stood at the window looking out for a time, then turned and began to wander along the shelves, picking up a book here and there and looking at it. There were bound volumes of an old magazine called *Good Words*. There was an old bound *Punch* with pictures of about the time of the Crimean War—elegant young men with long trailing whiskers, and girls with flowing skirts and little turned down collars. She put it back and looked at the upper shelves. Novels by Charlotte Yonge—*The Heir of Redclyffe, The Pillars of the House. The Channings* and *East Lynne* by Mrs. Henry Wood. Charles Kingsley—*Sermons, Hypatia,* and *Westward Ho.* Mrs. Markham's *History of England.* Miss Strickland's *Lives of the Queens.*

She was putting back a volume with rather a charming engraving of Joanna of Navarre, when the door opened and Miss Silver came into the room with a flowered knitting-bag on her arm. Just for a moment Sally had the feeling that she really was back in the past. Here was the old schoolroom, here were the old books. Miss Silver might so easily have been the governess for whom these things were waiting. She would sit down at the table and teach from Mrs. Markham's history.

Miss Silver smiled.

"You are looking at the old books, Miss Foster?"

Sally said, "Yes," and with the spoken word the past receded and the trouble in her thought was back upon her.

Miss Silver came up to her and put a hand on her arm.

"One cannot really talk standing up. Shall we sit down?"

"Are we going to talk?"

She received an encouraging smile.

"Oh, yes, my dear, I think so. These chairs are shabby but comfortable."

It was not until they were seated that she went on, and not then until she had taken a half-finished baby's bootee out of the flowered bag and begun to knit, her hands held low in her lap, her eyes fixed on Sally's face in the kindest and most attentive manner. The atmosphere was cosy and soothing, Miss Silver's voice agreeable in the extreme, but her words made Sally jump.

"I should like to talk to you about the return of Mr. Bellingdon's diamond necklace."

If Sally was startled, it was because she had a rather horrid feeling that the ground had opened in front of her, and that perhaps everything was going to begin sliding again. She said,

"You want to talk to me?"

Miss Silver coughed.

"I should like to ask you why the return of the necklace alarmed you so much."

"Alarmed me?"

Listening to her own faltering words, Sally thought they were enough to make anyone think that she had stolen the necklace herself.

Miss Silver was knitting briskly.

"You were so much alarmed that you were ready to faint. Mr. Moray noticed it and brought you some coffee. He also took your hand and held it, and when you had drunk some of the coffee the faintness passed."

Sally said, "Oh—" She wasn't at all sure that it wasn't coming on again. She leaned her head against the back of the chair and saw Miss Silver lay her knitting down upon her lap and dip into her knitting-bag, coming up with a small round box of Tonbridge ware. It had an inlaid pattern on the lid, and it unscrewed. She was unscrewing it now and holding it out to Sally.

"Pray take an acid drop, Miss Foster. You will find it very refreshing. It is, I believe, practically impossible to faint while one is sucking an acid drop, and it would be exceedingly inconvenient for both of us if you were to faint just now. There is also not the slightest reason for you to do so."

Sally found herself taking what Miss Silver had called an acid drop. The lemon flavour was certainly strong, and whether for that reason, or because of the practical course which the conversation seemed to be taking, she no longer felt as if everything was sliding away. She said,

"I don't faint—ever."

Miss Silver had resumed her knitting.

"It is not a practice to be commended. And now, my dear, what frightened you at breakfast this morning? No, wait a moment before you answer. It was something to do with the arrival of the parcel which contained the necklace. It gave you a shock which almost caused you to faint—and as you have just told me, you are not in the habit of fainting. I need not remind you that the necklace was taken from a murdered man. If the circumstances of its return have given you any clue to the identity of the murderer, you will be in no doubt as to your duty."

The words "no doubt" impinged on Sally's ear in an ironic manner. She was full of doubts. They blew about in her mind like veering winds, scattering her thoughts as if they were fallen leaves and making it impossible for her to order them. She looked at Miss Silver and said,

"No doubt?"

Miss Silver's answer was firm.

"I believe that you can have none."

After she had been silent for a little Sally said,

"You see, I know who you are."

"Yes, my dear?"

"I have a flat in Miss Paine's house—at least it was her house. David and I were helping her when she rang up Mrs. Moray to get your address, and when she rang up to ask you to see her. She didn't tell us why—but you can't help wondering—" Her voice trailed away.

Miss Silver's needles clicked.

"You wondered whether her death had anything to do with the theft of the necklace and the murder of Mr. Hughes?"

Sally nearly swallowed the acid drop. She sat bolt upright and exclaimed,

"But it couldn't—I mean, the necklace hadn't been stolen then—it wasn't until next day!"

Miss Silver turned the blue bootee.

"Miss Paine came to see me because she had seen two men meet in the Masters gallery. She saw them meet, and she saw one of them speak to the other. Owing to her proficiency in lip-reading she came into possession of evidence with regard to a crime which was being planned between these two men. She left the gallery and tried to think what she ought to do. She was very doubtful how her story would be received if she went to the police. She went back to the gallery, but the men had gone their separate ways. As you no doubt know, Mr. Moray's portrait of Miss Paine was on exhibition in the gallery. Unfortunately, as I believe for Miss Paine, one of the two men who was looking in her direction and whose share in a compromising conversation she had been able to read noticed the portrait and identified her with it. It is, of course, the portrait purchased by Mr. Bellingdon and entitled *The Listener*. The caretaker at the gallery, who is inclined to be talkative, poured out the whole history of the picture and of Miss Paine, mentioning that she was stone-deaf, but that no one would ever guess it because she was so good at lip-reading. The man to whom this information was given was the prospective murderer. He must have been considerably alarmed and have tried to recall just what information Miss Paine could have acquired. He would have had no difficulty in obtaining her address from the caretaker, since Mr. Moray was residing in her house. I believe that this man, who had already planned a cold-blooded murder, did not hesitate to take steps which would prevent Miss Paine from becoming a possible danger. I think she was followed when she came to see me, and again when she left me, this time most unfortunately on foot. As you know, she met with an accident which I cannot regard as fortuitous."

Sally said, "Oh—"

Miss Silver drew upon the ball of wool in the flowered knitting-bag.

"A cruel and cold-blooded conspiracy was entered into

and carried out. Mr. Garratt, who was to have been the messenger when the necklace was fetched from the bank, was incapacitated and Arthur Hughes was sent in his place. I believe what had been counted upon was that Mr. Bellingdon himself would fetch it. I believe the theft of the necklace was intended to screen an attempt on Mr. Bellingdon's life. But when it came to the point Arthur Hughes had to be shot because he had recognized the assailant. Yesterday there was another attempt upon Mr. Bellingdon's life. A wheel came off his car on a notoriously dangerous hill. He was known to be taking that road, and there is very little doubt that the accident was contrived. Now the necklace has been returned. I find this an extremely alarming circumstance."

Sally said, "Why?"

The word came out so faintly that she could hardly hear it herself, but Miss Silver answered her.

"It is someone in Mr. Bellingdon's household who is interested in his death—someone who would profit by it. The information necessary for the planning of the first crime could only have come from an intimate member of his household. Only someone who would benefit under his will would have the necessary interest. I believe that this person has a passionate desire to possess the necklace and was in a position to stipulate that it should be returned. The consent of any other associates could very well be influenced by the fact that the necklace would be extremely dangerous to handle and would have to be broken up, when a great deal of its value would be lost. Mr. Bellingdon is about to marry again. He will be making a new will. Until that will is made he must continue to be in great danger. If you know anything—anything at all—you must not keep it back."

The thoughts that had been clamouring in Sally's mind fell suddenly still. There was a quietness and a clarity. She was back in the dark passage at the North Lodge and heard Moira Herne speak to a man in the room behind her. There was a man in that room. What man? She hadn't seen him, and she hadn't heard his voice. He had been with Moira at the lodge, and he had talked with her in the dark front room where the blinds were down. Moira had come out of the room, and she had turned on the threshold and said, "You're sure it will come tomorrow—absolutely sure? Because I won't go on until it does—I can tell you that." When Moira stopped speaking there had been the murmur of a man's voice from the room behind her—just a deep blurred murmur of a voice that might be any man's. After that there was the bit about David, and Moira saying, "Come along, or I'll be late," and then her footsteps passing the threshold and going away down the flagged path to the drive. And the man's footsteps following—

She came back to the schoolroom, and to Miss Silver knitting a baby's bootee. The pale blue wool was a lovely colour. She felt suddenly able to tell Miss Silver what she had heard.

32

Miss Silver had a short interview with Inspector Abbott. It took place in the small room which they had occupied on a previous occasion. Her message having been conveyed to him, he found her very comfortably seated on a low armless chair with her knitting in her lap. At the moment of his entrance she was counting stitches and did not immediately look up. When she did so, it was to give him a welcoming smile and to say,

"I believe there is now no need to attempt any concealment as to the reason for my presence at Merefields, since Miss Foster informs me that Mr. Wilfrid Gaunt is perfectly well aware of it."

His colourless eyebrows rose.

"A tolerably efficient broadcaster, I imagine."

"He has a malicious tongue. I have no doubt that the situation here has given him an opportunity of exercising it at my expense."

"He has certainly exercised it. At least I suppose it was not Mr. Bellingdon who informed Mrs. Herne that you were what she politely stigmatized as a police spy."

Miss Silver pressed her lips together for a moment before saying,

"She is an exceedingly ill-bred young woman. I fear she may be something worse than that. I have been having a conversation with Miss Foster which I do not feel justified in keeping to myself. I would like to preface my account of it by telling you how reluctant Miss Foster was to tell me what she did, and how certain I am that she was both truthful and careful in what she told me. It was not until I imparted my conviction that Mr. Bellingdon's life was actually in danger that her resistance broke down."

"And just why did you suppose that she had anything to tell?"

Miss Silver pulled at her ball of wool, releasing two or three of the pale blue strands.

"You would not have needed to ask me that if you had been present when Mr. Bellingdon opened the parcel containing the necklace."

He said, "Oh, yes, I was going to ask you about that. He opened it at breakfast, didn't he? Was everybody there?"

"Yes, Frank."

"And what did Sally Foster do to make you think that she knew something?"

"She leaned back in her chair and turned so pale that I thought she was going to faint. Mr. Moray thought so too. He got her some coffee and took her hand under the table."

Frank Abbott laughed.

"That, my dear ma'am, has been done even when there was no risk of the girl fainting! But go on—you have me intrigued. Why did Sally swoon?"

Miss Silver told him, repeating the story as it had been told to her. When she had finished, he was interested but critical.

"Well, you know, on the face of it it's a fairly compromising story, but not in a direction which has anything to do with the police. When girl meets boy in a dark room at an empty lodge it isn't usually to discuss stolen necklaces or attempts at murder. As to what Sally heard Moira say—what was it again?"

Miss Silver repeated the words with prim accuracy. " 'You're sure it will come tomorrow—absolutely sure? Because I won't go on until it does—I can tell you that.' "

He nodded.

"Well, there you are. What does it amount to—something, or nothing? There's a lot of I-dotting and T-crossing to be done before you can make it mean anything at all. When the necklace turned up at breakfast next morning Sally Foster did a quick job of dotting and crossing and was very nearly shocked into a swoon. But suppose I put it to Moira Herne that she was overheard at the lodge and what about it, she's got quite a choice of perfectly good explanations open to her. 'You're sure it will come tomorrow? Because I won't go on until it does.' Well, that could mean an engagement ring or any other fribble the lady fancied. If she's short of money and not too particular how she picks some up it could be a cheque. Anyhow you may be sure that she'll have something up her sleeve."

Miss Silver knitted placidly.

"My dear Frank, I think you are overlooking a quite important point. If Mrs. Herne has a reasonable explanation to offer, it must reasonably include the identity of her companion at the lodge. If she refuses this, you would inevitably suspect that she could not rely upon him to corroborate the explanation which she offers."

He laughed.

"If she liked to keep the boy-friend anonymous she would have a perfect right to, you know. If she is carrying on an affair—well, it isn't our business, and she won't hesitate to say so. Come—you didn't suppose that a bit of hearsay like this could be used as evidence."

She continued to knit, and had now arrived at the last rows of the bootee. It passed through her mind that nature had provided pretty, idle young women with a corrective to lightness of conduct. The bearing and the rearing of a succession of infants had perhaps been overdone in the past, but the modern discovery of how to escape from it altogether did not always serve the ends of morality. It was merely a passing thought, checked by the timely recollection that Moira Herne was a widow. Or was she? St. Paul however, himself a confirmed bachelor, had recommended that the younger widows should marry and have children. A truly great and wise man. But if he had known Moira Herne, would he have considered her a suitable influence in the home? She feared not. Her answer to Frank Abbott's question was not sensibly delayed. She had thought disapprovingly of certain modern tendencies, considered St. Paul's attitude towards widows, and Moira's suitability for motherhood, while he was still speaking. When he stopped, her mind moved quickly to the point which he had raised.

"I do not believe that I had got as far as the question of evidence. I was thinking of how we could best arrive at the truth. In this connection the identity of Mrs. Herne's companion at the lodge would seem to be important. If he was with her in that front room, it should be possible to obtain his fingerprints."

"Oh, yes, that could be done."

"Then Sally Foster thinks that they drove away in a car which may have been in the lane or just inside the drive. Someone may possibly have noticed it."

His hand rose and fell on the arm of his chair.

"Dusk, and a thunderstorm going on? Not very likely, you know, but we'll see what can be done. Well, I must be getting on, or Crisp will suspect me of dalliance."

She said,

"One moment, Frank. I feel sure that Mr. Garratt knows something."

"What! Did he also swoon at the breakfast table?"

Her look reproved him.

"I will not go as far as that, but he certainly received a shock. I am convinced that he has some knowledge which is causing him distress."

"He certainly looks ill."

"He has something on his mind. I have felt increasingly certain on this point. In fact—" She laid down her knitting and rested her hands upon it. "Frank, I am extremely uneasy."

He was struck by the gravity of her expression.

"On what account?"

"On Mr. Bellingdon's account. I feel I should tell you that he has determined upon a course of action which may have serious consequences."

"Such as?"

"Another and immediate attempt upon his life."

"You really think his life has been attempted?"

"I feel more and more sure of it as the case goes on. The return of the necklace—"

He broke in before she could complete her sentence.

"Well now, why was it returned? And if it was going to be returned, why was it taken?"

"I believe that it was taken as a blind, the real object of the crime being the death of Mr. Bellingdon who it was believed would fetch the necklace himself if Mr. Garratt could be got out of the way. He *was* got out of the way, but Mr. Hughes was sent instead, and as he recognized his assailant he had to be shot."

Frank Abbott said,

"Well, you know that doesn't agree with one of the very

few bits of evidence we've got—Miss Paine's account of what the murderer said to the man whom he was meeting at the Masters gallery and who in all probability was the fence who was going to get the necklace out of the country. I can't give you his words *verbatim*, but they certainly did not give any hint that there was anything in the job beyond the theft of a famous and valuable bit of jewellery."

"And would you expect there to be such a hint? As I see it, this crime was planned from within the family circle. It was to be camouflaged as an ordinary jewel robbery. The man who played the principal part was someone equally at home in the family and in criminal circles. He was—he is—a man of bold and reckless character, willing to take a high risk for a high prize. He must be in a position to ensure that he will have his share in the prize. To speak plainly, I consider that he has a hold upon some member of Mr. Bellingdon's family and can be sure of his or her co-operation."

Frank leaned back in his chair.

"Well, it's a theory. Putting it on one side for the moment, what has Bellingdon done, or what is he going to do, that you think will send the balloon up?"

Miss Silver said,

"He is going to inform his household that he proposes to marry Mrs. Scott and alter his will."

Frank whistled.

"A very sporting effort! I suppose it hadn't your encouragement?"

Miss Silver coughed.

"I told him that in my opinion it would provoke another attempt, to which he replied that he would rather take the risk and get it over. He said that he was an impatient man and did not like to sit and wait for things to happen."

"Oh, well, I am with him there."

"So you see that the next few days may be critical. He has had an interview with Mrs. Herne, and I think it probable that he has informed her of his intentions both with regard to Mrs. Scott and to his will. She is not likely to keep them to herself. If Mr. Bellingdon dies before his marriage, the beneficiaries under his existing will must profit. If he makes a new will in contemplation of marriage, or if he marries Mrs. Scott, the old will ceases to be operative. The person whose interests are most likely to be affected is Mrs. Herne. The return of the necklace also points in her direction. If you take the words overheard by Sally Foster as referring to the Queen's Necklace, it would mean a determination on her part to secure it, and a refusal to go any farther unless she did so. I have no doubt that it is left to her under Mr. Bellingdon's present will. Now I ask you to consider the part played by the unknown man whom we have been speaking of as the murderer. He has a bold and reckless character and contacts in two widely different circles. His interests are so much identified with those of Mrs. Herne as to enable him to feel sure that he will participate in whatever she may inherit from Mr. Bellingdon. It seems to me that there can be only one person to whom these considerations would apply, and that person is Mrs. Herne's husband."

"My dear ma'am!"

She said,

"Oliver Herne was killed in a motor accident on the continent. He was a racing motorist and of a bold and reckless character. He may have taken one risk too many, or it may have suited him to disappear. According to Miss Bray he was heavily in debt. The car was burnt out. Mrs. Herne identified her husband's cigarette-case and signet-ring. I merely advance all this as a speculation. There is, as you know, another possibility. Meanwhile I think that every precaution should be taken."

33

It was not a day upon which anyone cared to look back. Visits from the police are not apt to leave a happy atmosphere behind them. Hilton went about with the air of one who has been tried almost past bearing and reported to Annabel Scott, for whom he cherished a considerable regard, that Mrs. Hilton was very much disturbed in her mind—the impression conveyed being that a severe social stigma had been placed upon them, and that they were in doubt as to how long it could be endured. The various women who came in to help opined gloomily over more than the usual cups of tea that once that sort of thing started in a house you never knew where it was going to end, supporting this theory with shattering tales of disaster.

Lucius Bellingdon disappeared at midday accompanied by Annabel Scott. They took her car, but not before Parker had practically gone over it with a magnifying glass.

David Moray made a first sketch for Medusa. If Moira had imagined that the sittings would provide a pleasant distraction culminating as and when she pleased in a more or less serious affair with David Moray, she was to be disappointed. He couldn't have been more impersonal if he had been painting a house. The way in which what he was pleased to call the planes of her face were constructed, the exact angle at which she was to turn her head, were a great deal more important than the fact that she had allowed her blank stare to melt into a beckoning one—a change which usually produced most gratifying results. When she followed it up by saying in an interested drawl, "You know, I'm not at all sure that I shouldn't like you to do me with snakes in my hair," he told her briefly that they weren't necessary, and that talking put him off. Even Sally Foster wouldn't really have considered a chaperone to be necessary. The mousetrap and the cheese might be there, but David's mind was entirely occupied by Medusa who had been a myth for three thousand years or so.

It was impossible to say what was the state of mind of Hubert Garratt or of Arnold Bray. Unquiet certainly, and apprehensive of what was still to come.

Miss Bray darned house linen and hardly ever stopped talking—her theme the shortcomings of the domestic staff, Mrs. Hilton having undercooked the joint at lunch and sent up pancakes which resembled scorched leather.

"Really, the least thing upsets them, and I shouldn't be at all surprised if they gave notice. Mrs. Hilton had just that kind of look in her eye when I *ordered* the pancakes this morning. She said we only had shop eggs and she couldn't guarantee them, which is quite ridiculous, because there must be plenty of eggs in the village, and anyhow their being grocer's eggs wouldn't make them *burn!*"

Miss Silver supposed not. Miss Bray sighed heavily.

"It was really a good thing that Lucius and Annabel weren't here—he does so dislike anything scorched. I suppose he has gone over to Emberley to see about his car. I hope he will be careful on the hill."

Miss Silver hoped so too.

Wilfrid, still clinging, compared Merefields unfavourably with the Morgue. Upon Sally protesting that they were, after all, still alive he replied that it was just this that put the lid on it.

"If we were dead, darling, each on our quiet marble slab, we shouldn't even know that we were being murdered one by one and the police visiting us from dawn to midnight. As it is, only the fact that for all I know you may be marked out as the next victim prevents me from sending myself a telegram to say 'Fly—all is discovered!' "

Sally looked at him ungratefully.

"I do wish you would go away and stop talking nonsense!"

"And leave you to the homicidal maniac who haunts these groves? Certainly not! Of course none of us really knows who the homicidal maniac is, which does add a spice of interest to an otherwise banal situation. I might be thinking that it may even be you, and you may be thinking that it might, strangely and impossibly, be me. How do you think I should look in the dock? Should one aim at an air of buoyant innocence, or wring the jury's heart, if it has one, by appearing to be crushed by 'man's inhumanity to man' as the poem says? If it makes all the ages mourn it might to the trick with the jury. Or do you think just plain straws in the hair and an impressive row of psychiatric experts to swear that my grandmother crossed me in my cradle?"

The day dragged on. It dragged worse than Sunday had done, because there was a horrid feeling of tension. Sunday had been boring but it hadn't been tense, at least not until most of it had been got through, but Monday managed to combine dullness and tension to a really remarkable extent. Humanity has done the best for itself that it knows how by arranging its time on an ingenious pattern of so many seconds to the minute, minutes to the hour, hours to the day, and so on and so forth through the weeks, the months, and the years, but the something which laughs at time and its measurements steps in and makes havoc of the careful plan by stretching the unendurable second to an endless length or leaping the intervening day, week, month, or year at breakneck speed.

For no one at Merefields was there any hint of breakneck speed. Lucius and Annabel, it is true, found the hours slip away with smoothness and ease, but then they were not at Merefields, and they delayed returning there for as long as it was decently possible. As they turned in at the south drive she said,

"Lucius, why do we have to go back? We could just go on past the house and out of the other gate and up to town. I can always go to Monica Bewley, and you have got your flat. We could get married in a day or two, and then whatever happens we should be together."

She was aware that he shook his head.

"I've got to get this business cleared up first. I'm not dragging you into it the way things are."

She wanted to say, "I'm in it, I'm in it, I'm in it." And, what then? He would only try and get her to go away from him, and that she would not do.

They walked up from the garage together, and just before they came to the house he put his arms about her and held her close. They did not kiss, they only stood like that holding one another with a feeling of nearness quite beyond the physical embrace. If this was for all the years to come, what wonderful years they were going to be. If this was their one moment never to be repeated, it must be savoured to the full.

They went in, and the tension in the house took them sharp and hard, as if they had walked into a stretched wire.

34

The party broke up early. Sally had made up her mind that nothing would induce her to stay another day. She took off her yellow dress. She got things out of a drawer and packed them. She laid out her London suit and the things that went with in and packed everything else. She should have felt a lot better after doing this, but she didn't. What was the good of leaving Merefields behind her if she had to leave David there with Moira Herne? He had gone back to watching her. And he might have been thinking about Medusa, or he might have been thinking about Moira. Whichever it was she was poison, and the dreadful thing about poison was that you could get to have a liking for it— you could in fact become an addict. When Sally got to this point she took everything out of her suit-case again and put it away in drawers or hung it up. Even if she died of a combination of boredom and Wilfrid she wasn't going to go away and leave David to become a poison addict.

Miss Silver engaged in her usual nightly routine. She removed the dark blue crêpe de Chine which was such a standby and put on the blue dressing-gown trimmed with handmade crochet, a very comfortable exchange since the evenings were chilly and though there was a fire in the drawing-room she really would have preferred to be wearing something warmer than silk. She removed her net, undid the neat plaits which disposed of her quite abundant hair, and proceeded to the thorough brushing which was her custom, after which she plaited it up, put all the pins back again, and controlled it with a net whose mesh was of dark brown silk instead of hair. From this point she would upon an ordinary night have proceeded to a more thorough undressing, to her nightly ablutions and the assumption of a cream Dayella nightgown made after a pattern some fifty years out of date and trimmed with a crochet edging similar in style but carried out in a finer thread than that which adorned her dressing-gown. But on this occasion after glancing at her watch she sat down in one of the chintz-covered chairs and composed herself for a vigil. She might be mistaken—she hoped very much that she was mistaken—but there lay heavily upon her mind the thought that during these hours of darkness some evil which had been planned was to be carried into effect. In these circumstances, she had resolved to be on the alert at any rate for some hours. Nothing of an unlawful nature would be attempted until the household had settled into sleep. It was now a little after half past ten. If the danger came from outside, it would not be set in motion whilst there was still traffic on the roads and among the lanes. If it came from inside, time would be allowed for the first and deepest slumber to lull every occupant of the house into unconsciousness. She would not, in fact, expect anything to happen on this side of midnight.

Having decided on a course of action, she set herself to occupy the time. There were letters that she could answer, amongst others a grateful one from Andrew Robinson, the husband of her niece Gladys. It appeared that Gladys was settling down again and had been talking of taking cooking lessons. This, if persevered with, would certainly add to the harmony of the Robinsons' home. As she commended Gladys's intention Miss Silver permitted herself to wonder how many marriages came to grief owing to the wife's incompetence in the household arts. Gladys, who would spend hours over her hair, her face, her nails, considered herself a martyr if she was expected to expend time or thought upon preparing her husband's meals.

The letter to Andrew was succeeded by an encouraging one to Gladys herself. By the time that Miss Silver thought it wise to put her writing things away it was close upon twelve o'clock. She opened her bedroom door and looked out into a corridor. The panelling upon the walls helped to darken it, but a low-powered bulb lighted the central landing to which the stairway rose. Miss Silver's door, barely ajar, gave her this prospect, but only for a moment, because quite suddenly the light at the head of the stairs went out, leaving an even darkness everywhere. Standing on her own threshold she opened the door to the length of her arm, turned off her own light, and listened.

There was no sound in all the house, no smallest sound. There were three ways in which the light could have been turned out—by a switch on the landing, by a switch in the hall below, and by turning off the current at the meter. The switch on the landing had certainly not been used. Anyone touching it would have been right under the light and directly in Miss Silver's view. The current had not been switched off at the meter, since her own light was still burning. It followed that the landing light had been turned off by someone in the hall below.

Miss Silver stepped into the passage and began to feel her way along the wall. Since she was wearing the felt slippers which had been a kind gift from her niece by marriage, Dorothy Silver, she could count on making no sound. She reached the landing and feeling her way by the balustrade leaned over it and listened.

35

There was no sound, and the darkness was unbroken. Yet someone had turned out the light, and it had been turned out from below. There was someone down there in the darkness, and the purpose which requires darkness for its pursuit is an evil purpose. Somewhere down there, out of sight and hidden in thought, this evil purpose moved to a premeditated end.

Miss Silver pondered gravely upon what her course should be. As she stood here she was in the very middle of the house. There lay beneath her the hall with its panelling and its portraits, and the rooms which opened from it. On either side of her stretched the two main corridors with the bedrooms which they served. To her left her own room and Miss Bray's, Wilfrid Gaunt's, two bathrooms, and the rooms occupied by Annabel Scott and Arnold Bray. To her right Sally Foster, David Moray, Moira Herne, two more bathrooms, and Lucius Bellingdon. If evil was intended to anyone in the house it would be to him. He had provoked a decision between himself and the unknown danger which threatened him, and strongly upon her every sense there pressed the conviction that this decision was at hand. She could wake him, acquaint him with her conviction, and very likely fail to induce him to believe in it. The light on the landing had gone out—she had no more to go on than that. If he did not believe her, she would have achieved nothing and the danger would merely be postponed. At the same time her decision must be swift. The main staircase was not the only means of communication between the ground floor and the one on which she stood. Towards the end of each of the bedroom corridors was a flight of stairs used by the staff. The threat to Mr. Bellingdon might come by either of these ways, the most likely being that which was nearest to his bedroom.

She felt her way to the stair-head, passed across it, and along the corresponding length of balustrade upon the other side. When she reached the entrance to the corridor she began to feel her way along the wall. One door, two doors, three doors were passed, and the next door on the right would be that of Lucius Bellingdon's room. There was no thread of light beneath the door, no sound when she laid her ear against the panel. With the most meticulous caution she tried the door and found it was not locked. This was what she had both suspected and feared. She had urged the precaution upon him, and he had laughed and said that no one could enter his room without waking him, adding that anyone who tried would get the surprise of his life. The apprehension which she had been feeling for the last few hours increased upon her. Anyone in his household would know that he was a light sleeper. Anyone in his household might have taken steps to ensure that he would not sleep so lightly tonight. And there were others besides Miss Silver who could walk soft-foot in the darkness and turn the handle of a door without making any sound.

Standing there unseen and unregarded she made a swift decision. She did not know, she had no means of knowing, what margin of time she could count upon. If the threat impended it might fall at any moment, or linger out an interminable hour. It might not even fall at all. In which case Miss Maud Silver would have exposed herself to some derisive comment. There are other risks than those of a physical nature. She dismissed this one as firmly as she would have dismissed the chance of a bullet or a blow and, turning, made her way back to the room occupied by David Moray.

He slept the sleep of the young and healthy, the curtains drawn back, the cold spring air pouring into the room. Neither the opening nor the closing of the door disturbed the dream in which he walked. It was an odd dream, and when Miss Silver's hand on his shoulder wakened him it vanished and left nothing that he could remember. He started up upon his elbow, saw her like a shadow between him and the window, and heard her say, "Hush, Mr. Moray." The dream feeling had come with him out of the dream. It made it less strange that a decorous elderly lady should be standing at his bedside in the night and telling him not to make a noise. He sat up blinking, and she said "Hush" again. He found himself whispering too.

"What is it?"

Her answer convinced him that he must still be asleep and dreaming.

"I believe that an attempt is about to be made on Mr. Bellingdon's life."

"An attempt—"

"Pray do not raise your voice or make any sound. I want you to come with me. I think it advisable to have a witness."

"To an attempt upon Mr. Bellingdon's life?"

There was a tinge of severity in her voice as she replied,

"That is what I said, Mr. Moray."

She was gratified to observe that he could move as silently as she did herself. She had occasion before this to remark that large young men often possessed this characteristic. They came out into the corridor, and he closed the door with a most praiseworthy absence of sound.

To David Moray the whole thing had an unreal quality. He had come up out of deep sleep and found himself moving in the darkness with no volition of his own. That someone was attempting or was about to attempt Mr. Bellingdon's life was the sort of statement which could only seem natural in a dream. His mind boggled and refused to deal with it. Meanwhile Miss Silver's hand was on his arm, her touch impelled him. Somewhere on their left she opened a door, drew him across the threshold, and partially closed the door again. The dampness on the air and the smell of scented soap informed him that they were standing in the bathroom immediately opposite Lucius Bellingdon's room. He bent to what he supposed to be the approximate neighbourhood of Miss Silver's ear and said on the lowest possible level of sound,

"What *is* all this?"

Miss Silver said, "Hush—"

Nearer to the door than himself, she had seen a momentary dancing spark at the head of the stairs. It danced, it slid to light the entrance to the corridor, and it went out again, but she had caught behind it the impression of a shadow that moved. One shadow, or two? She thought that there were two, but she could not have sworn to it. Or to anything at all except that dancing spark. There was a sense of something that was not exactly sound or movement. She took a half step back and drew the door with her until it was nearly closed. The movement which could not be distinguished as movement, the sound that was not quite sound, drew nearer and ceased. It ceased just on the other side of the bathroom door, and the door was three fingers' width ajar. Her hand was still on David Moray's arm, its pressure intensified. And right on the other side of the door a whispering voice said,

"Well, what now?"

There had certainly been two shadows, for one spoke and the other answered just above the edge of sound. The one that answered said,

"We go in."

David Moray put the flat of his hand on the jamb and leaned forward over Miss Silver's head to catch the whispered words. He thought that the person who had spoken first was a man, and that he spoke again.

"You're sure he won't wake?"

The other was a woman. She said,

"Well, I put two of those things in his coffee. He said how sleepy he was and went off early."

The man said, "It ought to do the trick. You open the door. If he wakes you can say you heard him call out in his sleep and came to see if there was anything wrong. Go on—get it over!"

The two who stood there moved. They crossed the corridor and came to the opposite threshold. The handle turned. They listened, and then went forward.

David straightened himself, stepped back, and opened the bathroom door. Miss Silver had released him. Her hand dipped into the pocket of her dressing-gown and came up with the electric torch which she had provided for this night's vigil. With her finger on the switch she moved quickly and silently across the passage. The door into Lucius Bellingdon's room had been closed but not latched. She pushed it and went in. The curtains were drawn back from the two large windows. The sky was not clear, but somewhere behind the veil of cloud there was a moon. They had been standing in the dark for so long that the room was quite visible in a kind of twilight. There was the great black mass of a wardrobe, a tallboy, the lesser bulk of a dressing-table, and away to the right the straight, plain outline of the bed.

Straight and plain but not unbroken. The head of the bed was against the right-hand wall, and on either side of it a black shadow stooped. David Moray, a step behind Miss Silver, found his mind groping. Two voices that had whispered in the dark, two shadows leaning together across the bed on which Lucius Bellingdon lay—he was conscious of these things, but he hadn't begun to think what they could mean, and before he got any farther than that Miss Silver made a quick step backwards and pressed down the wall switch which was just inside the door.

The room sprang into light, and he no longer had to think. He saw. There was a cut-glass bowl in the middle of the ceiling. The light dazzled in rainbows on its facets and shone down upon the bed where Lucius Bellingdon lay, straight and tall and very deeply asleep. It shone down upon the man and woman who leaned together across the low pillow and the sleeping face. They held another pillow between them, and when that sudden revealing light came on they had been lowering it. Just for an instant they were there like that, with outstretched hands and the pillow coming down. Then the picture broke. It was the man who had his back to David and Miss Silver. He dropped his end of the pillow and ran for the open window. He had a leg across the sill, when David's two hands came down upon his shoulders and hauled him back. They went down on the floor with a thump, the large Mr. Moray on top. After a passing glance Miss Silver spared them no more of her attention. She needed it all for Moira Herne who stood on the far side of the bed and stared at her as if she saw a ghost. Perhaps she did. The ghosts of dead hopes, dead plans, dead fortunes. After a moment she pulled the dropped pillow towards her, and as she did so Lucius stirred. He threw up an arm, muttered unintelligibly, and blinked at the light. Moira spoke. She said in a dragging voice,

"What do you want?" and Miss Silver said, "to stop a crime."

Lucius Bellingdon got up upon his elbow. He had the look of a man who is dazed or drugged. Moira spoke again.

"He was having a bad dream—he called out. I came in to bring him another pillow."

Miss Silver crossed the room, slim and upright in her blue dressing-gown. She put out a hand to the pillow which Moira had brought. The movement took Moira by surprise. She stepped back, but not in time. Miss Silver's hand falling from the linen cover was already damp.

It all took so short a time to happen. Of the two struggling men on the floor one lay prone and the other,

David Moray, was getting to his feet. If he was still quite at a loss to know why a man with a handkerchief over his face and two slits cut in it for eyeholes should have been trying to smother Lucius Bellingdon in his bed, he was at least quite sure in his own mind that that was what had been happening, and that if ever a fellow had asked for it, it was the fellow whose head he had just had the pleasure of banging on the floor. Though in no case at the moment to offer any further resistance, it was desirable that he should be well and truly secured. Looking back on it afterwards, David was astonished at his own temerity, but at the time it seemed perfectly natural to approach Miss Silver and not so much ask for as demand the cord of her dressing-gown. Since she immediately complied, he was able to tie his captive up and make a good job of it, by which time Lucius was on his feet and dominating the scene. It struck David forcibly that he showed no surprise, yet the scene must be considered an unusual one, including as it did one man barefoot and in his pyjamas, another unconscious on the floor, Moira Herne clutching a draggled pillow and looking like death, to say nothing of Miss Silver in the blue dressing-gown.

Lucius, however, looked at one person and one person only. He looked at Moira Herne, and she looked back at him.

The first impact of the shock was very great. There are things which the mind does not readily receive. If it is obliged to do so it cannot immediately accustom itself to the alien presence. The girl who stood there facing him with the naked stare of hatred was the child that Lily had brought into his house all those years ago. Lily had had no right to do it without asking him. Any man would have been angry about it, and they had quarrelled. But Moira had been a child in his house. He wondered now whether his anger and Lily's resentment were the parents of the hatred with which she looked at him. He had not loved her—was that the head and front of his offending? He wondered whether Lily had loved her either. If a child was starved of love, would hatred take its place? He did not formulate these things, he felt them. But something in him rose in protest. He had not been unkind. If it had been possible, he would have loved her. You cannot love at will, and even when she was a child it was not love that Moira wanted. She wanted to have her way, to be admired, to be deferred to. She wanted all the glittering toys of life. She wanted money, and she wanted power, and if they were not hers as a willing gift she would take them, and at any cost.

David got up from the floor. The man who remained there would not get away. The cord of Miss Silver's dressing-gown was strong. He dusted his hands and became aware of the group by the bed—the group by the bed and the silence in the room. It was broken when Lucius Bellingdon spoke. He said in his ordinary voice—and it seemed strange to all of them that there should be no change in it,

"What were you going to do?"

When Moira had no answer, Miss Silver gave one.

"You had been drugged, and that pillow is wet. They were going to smother you in your bed." Her tone was low and sad. It did not accuse. It stated a dreadful fact, and it carried a dreadful conviction.

Lucius turned away from the girl who had been his daughter. He spoke to David Moray.

"Who is the man?"

David said, "There's a handkerchief over his face."

"Take it off!"

The man on the floor was moving. There was an attempt to raise the bound hands, to struggle up. He had got to his knees, when the handkerchief was ripped away and there was nothing any more to cover his face. Most people had thought it a pleasant one, the face of an ordinary pleasant man—not dark, not fair, not anything very much at all—a face to pass in a crowd and leave no strong impression behind. But now it wasn't like that at all. It was informed by something that made it dreadfully different—hatred and the lust to kill. It was a face of a killer, and it was horribly and unmistakably the face of Clay Masterson.

What they all saw was there to see for the briefest possible space. There was a fading out, a smoothing over, a swift assertion of control. It was in a bewildered voice that Masterson said,

"Mr. Bellingdon, I don't know what all this is about. You were calling out—Moira said you were dreaming—she said she would get you another pillow—we came to help you—"

"With a mask over your face?"

There was no killer there now, only a young man with a deprecating smile.

"Well, sir, that was rather stupid, I know, but I'd come

to see Moira, and if I ran into anyone I didn't want to be recognized. You see, we weren't quite ready to give out our marriage."

Moira had let the pillow fall. When Lucius turned to her and said, "Have you married this man?" she said, "Yes." There was a pause. Then he said,

"What am I going to do with you?"

She tilted her head and looked up at him.

"You won't really like the headlines in the papers."

Miss Silver said,

"Mr. Bellingdon, this has been an attempt upon your life. In view of the other deaths which have occurred it cannot be hushed up."

Moira turned upon her.

"Hold your tongue, damn you! What's it got to do with you?"

Lucius came in harshly.

"I am not concerned with anything in the past. I have to deal with what has happened tonight. In the morning I shall report to the police and everything will be in their hands. For now, you and your husband will leave this house. You can go to your room and bring away whatever you can carry. I presume he came in a car. You can go away in it. Masterson will remain here while you fetch what you want."

She looked down at her green house-coat.

"I can't go like this."

"You have ten minutes. Make the most of them!"

Half way to the door she turned and came back.

"Look here," she said in her old drawling voice, "we might as well do a deal. Let me have the necklace and I'll clear off for keeps."

The blood rushed to Lucius Bellingdon's head. He swung round and picked up the hand-telephone from the table beside his bed.

"I give you ten minutes! If you're not out of the house by then, I shall call the police!"

"Well, you needn't be so cross about it," she said and turned again towards the door. Clay Masterson's voice followed her.

"Not very clever, my sweet. That damned necklace is about as safe as an atom bomb."

She said contemptuously,

"You haven't any guts. He won't prosecute." She went out of the room, and the door fell to behind her.

Lucius turned to Clay Masterson.

"There is no question of my prosecuting or not prosecuting, as you very well know. Murder isn't a private matter, and you have both done murder and attempted it."

"Prove it!"

It was the last thing any of them said before Moira came back. If the occasion had not been a tragic one somebody might have laughed. She had dressed, and she was wearing two fur coats and carrying a miscellaneous armful of suits and dresses. A crammed suit-case gaped in the doorway.

Lucius Bellingdon spoke to David, on guard over Clay Masterson.

"You can let him go."

The cord of Miss Silver's dressing-gown was unknotted, the crossed wrists were set free. Masterson stretched, went over to the door, and picked up the suit-case, forcing it to close. On the threshold he turned.

"Moira's right, you know, about the headlines and the general stink. And you won't be able to prove a thing. Better let dead men lie."

They came down to the car which waited at the turn of the drive. It stood in deep shadow, and in this shadow someone moved. Masterson dropped the suit-case and reached for and found an arm. Even in the dark it was beyond cavil the limp and undermuscled arm of Arnold Bray. He quailed, cried out, and tried to twist away, but Masterson held him.

"What are you doing here?"

"I wanted to see you. I knew you would come back to the car. I want my money."

"And what are you supposed to have done for it?"

"I did what you told me—I loosened the nuts on his car."

"And you will stand in the dock for it if you start blabbing!"

"I've got to have the money!"

"I haven't got it to give you. You'll have to wait for it."

The grip that held him had loosened. Arnold stepped back.

"You're clearing out—the two of you? I wish I had never had anything to do with you and your dirty work! For the last time—do I get what you promised me?"

Clay Masterson reached for him, swung him about, and knocked him sprawling amongst the bushes. Moira was already in the front seat, her armful of garments tossed in behind. He threw the suit-case in after them, slid into the seat beside her, and started the car.

As the sound of the engine died away, Arnold Bray got to his feet. He had a deep scratch on his cheek and quite a few bruises. His eyes were overflowing with weak vindictive tears. He shook his fist in the direction which the car had taken and cursed it. Presently he slipped a hand into his pocket and brought out three hexagonal objects. He could not see them, but it gave him great pleasure to feel them there. The fingers that ran over them came away greasy. He stooped down and wiped off the grease on the leaves and pine needles under the trees. He had taken off three of the nuts from Clay Masterson's off front wheel and he had loosened the others. He had, in fact, repeated exactly what he had done under Masterson's orders to Lucius Bellingdon's car. He had a long score to settle with Masterson. He thought that he was in the way of settling it. What?—he was to be the dogsbody, to do what he was told, to take the most damnable risks, and to get nothing—nothing at all? When he thought of the risks he had run, a cold sweat came out on him and trickled down his back. He lifted the hand which held the nuts and flung them wide and far among the bushes which bordered the drive. He had been a fool and he was getting a fool's payment, but he could do some paying too. Clay and Moira were gone and he could whistle for his money. But how far would they get before the wheel came off? If they had had to come away in all that of a hurry they would be making for the coast and a quick get-away across the Channel. That meant the Emberley road. Let Clay Masterson find out what it felt like to plunge down Emberley Hill on three wheels. Let him find out!

36

They were perhaps a quarter of the way down the hill, when Masterson became aware that there was something odd about the steering. He might have noticed it sooner if he and Moira had not been engaged in so violent a quarrel. If she had not been such a fool as to drag in the necklace, if he had not been such a fool as to tie that wretched handkerchief over his face, if each of them had had the sense to steer clear of the other, if they had never met—on some such mud-slinging lines recriminations were being bandied, until in their sound and fury normal perception was blotted out. It was only when the car swerved dangerously and his automatic attempt to right it failed that Masterson came back with a shock to the fact that they were on the most dangerous hill in the county, and that the car was out of control. Moira came to it no more than a panic moment later. She screamed, he cursed her, and the car ducked and swerved to the right.

They had not Lucius Bellingdon's luck. They were on the steepest part of the hill with a sheer drop into the old Pit quarry on the right. While the wheel which Arnold Bray had loosened went bounding on down the descending road the car lurched to the brink, hung there for a moment, and plunged to the rocks below.

The news came through in the early morning hours. Someone had seen the gap in the low bank and reported it. There was splintered glass on the edge, and a gold shoe which had belonged to Moira Herne. It must have been among the welter of things that she had thrown in at the back of the car, but just how it had been flung clear when everything else went down was one of those happenings which no one can explain. The Emberley police certainly did not attempt to do so. They came out to investigate, and they found the off front wheel at the bottom of the hill, and Clay Masterson and Moira Herne at the bottom of the quarry, both of them dead and the car mere scrap. From the police station they rang up Lucius Bellingdon and told him what they had found. Moira Herne was well enough known in Emberley. She was a careless driver, and had been before the magistrates there on more than one occasion—parking on the wrong side of the road, crossing against the lights, driving without due care and attention. There would be plenty of gossip as to why the wheel of Mr. Masterson's car should come off on Emberley Hill not much more than twenty-four hours after the same thing had happened to Mr. Bellingdon, and how it came about that Mrs. Herne was there with most of her clothes all thrown in loose as if she had left home in an almighty hurry.

Lucius Bellingdon took the news with a set face. He turned from the telephone and went to find Miss Maud Silver. She was in her room and she was packing. Their last interview had been strained in the extreme. He had set his mind upon an attempt at hushing up what had happened in the night, and she had told him that she could not be a party to it. If the attempt upon his life had stood alone it might have been possible, but so far from standing alone, this attempted crime was the fourth in a series police, but to withhold what information they possessed and Paulina Paine and the previous attempt upon himself. Whether it was possible to bring these crimes, or any of them, home to Clay Masterson would be a problem for the police, but to withold what information they possessed and thereby set so dangerous a criminal free to continue to prey upon society would not only be a moral offence, but would place each one of them in the position of being an accessory after the fact. Miss Silver's unswerving recitude of character forbade her to consider the possibility of such a course. The utmost concession to which she could force her conscience was to defer communicating with the police until she had left Merefields. Hence the packing interrupted by Lucius Bellingdon's knock upon her door.

It came at the moment when she had folded her warm blue dressing-gown and was disposing it lightly but firmly at the top of her suit-case. She said, "Come in!" without turning her head, supposing that one of the daily maids had come up to do the room. Lucius came a step or two inside the door, closed it behind him, and spoke her name.

"Miss Silver—"

She had straightened the bed, her suit-case was packed, her coat and hat lay ready to put on. If he had come with the purpose of trying to induce her to change her decision, he would find her inflexible. He would have discerned as much from her composed and resolute manner if he had had any thought to spare from what was on his mind, but her own, always alert and receptive, informed her immediately that he had not come to argue or persuade.

"Mr. Bellingdon—something has happened?"

On the brink of telling her what it was he paused to say,

"Yes."

She came towards him.

"What is it?"

His voice, his look, were stiff and steady as he said,

"They are dead—both of them—Clay and Moira. His car went over the edge on Emberley Hill."

Miss Silver said, "How?"

"A wheel came off."

"Mr. Bellingdon!"

He looked back at her with hard eyes.

"Someone had tampered with it. Someone had tampered with mine. I came to tell you that there is no need for you to go. You can ring Abbott up from here."

He turned and went out of the room.

37

Inspector Abbott was of the opinion that the elimination of Mr. Masterson and Mrs. Herne was, to use a favourite word of Miss Silver's, providential. His present use of it, however, drew from her a look of reproof which stimulated him to defend himself.

"A particularly cool and dangerous murderer, and one of the most callous young women I have ever encountered as his accessory before, during and after two murders and two attempted murders—and I don't suppose it would have been possible to get up a case against either of them! We might have nailed them on this last attempt, but you can't even be sure about that. The girl was in her own home—she had married Masterson secretly, and he was visiting her. By the way, I'm sorry the evidence about the marriage didn't come through yesterday—not that it would have made any particular difference if it had. But what put you on to the idea that there might have been a marriage?"

"The fact that whoever was acting with Mrs. Herne must be very sure of his hold over her. I felt convinced that there must be some legal tie. It might have been that Oliver Herne had survived the wreck of his car. Or Mrs. Herne might have made a second marriage. I asked you to ascertain if there was any record of such a marriage at Somerset House because I felt the urgent necessity of discovering the identity of Mrs. Herne's male associate."

"Yes, it would have been useful. But the fact that they were married could have been used to cover up this last attempt at any rate. Since they are both dead, it doesn't matter, but if it had ever come to a trial he had his excuse ready. He was in her room, they heard Bellingdon cry out, and they ran in to see what was the matter. Counsel for the defence could have made a lot of play with that, and there is no proof—absolutely none—that he shot Arthur Hughes, or that anyone pushed Paulina Paine. Of course we might have dug something up, but then again we mightn't. After that smash there's not much chance of an identification by Pegler. Bray, of course, comes into it somewhere as jackal, toady, what-have-you. I've thought all along that he was the most likely person to have tampered with Bellingdon's wheel. It's the sort of sneaking trick he'd be good at. No risk, no responsibility—just a few turns with a wrench and some easy money. But if he played that trick once, then he certainly played it again, and on his associates this time. Masterson probably tried to bilk him, and he wasn't standing for it. Of course there's no evidence there either, and never will be. An immoral suggestion, but I should say it would pay Bellingdon to give him a small allowance which would cease at his death or if Arnold ever showed up again. He's a slimy bit of work and best kept at a distance."

Miss Silver looked at him gravely and steadily.

"Whose work?" she said.

"You mean, what made him like that?"

"What has made any of them like that—Clay Masterson

—Moira Herne—Arnold Bray? Any criminal, at any time and anywhere? Small causes a long way back—small faults that were never checked and have grown into great ones and crowded out justice, humanity. As Lord Tennyson so truly says:

" 'Put down the passions that make earth Hell!
Down with ambition, avarice, pride,
Jealousy, down! Cut off from the mind
The bitter springs of anger and fear;
Down too, down at your own fireside,
With the evil tongue and the evil ear,
For both are at war with mankind!' "

Prone as he was to indulge his sense of humour in the matter of what he irreverently termed Maudie's Moralities, Frank was bound to admit the aptness of the quotation. After a slight reverential silence he said,

"How right you are." And then, "When are you leaving here?"

Miss Silver coughed gently.

"I am travelling up to town this afternoon. It will be very pleasant to be back at Montague Mansions. I can return for the inquest if my presence is considered desirable."

They were in the schoolroom at Merefields. He leaned back in a comfortable shabby chair and said with some accentuation of his usual coolness of manner,

"Well, you never can tell. We can find you if we want you, but I have a faint prophetic feeling that we're not really very likely to try. I may be wrong, or I may just conceivably be right, but when there is nothing to be gained by a public scandal about an Influential Person it is surprising what a lot can be kept out of the papers." He sat up with a jerk. "That, my dear ma'am, was a scandalously heretical observation and one which should never have been permitted to pass my lips. In fact I expect you to bury it in oblivion." There was a sardonic gleam in his eye as he added, "In point of fact I shouldn't be surprised if the inquest didn't result in a good many things being buried in oblivion."

"My dear Frank!"

One of his fair eyebrows twitched.

"Well, why not? Two people have been murdered, and

Lucius Bellingdon's life has been attempted. The people who conspired in that business are both dead. What point would there be in involving the wretched Bellingdon in a public scandal? My guess is that there will be a verdict of accidental death, and that that will be that. You are no doubt about to say that someone must have loosened the nuts on the wheel and so brought about the accident, and there will certainly be talk about the coincidence that two cars from the same garage should each have lost a wheel on Emberley Hill, one on Sunday afternoon and the other during Monday night. It certainly suggests a nut-twiddling addict on the premises, and as I said, if I was asked to pick anyone for the job I should plump for Arnold Bray. It's the sort of creeping, fiddling crime which would be right up his street. But how is anyone going to bring it home to him? I'm told there are no fingerprints in either case, so he either took care to wipe them off, or else he wore gloves for the job. So there's no evidence against him, nor against anyone else."

Miss Silver made a highly unprofessional remark. She said,

"Well, it would certainly save a great deal of trouble."

Frank got to his feet.

"To Arnold," he enquired—"or to the law?"

She smiled indulgently.

"Perhaps to both," she said.

38

There were two other interviews that day. The first was between Lucius Bellingdon and his secretary. It took place at the East Lodge in Hubert Garratt's sitting-room. Lucius walked down there and walked in. He found a grey-faced man sitting at his writing-table. He was holding a pen, but there was no writing on the sheet that lay before him. His eyes were fixed and he paid no heed to the opening of the door. There was a moment when his stillness and his ghastly look offered a suggestion against which Lucius reacted with vigour. He spoke his name loudly and harshly as he tapped him on the shoulder. Hubert turned like a man in a dream. He said in a vague, abstracted voice,

"She's dead—"

The hand on his shoulder weighed there heavily.

"Yes, she's dead. What's that to you?"

"Everything. Nothing."

"And what do you mean by that?"

"I'd have sold my soul for her. Perhaps I did."

"And just what do you mean by that?"

"It doesn't matter what I tell you now, does it? She's gone—everything is finished. You see, I've known all along that she never cared a snap of her fingers for me and never would. Why should she? I had nothing to offer her. There were always other people. There was Arthur—but she was through with him. And there was Clay. And she was all set to get off with David Moray. I know the signs by now. And whoever it was, or whatever she did, she knew I would hold my tongue. She didn't want me, but she knew she could count on me for that."

Lucius released him and stood back a pace.

"And just what have you been holding your tongue about, Hubert?"

Garratt said again,

"It doesn't matter if I tell you now—she's dead. You see, I've known all along that she was in this business somewhere. She knew that I was going to fetch the necklace, and she knew when, and she got that snuff out of the old snuffbox and put it on my pillow—"

"How do you know that?"

"She must have slipped down here sometime during the evening. I knew she'd been here because of the scent she uses. No one else who comes here uses scent, so I knew she had been here, and I wondered why. Afterwards I knew. She put the snuff there to knock me out, and of course it did—she could count on that all right."

"And why should she want to knock you out?" said Lucius Bellingdon.

Garratt's face twitched.

"She wanted to get me out of fetching the necklace. She wouldn't ever have cared for me, but I've always been around, and I suppose she didn't quite—didn't quite—" His voice petered out. He put up a hand to his shaking lips.

Lucius sat down on the edge of the writing-table. He said in a cool, hard voice.

"She didn't quite fancy putting you up to be shot at by Masterson? I've been around quite a long time too, but she doesn't seem to have had any scruples about me."

Garratt's hand dropped. He said on a startled tone,

"About you?"

"Yes, me. Wake up, Hubert! Who was the most likely person to fetch the necklace if you were knocked out? Me—every time. And I should have fetched it—I was all set to fetch it—but I was doing some garden planning with Annabel, and when I saw it was going to take a bit longer than I thought I sent Arthur Hughes instead. A last minute decision, and one that nobody knew about until it happened. So who do you think was really meant to be crossed off the list when the necklace changed hands? Not you, Hubert, and not Arthur, but me. That's been borne in upon me for some time now. Miss Silver got on to it right away, but I wasn't admitting it. I haven't admitted it now—not to anyone but you, and I think we'll keep it that way. They were flying for higher game than the necklace all the way through. I was to be got out of the way before I could marry Annabel and alter my will. My plans must have been obvious enough. So the bargain was made. I was to be eliminated, and Clay and Moira were to go shares in the proceeds. Marriage and a half share for him, the necklace and the other half for her. That of course is why it was returned—whatever happened, she had to have the necklace. Not many scruples about all that, are there?"

Hubert said, "She *wouldn't*—" but his voice fell away from the words and let them drop into a gulf of silence. It was so deep that it seemed to be bottomless, but in the end Lucius said,

"I don't know who loosened the nuts on my off front wheel yesterday afternoon, but it was someone who knew we should be running down Emberley Hill. Moira knew that, and what she knew Masterson would know, though in view of what has happened to them, I don't suppose they did the job themselves—that's pushing coincidence too far. I suspect Arnold, who is definitely in the jackal class, and I suppose we shall never know for certain unless he gives himself away. They were probably double-crossing him by going off without giving him his pay, so he repeated his performance for their benefit. Meanwhile the two of them had another trick up their sleeves, and it's thanks to Miss Silver that it didn't come off. Now this is for you, and it's to go no farther. Moira drugged my coffee last night, and she brought Masterson into my room between twelve and one in the morning to smother me with a damp pillow. I don't know what put it into Miss Silver's head that anything of that sort was on foot, but something did, and she brought David Moray along and caught them. Masterson came out with being married to Moira—a last gambler's throw—and I told them to clear out. They cleared, but they didn't get far."

He stopped, and there was a long pause. Garratt had pushed back his chair a foot or two. He did not look at Lucius. After a while he said in an exhausted voice,

"When do you want me to go?"

Lucius Bellingdon leaned sideways and picked up a pencil. He sat there on the edge of the table and balanced it between two of his fingers, his air one of intense concentration. Anything or everything might have hung on that delicate balance. All in a moment he tossed the pencil back on the tray from which he had taken it and said,

"Why should I want you to go?"

Hubert Garratt lifted one of his hands and let it fall again.

"I ought to have told you—about the snuff—I've been in hell. You wouldn't feel—you could trust me. I don't trust myself."

Lucius got to his feet. He said in a casual tone,

"Don't be more of a damned fool than you can help, Hubert. Be up at the house in half an hour, will you. There's quite a lot to do."

39

Sally had never been so glad to get away from a house in her life. She had never been so glad to get back to London. They traveled up together, she, and Miss Silver, and David, and Wilfrid Gaunt. Miss Silver said goodbye at the terminus, but Wilfrid insisted on making a third in the taxi which she had hoped to share with David. He not only accompanied them to Porlock Square but came in and up the first flight to Sally's very door, where she turned upon him.

"Wilfrid, I don't want you and I can't do with you. I want to unpack."

He leaned negligently against the jamb.

"Darling, you don't know what unpacking can be till you've seen me do it."

Aware of David moody in the background, Sally's tone sharpened as she said,

"Then go and unpack at home!"

He shook his head mournfully.

"Not a sympathetic atmosphere—not one that inspires me to do my best. Mrs. Hunable is definitely an earthy influence. Her father, so she tells me, was a market gardener. She has all the virtues of the cabbages amidst which she grew up, but she lacks charm. Now to watch you unpack—"

Sally put her key into the door.

"You are not going to watch me unpack—no one is! I'm going to light my geyser and have a bath. I feel as if it would take about a dozen baths to get rid of the feeling the last few days have given me."

Wilfrid appeared interested.

"How psychic of you, my sweet. Now just what sort of a feeling was it?"

Sally opened the door just enough to slide her suit-case inside and to follow it herself. She said,

"Slugs and snails and spiders and snakes!" And then she said, "For goodness sake go away, Wilfrid!" and she banged the door and shot the bolt on the inside.

David had already gone on up the stairs. He didn't look back either then or when Wilfrid heaved an ostentatious sigh and departed.

It was an hour or two later that Sally opened her door to find him on the other side of it. She had told herself that it would be Wilfrid if it was anyone. She had to change her expression rather quickly, but when she was about half way through she thought about its being a give-away, because she really had turned on quite a glare, and David might get ideas if it suddenly changed into a welcoming smile. Actually it would have been better if she hadn't stopped to think, because the colour rushed into her face, and blushing is just one of those things which you can't explain away. She stepped back, and David came in and shut the door behind him. Then he said, "I want to talk to you," and she didn't say anything at all.

Sally had some nice furniture. There was a very comfortable sofa with its back to the windows. She sat down in one corner of it and David sat down in the other. He repeated his previous remark.

"I want to talk to you."

Sally didn't say anything at all. She didn't seem to have any words, only bright elusive thoughts weaving soundlessly to and fro in the clear space that was her mind. There was a pause. Sally watched her bright weaving thoughts. They were there, and David was there. He looked very large, and he had a most portentous frown. He said,

"Why don't you say something?"

"I haven't got anything to say."

His frown deepened.

"As if that stopped anyone! The difference is, I have got something to say."

She waited for him to say it, but he just sat there not even looking at her, until at last he came out with,

"He's offered me a commission, but of course it won't be the same thing."

Sally said,

"Who has offered you what?"

"Bellingdon of course—a commission. But it won't be the same."

Sally put up a hand and pushed back her hair. If he had been looking at her he would have known it for a weather sign.

"David, if you want me to scream, you'll go on talking just like that. I haven't the least idea what it's all about."

He stopped frowning at the opposite wall and frowned at her instead.

"You would have if you were paying attention. What's the use of my coming down here to talk to you about it when you won't take the trouble to listen to what I say?"

Sally took hold of her temper with both hands and downed it. If he really wanted to talk to her . . . Something in her melted. Her eyes softened, and so did her voice.

"I really am listening. You were just being cryptic. What has Mr. Bellingdon given you a commission for?"

He shook his head.

"For is the wrong word. You've got the whole thing wrong. He has given me a commission to paint Annabel Scott."

She couldn't stop herself from putting out her hands to him.

"Oh, David!"

His corner of the sofa was too far away for him to take the hands—he mightn't have taken them anyway. He said in an abstracted voice,

"She's quite paintable. As a matter of fact it's beginning to grow on me. I've got rather a good idea for the pose. She took it the other evening quite naturally, and I thought then, 'If I was going to paint you I would do it like that.' And I believe I could—but of course it's not the same."

Sally had got there. She said rather carefully,

"You mean it won't be like doing Moira Herne as Medusa?"

He nodded.

"I could have done that and made something of it. I could still do it. I've got the sketches I made—but I can't use them. I told Bellingdon I wouldn't."

"Oh, no, you couldn't—not now! It would make the most frightful lot of talk."

David gave a gloomy nod.

"He was very decent about it. He's giving me this commission to paint Annabel Scott. I told him I'd like to paint him too. I would, you know. He's got the makings of a fine portrait. He said something about 'All in good time.' He wants Annabel first. They're going to be married, you know, right away."

The clouds were lifting over Merefields. Annabel would make a home of it. Sally was glad about that, and she was glad about David. Lucius Bellingdon could do quite a lot to help a young man with his foot on the ladder. If he made a success of Annabel's portrait, there would be plenty of other people with commissions for him. What she knew nothing about was the scene in Lucius Bellingdon's room when Moira had stood by his bed with a pillow in her hand and David had hauled Clay Masterson back from the window and thrown him. Whether Sally was ever to know about it or not, Lucius was not likely to forget it, and remembering, he would do what he could to repay a debt. His acknowledgement to Miss Silver had taken the form of a generous fee. In the case of David Moray there would be a commission for Annabel's portrait and the consequent mention of his name in circles where there is still money enough to keep the wolf from a painter's door. David would have been stupid if he had not been aware that the way up the ladder was now clear before him, but to the end of his days he would regret the lost Medusa.

These things lay between them. On the surface Sally said,

"I'm glad they're going to be married. They are just right for each other. I could be friends with her, but I don't suppose I shall ever see her again."

"I don't see why not."

Sally threw him a glance.

"I don't see why."

"When we are married—"

"When we are what?"

David said, "Married."

"Who said we were going to be married?" Sally hoped her voice wasn't shaking, but she had a horrid feeling that it was.

David sat at the other end of the sofa and frowned at her. All at once he crossed the gap, took both her hands in his, and said,

"We hadn't got down to saying things, but you knew. You've always known—haven't you? I have. I knew the very first minute when I ran into you on the stairs and nearly knocked you down and Paulina said you were her first-floor flat and your name was Sally Foster. And I said to myself then, 'Well some day it will be Sally Moray, because she's going to be my wife, and I'll always be able to say that I made up my mind in that very first minute.' "

"David, I don't see how you could!"

"It doesn't take me any time at all to make up my mind—not about important things."

"It's taken you time enough to tell me. I thought you were falling in love with Moira Herne."

"Her? I just wanted to paint her."

"How was I to know that? You never took your eyes off her!"

"You can't paint a woman if you don't look at her—at least I can't. Sally, I want to paint you—I've wanted to paint you all along! Only I was afraid if I did that I'd be saying all the kind of things I had made up my mind I wasn't going to say until I'd got on a bit."

He had his arms round her, and there was something in

his voice that tugged at her heart. She gave him the smile which he had always found undermining.

"What sort of things, darling! Nice ones?"

He nodded. It was getting difficult to speak.

Sally said softly,

"Why don't you say some of them now?"

ABOUT THE AUTHOR

PATRICIA WENTWORTH began her career writing historical novels. She wrote her first mystery, *The Astonishing Adventure of Jane Smith,* in 1923. Miss Maud Silver, elderly spinster-detective, was introduced in 1928 in *Grey Mask,* and her immediate popularity was so great that she became a regular in Wentworth mysteries. At the time of her death in 1961, Miss Wentworth had been writing for fifty years, producing over seventy-five novels.